FINDING HANNAH

M.A. PURCELL

POOLBEG
CRIMS●N

Published 2024 by Poolbeg Crimson. An imprint of Poolbeg Press Ltd, 123 Grange Hill, Baldoyle, Dublin 13, Ireland

Email: poolbeg@poolbeg.com

ISBN 978-1-78199-682-9

www.poolbeg.com

About the Author

M.A. Purcell lives in rural County Clare, well known for its traditional music heritage and the storytelling that continues to be nurtured in the hills and valleys of the Slieve Aughty Mountains.

On retiring from her job as a Respiratory Scientist, she took the plunge and fulfilled a long-held dream of writing a novel, which was published in 2023.

She lives on the family farm and when not reading or writing, enjoys a bit of easy walking, concocting aromatherapy blends, a sing-song with the East Clare Singing Club and sharing a glass of wine with friends.

Acknowledgements

Someone told me the second book is always the challenge. That anonymous observer may have had a point but hopefully, as points go, it may not be the most accurate assessment of the process.

That said, my amazing and supportive beta-readers, Margaret, Isabel, Majella and Fionnuala, were on the ball with their advice. It was a pity I ignored it! Girls, I hope ye won't get too much of a shock when ye realize this book bears little resemblance to the manuscript ye read and gave me such good advice on.

Thank you to the members of the team at Poolbeg, Gaye Shortland, Paula Campbell and David Prendergast, who provided the guidance and encouragement to bring this book to fruition.

Thanks a million to Rosa Ospina in the Dungarvan Tourist office, for her help in traversing that fair town. And thanks to Mark in the Wine Buff, Ennis, for generously sharing his knowledge of wine.

I want to say a special word of thanks to the readers of my first book. It was amazing and uplifting to hear people's reactions to it. Thank you to all the people who contacted me to say they enjoyed it and encouraged me to keep going on my writing journey. Thank you to my local libraries and bookshops for promoting it and to the many people who, after reading it, encouraged their families and friends to read it also. I hope you will read *Finding Hannah* with as much gusto.

And to my wonderful family – yeer delight and excitement was the icing on my dream coming true.

For Ann

Who believed that dreaming big should be the norm for all of us

PROLOGUE

The distinctive squeal of the front door opening drifted up the stairs. Hannah, her hand on the desk drawer preparing to open it, started. Her mum was gone nearly an hour – what could possibly have brought her back?

An uneasy shiver slithered along her spine. She tiptoed to the door, eased it open and crept to the banister overlooking the hall. Her body went cold. Larry, the creepy security guy from her father's office, was standing, still as a statue, inside the front door. His head was cocked as if he was listening to the house.

Hannah froze. She hardly dared to breathe. At last, he seemed to make a decision, softly opened the door into the lounge and padded through.

She turned and fled, feet light and sure over the floorboards, grabbed the backpack on the bed, stuffed in the last few bits any old way and hurried quietly upstairs to the top floor. The heavy oak door into her dad's study was never locked. She barely paused, opened it and slipped in. A glass outside wall on the left, with only the outline of the door, also glass, designated the area as a room rather than a continuation of the rooftop seating area on the outside but level with it. Concrete steps led down to a lush garden on the flat roof of the back extension, level with the floor below and the same height as the original building. She slipped the catch on the glass door, sidled through and carefully pushed the door closed so that it locked automatically. She drew a quick breath, bounded down the steps, crossed to the parapet that divided theirs from next-door and climbed up on it. The parapet was rounded and she wobbled a bit, lumbered as she was with the bag, but her sense of balance was good and she navigated it successfully, to jump lightly onto the next roof. It too was flat but sported a large, broad chimney on the area nearest to her home.

Hannah's legs were trembling. She landed with every sense screaming within her to hurry, hurry. She scurried around the chimney, aiming to get out of sight as quickly as possible, but immediately skidded to a stop. Against the far side of the chimney snuggled a small domed, much-patched tent.

As she hesitated a wild-looking young man erupted through the ragged flap and stood protectively in front of it. He relaxed his stance marginally when he saw her.

"Lost or what?" He grinned, showing even white teeth that made him look marginally more friendly than feral.

Hannah could feel her breath hitching. She moved further around the chimney, throwing an anxious glance over her shoulder. "Running for my life, more like. " Then, "I know you. You're the boy from the soup kitchen. Dave, David?"

"So what? I help out, just like you. You got a problem with that?"

"No. It's just – I really am running for my life."

"Dramatic or what?"

"No. It's true." She felt unwilling tears well, gasped as a sound clattered from the parapet. "Oh my God, he's guessed the way I've come!" Her eyes sent a mute appeal. "Please help me!"

The thud of someone jumping off the parapet sounded behind the chimney. The boy moved aside and swept open the flap of the tent. "*In. Quick.*"

She switched off all thought, dropped on her knees and crawled into the tent. The boy dropped the flap. Hannah found herself in a stale darkness. Odours she couldn't identify assailed her nostrils and a fug of old warmth surrounded her. She shivered on the instant thought that it was like being in an animal's lair.

The clatter of shoes sounded as someone rounded the chimney.

She held herself completely still, heard her new friend growl, "*Lost or what?*"

Larry's voice demanded, "*Where is she?*"

"*She?*" The boy made a scornful sound. "You're looking for a woman? On my roof? Mister, you're delusional if you think you'll find a female up here."

"Your tent?"

"What's it to you?"

"What's in it?"

"My belongings."

"We'll just see about that. *Whoa!* No need to pull a stunt like that."

"No stunt, mister. This here is a bona-fide knife and I know how to use it. My belongings are nobody's business but mine."

Larry snorted. "You're squatting on somebody's roof. I could make a whole lot of trouble for you. Answer the question and you'll find I can have a very poor memory when needed."

"I've answered your question. *My tent, my belongings.*"

"Not that one. Jesus, how specific do I have to be?" He continued slowly and more calmly. "Did you see a girl here a few minutes ago?"

"No. No girl here. Only me. This is my patch and I don't like visitors so I'd advise you to go back to wherever you just came from."

"If I find you've lied to me, I'll make sure you regret the day you were born."

"I live on a roof, mister. I don't need you to make me regret the day I was born. Now you go and get on with your day and I'll get on with mine."

Hannah heard the tread of retreating footsteps and the softer pad of the tent owner's runners following them.

There was a long beat of quiet. Then the flap was lifted.

"It's safe to come out now. I've watched him out of sight. Although I wouldn't trust him as far as I'd throw him. But he'd have to come back over the wall and we'd hear him."

"Thank you. I was afraid for my life."

"With good reason, I'd say." He watched her with hooded eyes. "You planning on ratting on me?"

"Ratting? No way! You just saved my life. But, when I can think straight again, I'll find some way to repay you."

"Don't make promises you can't keep, Hannah."

"You know my name!"

The lad shrugged. "You know mine. Everyone's on first-name terms at the soup kitchen."

"I guess, but please tell me your full name so I can find you when this is over and thank you properly."

The young man laughed and sketched a deep bow. "David Gilson at your service. And nobody, but *nobody*, calls me Dave. My name is David."

Hannah half-smiled. "Pleased to meet you properly, David," she said seriously.

"Why is the gangsta-dude after you?"

"I took something he thinks belongs to him."

"And does it?"

"No. It's my dad's. At least the information on it is my dad's. *He* stole it." She chewed her lip. "He's supposed to be my dad's head of security and instead of that he's planning to destroy the whole company."

"That's a big statement. Are you sure?"

"Well, even if I wasn't, I am now – the way he came after me!" she snapped.

"OK. No need to get your knickers in a twist." He studied her solemnly. "What are you planning to do now?"

"Go to Ireland, to my godmother."

"How are you going?"

"By train to Fishguard – that's in Wales – then by ferry. But, after that, I don't know ... my godmother is in County Clare ... that's on the other side of the country ..." Suddenly Hannah sagged and felt on the verge of tears. It seemed a lot simpler before her dad's dodgy security guy turned up.

"Breakfast," David said decisively.

"Breakfast?" Hannah echoed.

"Nobody can plan on an empty stomach."

"That's true, I suppose." Hannah bit her lip, then suddenly looked at David with wide, horrified eyes. "*Oh no! I'll have to go back!*"

"*Go back?* You can't."

"I must. I've left the money for the trip behind in my desk drawer. I had to run before I could finish gathering what I needed. *Shit! Shit! Shit!*"

He frowned at her. "You *can't* go back. Gangsta-dude is down there searching for you."

"Wait!" She grabbed her backpack, scrabbled in one of its pockets and produced a wallet. She pulled out some bank notes. "*Phew!* This will get me to Fishguard and I've already paid for the ferry."

"Right. Breakfast. I'll show you the –" A pebble clattered beyond the chimney. "*He's back!*" David dived at the tent and pulled out a backpack. "*Run! Here, follow me! I have an escape route!*"

Hannah followed him blindly, aware of a shouted oath somewhere behind the chimney.

CHAPTER 1

Lauren O'Loughlin paused to admire the wooden plaque attached to the wall beside the door. **TLCI** it said in bold black letters and underneath in neater script, **Tegan, Loughlin, Consulting Investigators**. She was tempted to pinch herself to make sure it was real but the bunch of roses in one hand and the keys in the other wouldn't allow her. She contented herself with opening the door, remembering at the last minute to press the fob on her key to disarm the alarm. She listened, counting the six beeps, and walked into the hazy, sunlit foyer. Hazy because the full-length windows that fronted the unit were draped in gauzy net that allowed the light through but preserved the privacy of anyone in the foyer.

They had been lucky. The middle unit in Knocknaclogga's small business centre had become vacant at the time Trout and herself were looking for a premises to set up their investigation agency. And it was perfect, with two offices where they could both continue their day jobs, a conference room to meet with clients and a kitchenette and bathroom cleverly tucked in the middle. The small foyer she was standing in would serve as their waiting area. She had sourced the four mismatched armchairs from the charity shop in town. Four, she thought, looked better than two for when they had clients. She refused to say *if*. Words had energy and she wasn't going to risk putting a negative connotation on their fledgling venture.

She dropped her keys into the bag hanging on her shoulder and picked up the vase of wilting sweet peas that was dropping petals on the stout oak table which would serve as their reception desk. Trout laughed at her efforts to prettify the office but she reckoned he was secretly pleased that she wanted to. *Trout*. She smiled, a soft dreamy look lightening the sharply drawn contours of her face. So much had happened over the past – what was it – six weeks? This was July, almost two months. She thought about their friendship as she discarded the sweet peas in the kitchenette, rinsed and refilled the vase and arranged the roses to her satisfaction.

It was difficult to maintain any sort of privacy in a small place like Knocknaclogga. She had no doubt they were the subject of intense speculation but so far no one had asked straight out if they were in a serious relationship. Or anything other than colleagues. What would they ask? A smile twitched her lips. Was he a boyfriend? She was a bit long in the tooth for a "boyfriend" and she knew only one person who would have the temerity to ask if they were friends with benefits. She replaced the vase and stood back, considering the question. They were exploring the possibilities, she thought – and each other, a little voice whispered seductively in her head. Well, she was more than willing to . . .

The door crashed open behind her and a Fury, with wild hair and bared teeth, tore into the foyer. "*Where is she? What have you done with her?*"

Lauren was grabbed by grasping hands and swung around to face the dervish.

"How could you do this to me, Lauren? You were always a jealous bitch but this is too much!"

The hands shaking Lauren were painfully tight on her upper arms. Shock was holding her immobile.

"I could kill you!" the voice screeched. *"You always wanted her for yourself, didn't you? Didn't you?"*

Lauren felt her teeth rattle and her head snap back, as the shrill, jabbering words pierced her ears. She attempted to bring her hands up but the woman's hold, if possible, tightened.

"What the hell's going on here?" Trout came behind the woman, chopped down on her arms, breaking her grasp, pinned them to her sides and lobbed her into a chair.

Lauren felt her knees buckle. Trout caught her. "It's OK. I have you." He hugged her tightly. "All right?"

She nodded, took a deep breath and looked at the woman who now had buried her face in her hands and was sobbing inconsolably – her cousin, Marina, who lived in London and these days rarely visited Knocknaclogga.

She disentangled herself from Trout and crouched beside Marina's chair. *"Marina?"* she said urgently. "Are you talking about Hannah?"

"As if you don't know!"

"What makes you think she's here?"

"She's missing! And where else would she be?"

"Missing?" Lauren felt her gut roil. "What do you mean *missing*?"

Hannah was Marina's only child and Lauren's precious godchild. She was, in Lauren's opinion, the best thing to come out of her cousin. Pun intended, she thought wryly. Her goddaughter was almost sixteen – funny, intelligent, and felt deeply about life and living.

"You know what *missing* means – gone, lost, nowhere to be found!" Marina tumbled her words together, shrill and panicked. "I haven't seen her since Friday morning and nobody seems to know where she is."

"Friday? That's what? Three, four days. How could you not see her for nearly a week? She lives with you!"

"Well, she was with her father for the weekend," Marina became defensive. "Or at least she said she was going to be. I had an appointment in Venice – I was away myself since early Friday."

Lauren, in her own mind, translated appointment into assignation. "You didn't check with Karl that she was definitely going to him?"

"*For God's sake, Lauren!*" Marina was getting shrill again. "Hannah has been making her own arrangements with her father since she was fourteen. I had no reason to doubt this was any different."

"Are you sure she's missing? Maybe she's staying with friends."

"I'm not stupid! You think I haven't checked with her friends? Nobody has seen her and . . ." her face crumpled, "she didn't go to school on Friday."

"Not go to school? Jesus Christ, Marina, today is Tuesday."

Marina glared at her. "If you're party to this, Lauren O'Loughlin, I swear I'll never talk to you again."

"Why in God's name do you think I'd be party to whatever is going on?" Lauren felt herself losing her first flash of concern and getting annoyed. Marina borderline hysterical was something she was familiar with, but this was something new.

"You two are always planning things!" Marina's voice rose again. "*You knew she wanted to come to Ireland and you've gone behind my back and brought her over! How could you be so cruel, Lauren?*" Her hands shot out to grab Lauren again.

Trout was faster. He shoved his arm between the two women, effectively blocked the move and said quietly, "This is getting us nowhere. If you want our help you need to tell us what happened, coherently and without wild accusations."

"Who are you?" Marina looked up at him, her eyes seeming to register him for the first time. She straightened herself, rooted in the pocket of her smart trench coat and produced a folded square of matching cotton with which she patted away the tears on her face.

"This is my friend, Thomas Tegan. Trout, this is my cousin Marina."

Marina's voice took on a husky note as if she was bravely coping under extreme circumstances. She turned her tear-drenched eyes and looked pathetically at Trout. "I am telling you what's happened. Hannah's missing. If she's not with Lauren, where is she?" She turned back to Lauren. "Please tell me she's with you! You know I didn't mean all those things I said."

Lauren took a deep breath and tried to dismiss the hurt. Hurtful sayings were Marina's stock-in-trade. She always claimed she didn't mean them. "She's not with me. I haven't even heard from her lately." She tried to recall when she last talked with Hannah. They emailed regularly and phoned often but, now she thought about it, it was at least three weeks since they'd talked. Their last email exchange was, if she remembered correctly, all about books Hannah was reading, snippets from school, and teasing about what the word *partner* really meant, from Hannah's side. The excitement of setting up TLCI and working towards her PI licence from hers. There was nothing there to suggest that her godchild was planning a disappearing act. She had a feeling there was something Marina wasn't telling them. She frowned.

"What makes you think Hannah is in Ireland?" she asked.

"And what makes you think that she hasn't just run away?" Trout said.

Both women stared at him.

He shrugged and added in that reasonable tone he sometimes used, "She's the right age for it."

CHAPTER 2

A loaded silence stretched between them. Trout heard the steady tick-tick of the sunburst wall-clock that Lauren insisted they needed. He had his doubts. Generally, people who employed private investigators didn't need to be reminded that time was ticking. He studied the cousins, searching for traces of the bloodline that connected them. Lauren was frowning, her eyes the fathomless, grey-green of an Irish lake in the mist. Her red-gold curls hung loose in a bob that skimmed her shoulders. She didn't often leave her hair loose when she was working. Just as well, he thought, feeling the itch to run his fingers through its silky strands. She was gnawing at her bottom lip, watching her cousin with wary apprehension. A sprinkling of freckles highlighted the paleness of her face. He could see she was more worried about the missing girl than she wanted to admit.

Marina was glaring at him, but her fury couldn't mask the fear in her eyes. Blue eyes, he noted automatically, skillfully enhanced to give her a wide-eyed look. He wondered that someone so distraught still took the time to primp and paint herself into an unnatural prettiness. Still, that was people – her persona probably depended on the make-up, perhaps it even hid a less confident person. Although he doubted that as fast as he thought of it. He studied the gamine face framed with hair the colour of a fresh chestnut and noted that ugly red splotches of fear showed through the flawless make-up. As he listened, he realized that the anguished words spewing from them made a mockery of the flirty, fire-engine-red lips.

"Hannah would never run away – she's not that type of a child – Lauren will tell you – she's nearly too bloody sensible, if anything – that's why it's inconceivable that, that . . ." She was gobbling her words again, teetering on the brink of hyperventilation. Her eyes flooded with tears as she looked at Lauren. "You see, I was so angry but I *wanted* her to be here with you! The other thing can't be true! It's too awful!"

"Other thing? What 'other thing', Marina?" Lauren asked.

Trout stared, suddenly realizing that there was much more to this than Marina's wild accusations. Time to take control.

"Lauren, will you take Marina into the conference room, please?" he said, exchanging a meaningful glance with her over Marina's head. "I'll give Brendan a call and ask him to fix us some coffee. I saw him prepping the machine as I passed – it'll be faster than trying to brew a pot."

"What about Hannah?" Marina had launched herself out of the chair, nearly toppling Lauren, still crouched by the chair, in the process. "You *have* to find her, you *have* to!"

"We have to know the details of what happened before we can start looking for her." Trout held out a hand to Lauren and helped her to stand.

"Come on, Marina," she said. "Trout is right. He'll get us coffee and you can tell us what the hell's going on." She curled an arm around her cousin's waist and steered her towards the room at the back of the building.

Trout already had the phone to his ear as he called after them, "Who's in the car outside?"

"Car? The driver, chauffeur, whatever you want to call him." Marina waved a dismissive hand.

In his ear Trout heard, "Sallins'. Good morning, Mr Tegan – have you a job for me?"

"I need three large coffees, Brendan, please. I'll be over in a couple of minutes for them."

"Yes, sir, immediately." Brendan was the eldest of the Sallins children and since he had assisted them earlier in the year was campaigning hard to become part of the TLCI team. His parents owned the shop next to the business centre. He added in a rush, "I could pop across with them if you like."

"Thanks, Brendan." Trout smiled at the young man's enthusiasm. "I'll come over. There's a car I want to check out."

"Is that the current-year Merc with the tinted windows parked outside your office?" Brendan prided himself on his knowledge of cars. "It's an S-class, diesel, three-thirteen horsepower, automatic transmission with all-wheel drive. It's a super-cool car. The chauffeur has a uniform with Luxury Drives embroidered on the lapel."

"Has he now? How did you learn all that?"

"I walked around the car and had a chat with the driver. He said he was a chauffeur."

Brendan had an unmistakable note of pride in his voice.

"Well done, Brendan. I appreciate your efforts but would prefer if you kept a lower profile."

"Only being a nosy teen, Mr Tegan. Everybody knows we're like that. I'll have that coffee ready for you in a jiffy."

Trout laughed in spite of himself and headed out the door. The car, a large, silver-grey saloon, was indeed a Mercedes S-Class and he reckoned the rest of Brendan's information was equally correct. He stopped by the driver's window, smiled and waited while the worried-looking young man opened it. Trout reckoned he was in his late twenties, early thirties, with black hair and wide blue eyes that watched him warily as the window descended.

"Marina is likely to be with us for a while. If you'd like I can get Brendan in the shop to bring you a coffee and roll or perhaps you'd prefer to walk over and get something yourself?"

The young man looked at him, looked at the door to the office and back again. "Mrs Offenbach said to wait for her."

"As I said, she'll be some time." Trout shrugged. "It's up to yourself. I'm Thomas Tegan. I'm a private investigator and my colleague is a cousin of Mrs Offenbach. Look, I'll tell Brendan to bring you a coffee and you can decide then if you want to stretch your legs."

"Thanks."

"Do you have you a name?" Trout enquired mildly.

"Eoin. Eoin Laverty."

"Have you driven Mrs Offenbach before today, Eoin?"

"No." The driver hesitated, seemed to see something in Trout that gave him confidence and added, "Luxury Drives is the company Karl Offenbach uses if he's travelling in Ireland. I believe it was his secretary arranged for Mrs Offenbach to have the use of a car and driver for as long as she wants."

"Good to know. I'll tell her I talked to you and that you'll be here when she's ready for you." Trout nodded and continued across the compact car park and on to the forecourt of Sallins' shop.

Brendan met him at the door, four take-out cups in a cardboard carrying-tray. "Three coffees and I've put milk in the fourth cup," he said, handing it to him. He half-turned, grabbed a paper bag from the counter and thrust it towards Trout. "And here's some of those pastries that Lauren likes as well."

"Perfect. Thanks, Brendan. Put it on my tab and will you bring a coffee up to the driver, please? Eoin, he said his name was – he might even agree to having a bite of breakfast, if you ask him." Trout winked.

Brendan beamed. "Cool, Mr Tegan. I mean, of course I will."

CHAPTER 3

Lauren and Marina were sitting at the glass-topped, round table she had considered would be less intimidating for interviews than a solid wooden structure. Now, as she contemplated Marina's orange Birkenstocks through the glass, she was questioning that decision. She acknowledged the Birkenstocks had thrown her when she first saw them. She had often heard her cousin proclaim she wouldn't be seen dead in such an ugly shoe. Then she remembered reading in some fashion magazine that they were the summer sandal all the fashionistas were wearing. Her cousin was nothing if not a fashionista, and they complimented her oatmeal-linen, cropped pants and multicoloured top to perfection. Marina had discarded the trench coat and it lay now on the back of her chair, the perfect foil for the swirling colours of her top. Lauren feared her own well-worn flip-flops and pretty cotton dress looked drab in comparison – though she had thought the yellow shift-dress cool, comfortable and business-like only a couple of hours earlier. She had to remind herself, with a hidden sigh, that the petty jealousies of their childhood were far in the past. Not that Marina made it easy . . .

Marina, so far, had wavered between contrition, petulance and anger while they waited for Trout. She had started with "I suppose you'll be blaming me for this mess", her tone implying the unsaid 'as usual'. And she had rushed on before Lauren could say anything. "Heaven knows I wouldn't win any mother-of-the-year prizes but Hannah knows that I love her and want the best for her." The tears shimmering at the edge of her eyes gave her a lost look that Lauren knew only too well.

"Nobody's blaming you for anything." Lauren did her best to keep her tone level but the edge was there nonetheless. "Anyway, until we know exactly what's happened, we're in no position to make any judgement." Suddenly appalled by her own lack of empathy and a stab of fear for her godchild's safety, she softened her voice. "Was Hannah behaving differently lately – was she struggling at school, depressed, anxious, any change of behaviour?"

Marina jerked up her head. "You'd be more likely to know that than me. Every time I turned around, she was talking to you or had emailed you or wanted to come and live with you."

The bitterness stung Lauren and for a long moment she stared at her cousin. She thought of and discarded various responses and finally settled on, "We didn't talk that often."

"Like hell you didn't! All I heard was Lauren said, and Lauren thinks, I wonder what Lauren would do!" The tirade seemed all the more vicious as Marina sat bolt upright, unmoving, as she spewed the words at her cousin. Finally, she grabbed the orange tote she had dropped on the floor beside her chair, scrabbled within its capacious interior and howled, "*Damn it! Where's my cigarettes?*"

Lauren shook herself out of the trance she'd retreated to, and said, "You gave them up."

"But I need something now. Do you have you any?"

"No."

The bald answer had caused Marina to focus on her cousin. "I'm taking it out on you and I shouldn't. I want you to help. Hannah trusts you. We'll talk of something else while we wait for that delicious man to come back. What's he like?" She slanted a sideways look at her cousin. "He's a serious bit of OK, Lauren. I wouldn't mind a nibble there. "

Lauren had felt a surge of heat flash through her. This was the story of her relationship with her cousin, forever. What Marina wanted, Marina got. Well, they weren't kids any longer and she wasn't going to let her pampered cousin walk all over her, no matter what her trauma was.

"Hands off, Marina. He's mine," she said.

They had sat in silence since.

Lauren breathed a sigh of relief when she heard the outer door open and close, heralding Trout's return. She rose, needing to retrieve her laptop to check for definite when Hannah was last in contact with her.

"I'll just get my laptop," she muttered, brushing past Trout as he entered without meeting his eye.

She felt his speculative gaze and wondered what she would tell him when they reviewed the case later. She half-paused. It was a case. She had no doubt of it. Her godchild was missing and TLCI would have to find her. It took her a minute to remember that she had left her bag in the kitchenette when she'd arranged the flowers. *God!* It seemed hours ago. She found it and hurried back with a new sense of urgency.

"Right, Marina," Trout said as Lauren sat down. "Let's put aside wild accusations and speculations and have the real story – including 'the other thing' that is too awful to contemplate."

In a fluid sequence Lauren opened her laptop, input her password, accessed a word document and wrote the date in the top left-hand corner.

"Right. Start at the beginning," she instructed her cousin, "and leave nothing out."

Trout, in the process of handing Marina the cup of milk and a pastry, said, "Lauren will take notes that we can use to refresh our memory as the case progresses."

"But where is the beginning?" Marina shook her head to the milk and pastry.

"When you last saw her – Friday morning, you said?" Trout added a dash of milk to the third cup and placed it beside Lauren with a pastry before settling himself into the chair on the other side of her, with Marina in his direct line of vision.

Marina locked her eyes on his and spoke through trembling lips. "Yes. Friday morning. I was going away for the weekend. Hannah was still in bed when I left."

"When was your trip arranged?"

"Wednesday. Hannah told me that morning that she was going to stay with her father for the coming weekend. I arranged it then."

"How can you be sure it was Wednesday?"

"It was the same morning JoJo went to stay with her friend for some days. That was definitely Wednesday. JoJo had it arranged since May and I saw it every time I looked at the year planner."

"Who is JoJo?"

"JoJo?" Marina frowned at Trout. "JoJo is – I suppose you'd call her our housekeeper but she's a lot more than that. She's Irish and started out as my nanny years ago and lived with us all over the world, wherever my parents were posted. She came to me full time when Hannah was born and moved back to the Mews with me when Karl and myself parted ways."

"Karl is Karl Offenbach, your husband?"

"Ex-husband."

"What does he do?"

Marina stared at him. "You've never heard of Karl Offenbach?"

"Not that I can recall."

Now Lauren's stare joined Marina's. "Karl is the owner of KOE International," she said.

"*KOE International?* That's one of the biggest finance companies in the world." Trout looked between the two women. "Are ye seriously telling me," he said slowly, "that Hannah's father is one of the richest men in the world?"

"You could say that," said Lauren.

"I suppose he is – I never think of him like that," said Marina.

Trout took a deep breath but, before he could say anything, Lauren said, "Marina's father worked in the British Diplomatic Service as a troubleshooter for the foreign office."

"*Holy shite!*" He turned narrowed eyes on Marina. "And what do you do?"

"Me?" She shrugged. "I'm just a stay-at-home mum."

"In greater Belgravia, with a jet-setting lifestyle," Lauren added dryly.

"*Jesus Christ!*" Trout exploded. "Why didn't you say so sooner? This puts a completely different complexion on Hannah being missing!" He was on his feet, words pouring out of him. "How can you be sure she isn't kidnapped? Have you contacted the police? Does her father know?"

"Sit down, Trout," Lauren said firmly. "Let Marina tell us what happened. Marina, what made you seize on the idea that Hannah was here? And come here to attack me? When there were all these other possibilities?" Her gaze challenged her cousin.

"I'm so sorry, Lauren," Marina sobbed. "I was so terrified by the other possibilities that I convinced myself she just came here to you."

"Back to the facts," Trout directed. "Hannah told you on Wednesday that she was going to stay with her father on the following weekend. What did you do then?"

"I made an arrangement to meet a friend in Venice." Marina sounded guilty.

"Would you normally go away for the weekend when Hannah goes to stay with Karl?" Lauren asked.

"Often, yes."

"Would Hannah be aware of that?"

"Yes, she would – and she certainly knew I was going to Venice – I mentioned it to her." Suddenly she erupted. "*Don't you dare judge me, Lauren O'Loughlin!* I'm here looking for your help. There was no way I could have known Hannah had an agenda of her own."

"So she had her own agenda," Trout said. "One that she needed both yourself and JoJo out of the way to put into operation."

"Yes," said Marina, sounding utterly defeated.

CHAPTER 4

The silence grew. Out of the corner of her eye Lauren saw Trout stir as if to say something. Without removing her gaze from her cousin, she raised her hand slightly to indicate he should keep quiet. In her peripheral vision, she saw him sit back.

Marina took a sip of coffee and grimaced. "I actually prefer tea," she said. When her comment elicited no response, she sighed. "Hannah did tell me on Wednesday that she was spending the weekend with her father. I truly had no reason to doubt her or even wonder if she had some plan of her own." She stared at the take-out cup, a faraway look on her face. "She was still in bed when I left on Friday morning. The flight was at seven, so I suppose I was leaving around six or a little before. I just popped my head in to whisper have a good weekend. She half woke up and wished me *bon voyage*." She ran a red-nailed finger round the lid on the cup. "I came back Sunday evening. I'd intended to stay longer. But I was uneasy and the trip was not going as I had hoped, so I bailed out." She paused gave a small, bitter smile. "I'm sure, Lauren, you'll be able to tell your friend that's my modus operandi. When the going's not to my liking, I leave." She shrugged. "Whatever the reason, I came home a day early to an empty house. JoJo was still away and there was no sign of Hannah. It wasn't that late but I thought she

should have been home. At that stage, if I was anything, I was cross."
She looked at Lauren. "Karl wants me to return to St John's Wood."

"Oh!" Lauren returned her look. "How do you feel about that?"

"I'm not sure." Marina made a face. "We get on so much better apart than we ever did together, but . . ." She shrugged. "We seem to spend more time together divorced than we did married. It suits us, well, it suits me anyway. Why jeopardize what's working?"

"Hannah?" Lauren queried with a slight quirk of her brow.

"Hannah adores her father."

"She's only fifteen. Cut her some slack."

"You'd take her side no matter what."

"That's not true. I've always been there for both of you."

"Has any of this a bearing on Hannah's disappearance?" Trout's question cut through and broke the potential argument.

A small silence followed.

Marina pushed the coffee cup away and leaned her elbows on the table.

Lauren followed her gaze and saw she was rubbing her thumb over a ring on her right hand. It looked like a band of rubies, the stones graduating from a large, central stone, going all the way around the ring. The purple-red of the stones caught the light, showy without demanding to be seen. Lauren was well aware that rubies could be just as expensive as diamonds, if not more so.

"Hannah knows that Karl and myself have a complicated relationship. He stays in the Mews with us sometimes – and when he's entertaining business associates I act as his hostess in his house in St John's Wood. The arrangement has served us well." Her voice sharpened. "I don't know what's come over him lately. He knows I want Hannah to have as normal a childhood as possible and she just can't have it, not in that mausoleum."

"I don't remember the house being that bad," Lauren couldn't resist saying.

"It's not just the house, Lauren. It's the whole thing. The house is the trappings but you've no idea what people expect from you when you have an address like that. And the attitude you have to maintain when you live there. It's suffocating. I didn't, *don't*, want that for Hannah." And, in a rare moment of honesty, she added, "Nor me either. I hated it. And it had occurred to me Karl might try and get her on his side." She twisted the ring round and round, watching the play of light on the stones. Suddenly savage, she said, "The whole weekend had been a disaster and to top it off Hannah hadn't returned as she was supposed to. I worked myself up into a bit of a state and rang Karl. It took a few minutes for me to realize that, firstly, I'd woken him up so he couldn't be in Britain and, secondly, to accept that Hannah wasn't with him. He was quite calm really, considering it was something like three o'clock in the morning where he was. He told me she'd be back and let him know when she was and basically hung up."

She looked at Lauren. The two of them could have been alone having an intimate catch-up, such as they often had.

"I was furious, Lauren. And extremely worried. She'd told me she'd be with Karl and I believed her, and she's only fifteen."

"You were fifteen once," Lauren said.

"That was different. Hannah had no reason to rebel. Not like I did."

"We'll have to agree to differ on that one." Lauren had stopped typing and was watching her cousin, a mixture of sympathy and irritation on her face.

"I searched Hannah's room to see what she'd taken with her when she left. Her rucksack was missing and possibly a couple of pairs of jeans. How would I know with jeans – she has so many of them. I couldn't find two of her favourite tops and I knew she'd have worn the new purple Docs she'd bought the week before. There was nothing more missing than she'd have taken with her if she really was staying with Karl. She likes to keep some stuff in his house – that way she needn't worry about carrying too much with her." Round and round, she twisted the ring. "That's when I found the note. It was on Missy Lu's lap."

"Missy Lu? I thought she'd have well outgrown a rag-doll by now." Lauren sounded as if she was breathless.

"Far from it. Missy Lu sits on her pillow during the day and retains pride of place regardless as to what her friends might think. In actual fact, I think most of them envy her having the aplomb not to care what they think." She lapsed into silence.

Lauren stared at her, looked at Trout.

He cleared his throat. "What did the note say?"

Marina pulled the orange tote onto her lap, reached inside and produced a small diary. She held it protectively in her hand before flicking it open and extracting a folded piece of paper. She looked at it for a long moment then leaned forward and handed it across the table to Trout.

He opened it carefully and held it so Lauren could read it with him.

It was written in purple ink.

'*Hi Mum, just so you won't be worried. I'm going to disappear for a few days. I've got wind of a plot to undermine Dad's work with the monetary commission by someone who plans to kidnap me. I thought rather than give them the opportunity I'd make myself scarce. Once I find somewhere safe, I'll be in contact. Don't worry. Love you, Hannah*'

Unbelievable, thought Trout, unable to grasp how Marina could come and subject them to such hysterical antics instead of handing them this message first thing.

"What the hell was she thinking of?" Marina said but there was a tiredness to her words, as if she'd said them all before. "I didn't believe it. I thought she had made it up, to cover up the fact she was coming here to you, Lauren. It wasn't at all like her to lie but, if it were true, she would just have told Karl, wouldn't she?" She looked at Lauren, pleading with her to agree.

"I would have thought so, yes – but, on the other hand, I can't imagine Hannah lying like that." Lauren reached out a hand and caught Marina's. It was icy cold. "So what did you do?"

"I rang Karl. He was fully awake this time, told me hang tight and got on to a friend of ours in Scotland Yard. Clive Ramsbottom. You remember Clive, Lauren? I tried to set you up with him once. I was shocked that Karl accepted that Hannah's message was credible. When Clive arrived, we got back on to Karl and tried to figure out what to do. It was Clive suggested we keep it as low-key as possible. He pointed out that if Hannah had, as she put it, got wind of something, she must have overheard it. So it would be safer not to alert whoever was planning the kidnap that she was out there and possibly vulnerable. He made some discreet enquiries. He contacted the hospitals. Nobody meeting her description had been admitted."

Marina had gone into a detached, almost resigned state that Lauren recognized as a precursor to a complete melt-down. "It's OK, Marina. You did what you had to do."

"There was nothing I could do. Then he got me to contact JoJo and Hannah's best friend Ruth again – I already had, of course – they still had no idea where she is. In fact, both suggested she might have gone to you." The dullness in Marina's voice was worse that her fury. "Then Clive found the Irish connection and that convinced me she had come here."

"The Irish connection?" Trout asked with a frown.

"Yes. Clive found out she had come here – so he said he would continue his discreet investigation in the UK but our best chance of finding Hannah had shifted to Ireland."

"He verified she had come here?"

"Not exactly – he discovered that a girl, who could have been Hannah, boarded the Fishguard-Rosslare ferry on Saturday as a foot-passenger."

"Could have been?" Trout's frown deepened.

"The girl gave her name as Louise Hayden. She had a provisional driving licence as ID but a disturbance of some sort meant that the officer checking only gave hers a perfunctory look as he had to hurry away to check out whatever was going on."

"Louise Hayden! Oh, how clever!" Lauren couldn't help the note of admiration in her voice.

Trout looked between them. "Who is Louise Hayden?"

"Hannah's full, registered name is Hannah Louise Hayden Offenbach. Hayden was my maiden name." Marina burst into tears.

CHAPTER 5

Trout left Lauren to comfort Marina and moved into the foyer, from where he rang his sister. He stood in the doorway, looking at the stand of trees across the road. Lucy and her husband Brose owned The Village Inn, a small hotel, just beyond his sightline, perched, like an eyrie, overlooking the village.

"Luce, have you a couple of rooms free?"

"Yes, I have, hang on –"

Trout could hear Lucy turning the pages of the big desk-diary she used for bookings.

"For how long?"

"A few days, a week, maybe longer, I can't say. But immediately. It's for Lauren's cousin Marina. She's here now."

"Marina Hayden? Who married the big-shot businessman?"

"Yes, her. And he'll be arriving himself at some stage, possibly tomorrow. They're divorced so separate rooms."

"There's divorce and there's Marina Hayden, from what I hear," Lucy said cryptically.

"I'd say have two rooms ready in any case."

"Right."

"Tell you what, we'll all come up for breakfast. Lauren and myself have a long day ahead of us and we can leave Marina in your kindly care."

"What? I can't be expected to baby-sit her!"

"Tut-tut, Lucy. That's no way for a proprietress to speak of a guest. We'll be with you shortly."

"OK."

"Oh – I forgot – there's a chauffeur as well but I don't know what his story is."

"Right. Get yourselves up here and we'll get things sorted."

"Thanks, sis."

Now that they more or less knew what they were dealing with, Trout was anxious to get started. His mind was clicking through possibilities but until they had dealt with Marina they weren't free to pursue any of them.

He returned to the conference room and felt a flash of relief to see Marina's tears had dried and the two women were talking calmly, although it looked intense.

"I've arranged a couple of rooms in the Inn," he announced. "I presumed you'd prefer to be here, on the spot as it were, rather than going into town."

"Good idea. Lucy will take good care of Marina." Lauren flashed a smile at Trout. "Come on, Marina, we'll get you up there and settled."

"I've ordered breakfast there," said Trout. "It's only ten o'clock so we're not too bad for time. I'll put a few things in motion here and be up after you. Marina's car is waiting outside."

"OK." Lauren closed her laptop and stuffed it into her bag. She raised an enquiring eyebrow at Trout and gave a small jerk of her head towards her cousin. "Marina tells me Karl is en route."

Trout nodded. "I figured as much. I've booked him in as well."

Lauren slung her bag over her shoulder and hauled Marina to her feet. "Come on, Marina. Let's get this show on the road."

Marina looked at her dully. "What are you going to do?"

"Whatever it takes. But first I want to get you settled with Lucy. She'll take care of you until Karl arrives."

She steered her cousin across the foyer and out into the late-morning sunshine. The silver Merc was waiting. The driver hopped out when he saw them coming and opened the back door.

Lauren went to climb in after Marina, then stopped and smiled at the driver. "Hi there, I'm Lauren, Marina's cousin." She thrust out a hand and the young man, with a surprised look, shook it.

"Eoin," he said.

"Good to meet you, Eoin. We're going to The Village Inn, it's not far – you'll see it on that hill behind the trees when you pull out. Take the next left – you can just see the turn-off on the bend." She indicated where she wanted him to go. "A couple of hundred yards beyond that you'll go right again and that'll take us right up to the Inn."

"Yes, ma'am."

"Less of the ma'am now, Eoin. You can call me Lauren – we're all in the same boat here." She settled herself in beside her cousin.

Eoin closed the door with a gentle *thunk* and, in seconds, the big car was moving off, the powerful engine almost silent to the passengers in the back. Lauren waved out of habit at a grinning Brendan as they passed the shop, then realized that her difficulty in seeing him properly was due to the tinted windows and that it was unlikely he could see her. Nevertheless, Brendan gave the car a thumbs-up as they passed.

"This is like a bad dream," Marina muttered. "I'm so frightened, Lauren. What will I do if anything has happened to Hannah?"

"There's no point in preempting things. Our priority now is to find Hannah. She's a resourceful girl and, if she felt she needed to lie low for a while, I've no doubt she found a way of doing it that is both safe and beyond most people's imaginings. After all, the Haydens are blessed with brains as well as beauty."

Marina laughed as Lauren had intended her to. "Add Karl's acumen to the mix and world dominance looks a possibility."

"That's the spirit."

"But, Lauren, if she's that good how will we find her?"

"We'll find her because we know her. We know how she thinks and more importantly we know where she comes from."

"Do we?"

"The first thing you thought of when you saw that note was Ireland, wasn't it?"

"Well, yes, but she's always banging on about coming to you."

"But how many of her friends know that?"

"Well, her best friend Ruth would – she even suggested she might have come here – but Hannah certainly wouldn't mention it to the rest of those harpies who call around for her."

"You see, only someone who really knows her has that knowledge. We'll find her." And if Lauren had her fingers crossed out of sight of her cousin, no one needed to know that but herself. "Look! There's Lucy waiting for us."

Lucy Tegan, now Lucy Worrell, bounced down the steps and had the back door open before Eoin had the car fully stopped. She pulled Marina into a brief hug, winked at Lauren and propelled her guest up the three steps to the open door of the Inn.

"Welcome, welcome! Trout ordered breakfast but I thought you might enjoy something more lunch-like so I've set out a few bits and Brose has made the most amazing shakshuka that will cover either meal."

She ushered them across the stone-flagged entrance hall and into the dining room. A table by the window was set for four and laden with a bowl of fruit, a platter of cold meats and cheese, various breads, a carafe of coffee and a pot of tea.

A compact, muscular man, more than a hint of a belly protruding from his chef's apron, was adding a dish pulsing steam that sent the aroma of herbs and spices straight to Lauren's stomach, which rumbled in anticipation. He turned and beamed at them.

"Food to set you up for the day, just as Trout ordered."

"Brose, you're a genius," said Lauren.

"I know, lucky for you. And Lucy tells me this is your cousin." He smiled at Marina. "You're very welcome to The Village Inn . . ." He quirked an eye towards Lauren.

"Marina, Marina Offenbach. Marina, this is Lucy's husband Ambrose Worrell."

Marina stared at him as if she was finding it hard to assimilate what was going on. "Pleased to meet you, I'm sure," she said vaguely.

"Food will help." Lauren pulled out a chair for Marina and Lucy steered her into it. "When did you last eat, Marina?"

"Eat? I don't know. Maybe yesterday."

"Bloody hell! Your blood sugar is probably on the floor. Here!" Lauren pulled off a chunk of warm focaccia, dipped it into the shakshuka and held it out to her cousin. Marina nibbled a corner – then, her eyes widening, she took the whole chunk and popped it into her mouth. Lauren ladled out the egg, tomato and veg mix, added bread and placed the plate in front of Marina. She poured coffee for herself and her cousin who was now eating hungrily, then served herself and tucked in with equal concentration.

Lucy gave her a thumbs-up, mouthed "I'll be in the kitchen," and melted out of sight.

Trout hurried into the dining-room, gave the table an appreciative glance and, without more ado, poured coffee, loaded a plate and tucked in.

They ate and drank in silence.

After Lauren mopped up the last of the sauce on her plate, she rose to her feet. "I'll ask Lucy to fill a couple of travel mugs with coffee for the trip."

"Good idea."

"Where are you going?" Marina came out of her trance and sent a panicked look from one to the other.

Lauren looked at Trout.

"Rosslare," he said. "If Hannah was on the Fishguard ferry, her destination was Rosslare. That's where I expect we'll pick up the trail."

"I'm coming with you," said Marina.

"No, you're not." Lauren spoke calmly but in a tone that brooked no argument. "You need to stay here in case she turns up in Knocknaclogga before we get back."

"But what will *I* do?" Marina asked.

"I was thinking – something must have spooked Hannah, maybe in the last week, ten days max. I think you should write down everything you can think of that was unusual, things she might have said, questions she asked. Anything that made you wonder."

Marina was frowning. "I'm not as good to write as you are."

"We don't need a publishable book! We just need what stuck in your mind about Hannah in the last week or so – before you went away. And you'll have to deal with Karl – we'll probably be coming and going."

Again, she looked at Trout. He nodded.

"I'll get Lucy," he said. "The sooner we get going, the sooner we'll find Hannah."

CHAPTER 6

Even with the motorway and the powerful Lexus eating up the miles, it took a good three hours to reach Rosslare. Trout and Lauren discussed the case from all angles on the way.

"What's Hannah like?" Trout had asked during a lull in the conversation.

"Hannah? Oh my God! She's amazing." Lauren appreciated the chance to talk about her godchild. "She's an interesting mix of Marina and Karl – you could nearly say the best of both of them. Mostly she's so rock solid you'd feel like doing something to lighten her up, but she can be more than a little fey at times. She wants to be an investigative journalist and her ambition is to win a Pulitzer."

"Surely that's an American award?"

"Technically it's awarded in America for achievements in America but that's not an issue in Hannah's mind. She's already an American citizen because of Karl and she figures she'll enroll in Columbia to do her post-grad work. She has a grand plan that is constantly changing." She thought for a minute. "Do you know much about children and teens?"

"Not a lot. Lucy and Brose's three never seemed to give them too much trouble and, while friends always seem to have child-centered drama going on, by and large it is of the storm-in-a-teacup variety."

"My family were poor breeders." Lauren kept her tone light but the underlying tinge of regret was plain to hear. "Mam was an only child and Dad had only the one sister, my Aunt Marianna. Between them they managed to produce just myself and Marina." She cast her mind back over the years and said thoughtfully, "Marina was in boarding school from a very young age and spent most of her holidays with us. My overriding memory is my mother warning me that we must mind poor Marina, that she needed all the support we could give her."

"Why?"

Lauren shrugged. "Who knows, really? Marina has always felt particularly hard done by. She's adamant that she was an impediment to her parents' life." She smiled. "I had to look up the word *impediment* so it sort of stuck with me. Nothing we could say would convince her otherwise. And, in my memory, every time she turned up in Knocknaclogga, it was as if the universe was expected to revolve around her." She looked sideways at Trout. "Don't get me wrong – we were both only children and we loved being together but Marina was way more precocious than me and, as we got older, seemed to expect me to bail her out of whatever escapade she'd landed us in."

"I can see how that would happen. She was very lucky she had you." Trout smiled as he glanced at her. "How did you manage to survive unscathed?"

"Eventually we moved in different circles. I couldn't see the point of her lifestyle and she thought mine was boring."

"And Hannah? You tell me she's fifteen and Marina is your age?"

"Marina and Karl have been on and off since college. And when I say on and off, I mean their first marriage was when Marina was twenty-one."

"First? They got married more than once?"

"Three times, with numerous engagements in between. Marina always swore she'd never have children so that was one of the barriers that kept them swinging back and forth with each other. Eventually, Karl said he had resigned himself to the situation and he persuaded her to retie the knot, till death do them part. Obviously, he still didn't know Marina as well as he thought."

"And when did Hannah come into the picture?"

"Marina told me they usually had the most amazing honeymoons, and that the last time she might have thrown caution to the winds once or twice. Anyway, two months later she thought she had a bug and, when she got it checked out, discovered she was pregnant."

Trout whistled softly.

"To be fair to her, once she got over the shock, she embraced the whole concept and she was determined her daughter would never feel she was unwanted. I've never, ever, heard Hannah complain about being unloved. In spite of what people might have expected, Marina's been fairly consistent in her parenting and she has JoJo to take up the slack – JoJo is the glue that holds that household in harmony. So, all in all, they rattle along fairly well. Karl comes and goes. Hannah adores her father and can't understand why her mother isn't with him, considering he often stays with them, *en famille* as it were, when he's in London." Her voice trailed away. She shook herself. "That's not really true . . . she knows well that Marina and Karl work much better apart than together."

"So, basically, you're saying that Hannah is as well-adjusted as any fifteen-year-old?"

"Yes, when you put it like that. Marina told me, while you were organizing the rooms with Lucy, that when Karl rang Hannah on Thursday evening, she was full of plans for going to a concert with some of her friends. She didn't mention that Marina was going away and simply said she was fine when he enquired for her. She hadn't said anything to Marina about a concert or going out with friends."

"That would definitely suggest that she had plans of her own that she didn't want either of them to know about," Trout said. "So, whatever spooked her happened long enough before then for her to have some sort of a plan cobbled together. Say a week, maybe only a couple of days. We must find out if Marina or Karl can pinpoint anything that Hannah was upset about."

"Well, you heard me pressing her to write everything and anything that seemed unusual down. Marina usually is inclined to think the girl hasn't an underhand bone in her body. I, on the other hand, accept that Hannah is who she is, while Marina conveniently forgets that in some ways she's a regular chip off the old block. Many's the time Marina ran rings around her own parents, another handy bit of amnesia she subscribes to."

"Anything else you can think of that might help us figure out what's going on? Speaking of which, are you satisfied that the note was genuine?"

Lauren turned startled eyes towards him. "It never occurred to me that it wasn't."

"Did you recognize the writing?"

"Yes. I'd say it was definitely Hannah's. Do you have doubts?"

"Not really – just covering possibilities. From what I could see the writing flowed freely so there was no sign of coercion – and, for all that it was brief, it said what it had to say and left it at that."

"That's a style Hannah has been cultivating: brevity. She believes that long-winded articles will be the death of journalism. She considers that less is better but make it count."

"Well, she certainly managed that. Can you think of anyone she might have confided in, apart from her friend Ruth and JoJo?"

"No – if she didn't tell Ruth, she didn't tell anyone. Look! The sign for Rosslare. What exactly are we looking for here?"

"Proof that she's actually landed in Ireland, whether she's with someone or alone, perhaps even pointers as to what direction she might have taken."

"You think she might be with someone?"

"It's a possibility we can't afford to overlook."

"And we'll start where?"

"Where all good investigators start, at the most obvious point."

Lauren looked at him. His profile was set, determined, as he changed lanes.

CHAPTER 7

Lauren looked around with interest. A huge *Welcome to Rosslare Europort* loomed on her left as Trout approached a roundabout that would take them to a car park close to the Terminal building.

"*Wow!* I don't remember it being this big!" she said.

"You've been here before?"

"Years ago, but it's changed completely."

"There's been a fair bit of development over the years and a huge expansion since Brexit. It's one of the foremost RO-RO ports in Europe now."

"RO-RO?"

"Roll On, Roll Off. I think the sailings to Europe have increased by three or four hundred per cent. And they're adding a one-stop clearance point that's making it very popular with freight carriers."

"I was a walk-on back in the day. You could get a train almost to the terminal, walk for a couple of minutes and you were at the boarding area."

"You still can."

Lauren turned to Trout. "I had almost forgotten. Hannah and myself travelled the route a couple of times when she was younger. It was a real adventure for her – she loved to experience different things."

"So she's familiar with the route – that's good. I wonder when exactly she travelled? The length of the train journey from London to Fishguard varies greatly, depending on the time of day and the number of changes – anything from five hours to twelve, believe it or not! I had a quick look before we left. A coach would be the better option – if she could book a place at short notice – seems to be about five hours." Trout pulled neatly into a parking space. "Could she have got a lift, do you think?"

"Who knows? Unlikely. Unless the driver was travelling too." Lauren unclipped her belt and climbed out, giving her muscles a grateful stretch.

"Hopefully we'll get some answers here." Trout got out and in his turn stretched his shoulders. "If we get a look at her walking off the ferry under her own steam, we can rule out a kidnap situation. Then we can concentrate on tracking her movements."

"It's horrible to think she's missing and may be in danger." Lauren couldn't keep the wobble from her voice.

"Hey, chin up! TLCI is on the job." Trout moved around to join her on the other side of the car. He slipped an arm around her shoulders and together they started towards a large building on the port side of the car park.

"You're right. Just for a moment I let the fear overwhelm me. I'm OK now. Where are we starting?"

"Security office. I believe the Railway Authorities have installed a top-class smart security system."

"Railway Authorities? Surely you mean the Port Authorities?"

"No. Rosslare is unique in that it's operated by Iarnród Eireann. The Fishguard and Rosslare Railways and Harbour Company actually own the port under some act or other from the 1890's. It's an amazing facility to have and it has been going from strength to strength over the last few years."

"The crossing isn't too long either – three or four hours. Departure times can vary according to weather apparently but usually there's an early-morning one-thirty sailing and an afternoon two o'clock one."

"So, if Hannah got the sailing on Saturday, would she be more likely to get the late-night early-morning one or the afternoon one, I wonder?"

"Depends on how she got to Fishguard. And, if she had to get her provisional driving licence it would have taken up some time on Friday. She may not have made the early-morning one."

"You don't think she had a licence already?"

"She'd surely have mentioned it. She still got childishly excited about grown-up things like that."

"Right. Afternoon it is. The two o'clock sailing gets in at half five, so we'll start with that one."

"Well, here's hoping we'll get some sort of answers here."

"Will they tell us?"

"We'll find out."

They had reached the building, fronted with opaque glass, set with tall doors of the same material sporting a key-pad intercom with a printed notice: **PRESS ONCE.** Trout obliged. A disembodied voice asked him to state his business.

"Thomas Tegan and Lauren O'Loughlin to see Security."

"In what capacity?"

"Following up on a recent query from the British Metropolitan Police."

"Do you have an appointment?"

"No."

There was a long beat of silence. "I will send someone to talk with you. Please wait a moment."

Trout raised an eyebrow at Lauren but made no comment. In a few minutes they could see a shadowy figure approaching. The glass slid apart to reveal a trim, bearded man, above medium height, in a crisp white shirt with narrow navy epaulettes and *Chief Security Officer* embroidered on the pocket.

"Thomas, me old segotia! I had to come and see for myself if it was you."

He held out a hand and Trout grasped it, saying, "Jarlath! So this is what 'rolling in clover' means?"

The two men shook hands heartily.

"Sure, you know yourself. I didn't last six months gardening. It got so bad I was tailing the cat to keep him from killing the birds. At that stage I knew I needed something to occupy myself and here I am." He looked at Trout slyly. "I hear you didn't even make it out."

"Something like that, only I went the PI route. TLC Investigations. This is my associate, Lauren O'Loughlin. She's studying for her licence on the job. Lauren, this is an old friend and ex-Garda colleague of mine, Jarlath Considine."

"I'm very pleased to meet you, Lauren. Both of you are very welcome. Come in and see my domain and you can tell me about this query from over the pond. Can't say I remember one in the last few days. And I'd be supposed to know."

He led them across an airy strip of tiled floor, past a tall curved desk where two women were busy answering phones, and up a flight of steps to a long balcony. At this level the glass was clear and bright sunlight augmented the recessed lights in the ceiling. A row of computer stations, manned by young men and women in a similar uniform to Jarlath's occupied the area along the wooden railings and further over a double row of monitors showed different aspects of the port – its buildings, car parks, freight terminals, a couple of ships in the distance, and people patrolling, scurrying about and generally carrying out their work.

"This is some set-up." Trout's voice was full of real admiration.

"Not too bad." Jarlath looked around him with no small degree of pride in his voice. "I had to learn a lot about the technical stuff. It's always a good idea to have some idea about what these computer geeks can do. I may not be as fast as the young ones," he indicated the row of desks along the balcony, "but, I can hold my own." He winked at Trout. "And I know most of the jargon. Now what can I do for you?"

Trout gave him a potted version of their task and Jarlath listened with total concentration.

"I see," he said at the end, fingering his beard. "We haven't heard from this Clive gent but then we wouldn't if they're trying to keep it on the low-low. But someone tried the same stunt as yourselves here on Saturday."

"Stunt?"

"Yeah. Some gent, American accent, tried to throw his weight around and demanded he see the footage of the incoming ferries. He stepped on my assistant's toes big-time." He tapped his nose. "We know what happens when some *amadán* treads on our toes, don't we?"

"Lucky for us that he was a bad-mannered git," said Trout. "I presume your boy sent him packing?"

"*Damn right he did!*" Jarlath tapped his fingers on the desk, looking thoughtful. "You know, I heard the lads talking about some incident – something odd that happened with one of the incoming passengers – when customs were examining passports."

"As in a diversion?" Trout asked.

"Something like that. Let me see." His eyes twinkled at Trout. "You know, Thomas, there's all sort of regulations around showing data footage to the general public, GDPR and all that, but there's nothing to say a man," he nodded to Lauren, "or a woman for that matter, can't show off a new toy to a pal." He indicated the bank of monitors. "This here is the latest in smart technology." His voice was clear, pitched at a normal level. "We monitor the comings and goings of the whole port area. We can communicate with any of our people at the flick of a switch and we store the recorded data for the regulatory ninety days unless we feel we need something for further down the line. That's part of the young ones' jobs, to snip and store information that might be needed in the future. Otherwise, the computers automatically overwrite what's on the files. It's very interesting. I'll show you how it works." Jarlath fiddled around with a dashboard that looked as if it could belong in a space ship. "Look at the screen in the far corner."

A separate monitor came to life. The long sleek line of the ferry approaching filled the screen. Another series of taps and the screen showed a steady stream of passengers moving along much like they would in an airport queue. A customs officer checked various forms of identification.

"Do people not need a passport?" Lauren queried as she watched the different documents being produced.

"Not between Britain and Ireland. It's advisable but any form of photo ID is acceptable as long as it's official." Jarlath's eyes were on the screen as he spoke. "Here we are now," he said softly.

A young girl was approaching – medium height, slim, wearing a yellow shirt over a vibrantly coloured T-shirt. A high pony-tail of what looked like dreadlocks hung from the back of an orange baseball cap and oversized dark glasses covered her eyes. She carried a medium-sized rucksack, set square on her back.

Lauren drew in a sharp breath.

"You reckon it's Hannah?" Trout asked softly.

She nodded, her eyes glued to the screen.

The girl handed the officer a small card that looked like a driving licence. He indicated that she take off her glasses. As she did so a commotion behind her distracted the man's attention. He glanced at the card, back at the girl and motioned her to move on. She replaced the glasses and hurried forward. A young man picked himself up from the ground where he had fallen, having apparently tripped over his backpack which he had placed on the ground by his feet. He had disentangled himself from it and now carried it awkwardly towards where the custom officer was watching him carefully. A beautiful golden Labrador came sniffing around him and moved on to the next in line. The lad, beanie pulled down low on his forehead, kept his head down, held out a passport and was duly allowed through. The girl behind him in a nondescript jacket and camouflage pants, dirty-blond hair straggling around her face, hurried after him as if it was important to keep him in sight. She adjusted her rucksack on her shoulders and passed through without incident.

Jarlath tapped some more and the same three next appeared on the walkway to the station, situated a short distance from the port. They had stopped as if to plan a next move. The girl in the yellow shirt looked directly at the camera and said something to the young man. He draped an arm across her shoulders and turned her away, without looking where she indicated. He said something sideways to the other girl and they moved forward together.

"What do make of that?" Jarlath asked Trout. "Nine people out of ten would have looked where she indicated. That young man didn't. And that raises some interesting questions."

"He's someone who knows better than to look straight at a camera. A professional of some sort?" Trout sounded grim.

"Who knows these days?" Jarlath shrugged. "These young ones know every trick, between the television and the internet. Any Google search will teach you something as simple as that."

CHAPTER 8

Trout and Lauren left soon after but not before Jarlath had made a call to his fellow security officer at the train station.

"I'd say your best bet is to go straight to the station. That's where that path leads and where the majority of foot passengers head for. It's only seven or eight minutes away and I've asked Bob Rackett to pull up the CCTV from Saturday evening. You might be lucky and see where they went."

They thanked him profusely but he waved it away. "Let me know how you get on. I've a granddaughter about the same age as that little girl and I can easily imagine how I'd feel if she went missing."

He had also told them that while there was a car park at the station, they'd have walked there, done their business and be back again in the time it would take them to go there by the road. They took him at his word and followed the well-marked path to Rosslare station.

It was smaller than Trout expected. A ramp took them straight onto a single platform. He looked around. There was no ticket office but a man and a woman in rail-staff uniforms were talking near a door marked EXIT.

As they approached the man detached himself and came to meet them.

"Mr Tegan, Ms O'Loughlin? Jarlath told me to expect you. Bob Rackett." He shook hands with each of them in turn. "We've set up the relevant recording and I think we've isolated the piece you want. This way."

He indicated a door marked **PRIVATE** on his left, and led them into a dingy, cluttered area that seemed to serve every purpose from Lost and Found to staff break-room. At the far end a large, single screen divided into squares showed different aspects of the stations. The pictures flickered continuously as they picked up different activities.

Lauren thought it would give her a headache in no time, but watched politely as Bob Rackett's unwieldy-looking fingers pecked at a keyboard, set on a shelf at chest height. The screen morphed into a grainy footage of people milling around in all directions. Some were disembarking from a train, recently pulled in to the platform. These, for the most part, hurried towards the ramp, while a straggling stream of humanity came against them from the port side and hurried towards the train.

"The afternoon boat-train," Bob said.

The three young people, last seen on Jarlath Considine's hi-tech system, came on to the platform and looked around with a bewildered air.

Lauren let out a breath she hadn't realized she was holding.

Bob looked at her. "These the ones you're looking for?"

"Yes. Do you know where they went?"

"That's difficult to say, but look at this."

There was no sound but the picture pantomimed a discernable story. Where's the ticket office? the motions of the girl in the oversized shirt seemed to ask. The nondescript girl pointed to the ticket machine. The young man, beanie still in place, kept his head down as if listening to the girls. He indicated to where Bob himself could be seen, near the exit. Hannah, for Lauren was sure she was the girl in the loose shirt, gestured towards the ticket machine and turned, as if to go towards it. Then she went completely still, turned back with an agitated motion of her hand and looked as if she was preparing to run. The young man raised his head. For a second, they got a glimpse of a smooth face with narrowed eyes. He caught Hannah, in what looked like a fierce grip, said something and moved to stand directly behind her. The other girl moved beside them. Together they formed a shield around Hannah. All three moved forward casually with no discernable haste, mingled with the disembarking passengers and headed back the way they'd come. They disappeared down the ramp.

"What spooked her?" Trout was studying the frame, trying to see anything that looked different from before.

"Maybe this." Bob went back a couple of seconds and stilled a shot of the exit doors, where he himself stood, casting his eye over the comings and goings of the station. Beside him, coming in from the outside, almost level with him in the picture, was a man in a grey three-piece suit, a cannon-ball head set on wide shoulders, a Clarke Gable moustache outlining thin lips. He stopped and surveyed the crowds with narrowed, searching eyes. Bob restarted the video. Still the man stood, scanning, assessing. Once or twice his eyes lingered to examine a someone among the hurrying people with an intensity that sent a shiver through Lauren.

"The youngsters recognized him, at least Hannah did," Lauren said slowly.

"And they were of the opinion that he's trouble, whoever he is," Trout said, his eyes riveted to the screen. "Any chance of getting a picture?"

"Sorry, mate. You're only seeing this as a favour to Jarlath."

"No worries." Lauren grabbed her phone from the top of her bag, had the camera open in a flash and started clicking a series of photos.

Bob half smiled and, without being asked, scrolled to the three youngsters and stilled it where the picture was marginally clearest.

"Shark-eyes stayed until the train pulled out," he said. "Before he left, he quizzed me about any girls travelling alone. Claimed he was to meet his niece off the boat and seemed to have missed her." His dry tone conveyed what he thought about that query. "I wouldn't like to cross the same gent, considering the way he stomped out of the station when I couldn't help him."

"Did you see the look on Hannah's face?" Lauren had a catch in her voice. "She was absolutely terrified."

"On the other hand, her friends seem to be both savvy and protective." Trout thought for a minute, then turned to Bob. "Any idea where they could have gone?"

Bob shrugged. "All I can tell you for sure is that they didn't come back onto the concourse. If I was a betting man, I'd say they hitched a lift." He turned back to the screen, fiddled with the keyboard and the multiple screens loaded back on the monitor.

"Except they'd want to get off the road fast," Trout said.

"And three of them would find it hard to get a lift," Lauren said.

Bob looked at Lauren. "It would depend. Maybe they got lucky and got in with one of the freight guys. Once those big lories are through the checks there's nothing to stop the drivers picking up somebody and those sleeping cabs are quite roomy. They might not take them far but all the young ones needed was to be off the road when the Shark passed."

"How far is Rosslare town?" Lauren was trying to imagine what three, frightened young people under such pressure might do.

"Not too far if you've transport but it would take the best part of two hours to walk it." He didn't try to hide his scepticism. "Although . . ." He stared at the ground.

They waited.

"It would be a long shot," he muttered. He raised his head and said, almost reluctantly, "There's a hippie commune." He stopped, thought some more, seemed to come to a decision. "There's a footpath from the East Freight Park. If they went that way, and if they noticed the footpath . . ." Suddenly frustrated, he growled, "*If, if, if.*" He took a breath and continued, measuring each word. "The footpath goes onto a rough hill that overlooks the sea. A couple of years ago, more than a couple, while it was still privately owned, a blow-in with more money than sense bought the hill. About ten acres. He definitely had more money than sense, or so we thought at the time. He was going to live off-grid and create a latter-day Nirvana." Bob smiled, a mere twitch of his lips. "Whether it's Nirvana or not, he divided it into plots, stuck in any old thing that a person could live in, if they weren't fussy. He rents them out and by all accounts is rarely without takers for his 'alternative accommodation'. His description, I might add."

"What sort of 'things'?" In spite of herself, Lauren was fascinated.

"Over the years he's built a couple of log cabins, but he started off with a decommissioned bus, a couple of yurts and an old freight container that he managed to make into a dwelling of sorts. Of course, the rent's nominal and the facilities basic, but apparently he more than gets by. Anyway, I'm just telling you that's where the path goes. There's a contingent of permanent residents and they tell me anybody who wants to stay for a couple of days is always made welcome."

"They'd have tried to stay off the main road," Lauren murmured.

"There's only the one road really." Trout turned to Bob. "How long would it take to get to this Nirvana place?"

"You'd have to walk but you could take the car to where the path starts in the East Park. Fifteen minutes from there."

Trout looked at Lauren who was gnawing at her bottom lip. "It's worth a chance."

She took a deep breath and said quietly, "We'd better check it out. Then we can concentrate on the freight rigs that passed through on Saturday." She added under her breath, "If we need to."

CHAPTER 9

The path was a narrow but well-trodden trail that led upwards into thick scrubland. Trout and Lauren looked at it for all of ten seconds, then looked at each other.

"How long is a long shot?" Trout asked.

"It's a hell of a lot shorter than having to come back if we can't find any trace of them." Lauren had a set look on her face. She squared her shoulders and set off with scant regard for the fact that her dress and flip-flops weren't the most suitable gear for hiking in.

Trout set out after her, marvelling for the umpteenth time at how lucky he was to have found her.

They walked in silence as all their breath was needed for the climb. The trail started to rise almost immediately and climbed at a steady gradient within a thicket of furze, sallies and holly. Although the path was well defined it was impossible to see what lay to either side due to the density of the tangled vegetation. Likewise, ahead. The path twisted and curved, keeping the way forward shrouded in foliage. It was very quiet. An occasional bird pipped or some small out-of-sight animal rustled. Even the hum of the traffic from the port became muted. They hiked steadily upwards, enclosed in a hushed world with only dappled sunlight to accompany them, unaware that they had reached the top until Lauren took a step forward and found herself on the edge of a large clearing, outlined by a semicircle of the scrub and shrubbery they had travelled through.

Directly in front of her, a substantial log cabin seemed to float suspended between the sky and the sea. She gasped and closed her eyes to give them a chance to adjust to the brightness. When she opened them, it took her a moment to realize that the cabin was situated in a way that supported the illusion, whereas in reality it was well back from the edge of the cliff, with the sea spread out behind it like a cloak of azure silk floating from the shoulders of a giant.

Trout moved to stand beside her. "Nice view."

"You wouldn't want to suffer from vertigo."

"There is that. Looks like we've got a welcoming committee."

Lauren glanced around. Wraith-like figures in greys and greens and browns had appeared, silently and insubstantially. At first, they seemed almost indistinguishable from the bushes. Men with long straggling hair and even longer beards. Women in every type of clothing from long floaty dresses to sparkling silver mini-skirts to loose tunics over skintight leggings. Children peeped out from behind and between the adults.

It could be a scene from a by-gone era or a post-apocalyptic prophecy, Lauren thought, wondering if she was dreaming, or more likely hallucinating. Some of the adults moved further into the clearing and took substance from the sunlight, but as yet no word was spoken.

"Hi, Lauren. You're a long way from Knocknaclogga." A lazy male voice floated on the air towards where herself and Trout stood immobile.

Lauren started, then scanned the faces. One in particular claimed her attention. Large protruding eyes, startling blue, watched her from over a hooked nose. Fleshy lips, very red against a wispy grey beard, grinned at her. Exophthalmic, she thought – I know those eyes.

"Jazzer? Fancy meeting you here," she said faintly.

"Hi, Lauren." A low husky voice preceded a tall, slim woman as she moved with the grace of a dancer away from the crowd.

"V, good to see you. Are yourself and Jazzer gigging here?"

"Yeah. We're here for the Moon-fest at the weekend. Thought we'd have a couple of days' holiday while we're at it." V turned luminous eyes and regarded Trout intently. "This the guy you're hanging out with?"

"You could say that. Trout, I want you to meet V and Jazzer – they play the most amazing music."

"Pleased to meet you." Trout nodded.

"Don't mind these." Jazzer waved a hand at the people still standing on the verge of the scrub. "Simple curiosity. We all like to know who's gracing us with their company. Everybody hears the song of the scrub when someone arrives." The bulbous eyes twinkled at Lauren. "I've composed a piece that captures the sound. Maybe I'll play it for you later."

"I know you like music, Lauren, but I wouldn't have thought this would be your scene." V was looking at Lauren with a shrewdness that belied her casual words.

"You're right. We're looking for my goddaughter."

"You think she might be here?"

"We don't know. What we do know is that she arrived on the ferry with two friends Saturday evening. She got a fright when she saw someone unexpected at the station, someone that we think she was rightly afraid of. We're thinking herself and two friends might have walked in this direction."

V nodded. She looked at Jazzer. He nodded back.

"I've the kettle on," V said. "A cup of tea will revive you after the climb." She turned and, without waiting to see if they followed, swayed her way onto a path and out of sight.

Lauren and Trout moved to follow her. Jazzer fell in beside them. The others melted back into the bushes but now the air was filled with sound, soft talk, a snatch of a song, children laughing. It still had an air of unreality about it but Lauren felt more comfortable when she had Jazzer and V to vouch for them.

"I didn't see your van in the car park, Jazzer," she said.

He laughed. "Wasn't sure it would make the trip. We hitched a lift with Calamity Jane and Nutcase."

"They're the Crustys from over Dreeny way, right?"

"Yeah. Good people. You've met them at the market a couple of times."

"I have. Jane makes the most amazing sourdough bread." She slanted Trout a look. "Just don't buy the brownies if you're shopping at the market. It's on in the village hall, first Saturday of the month." She smiled mischievously. "The brownies are special order only."

"We won't be offering you brownies with your tea." Jazzer gave Lauren a wink. "Here we are."

The path ended at a small clearing where a structure, which from the outside looked somewhat like a giant copper cylinder with a lagging jacket around it, stood in the background.

V was lifting a steaming kettle from a crook over a fire-pit. "Sit."

She waved them towards a couple of deck chairs. There was also a three-legged stool and a director's chair as well as a flimsy-looking foldable table. Trout and Lauren sat where she indicated. She poured the water into a large ceramic teapot. The unmistakable scent of chamomile drifted in the air.

"Since Jazz gave up the caffeine, we only use herbal tea." V's husky voice held a trace of laughter. "Hope you can tolerate it."

"I like chamomile tea," Lauren grinned, "and yours is always so fresh and lovely."

Trout indicated the structure behind them. "Is that a yurt?"

Jazzer, in the process of placing four mugs on the table, said, "Yeah. Cool, isn't it? Want to have a look inside?"

"Yes, please." Lauren was on her feet in an instant. Trout followed her more slowly.

Jazzer lifted a flap and indicated they should enter. It was surprisingly spacious inside, circular, with an intricately patterned wooden floor. The walls were lined and swagged with what looked like woollen blankets, the edges tucked securely into a narrow strip of skirting board. A double mattress with a gorgeous patchwork quilt sat on a wooden dais taking up the whole left side. A black-and-white sheepskin rug covered the floor beside it and a carved wooden chest took up the space between the door and the bottom of the bed. A free-standing rail for clothing, an old-looking chest of drawers and stacked wicker baskets followed the curve of the interior almost back to the door on the right side. A large beanbag lay in front of them as if wondering what it was doing there.

"The winter yurts have a stove but this one doesn't need one. It's very warm and comfortable." Jazzer was looking around it with a delighted air.

"It certainly looks it," Lauren agreed.

"Romeo keeps the place in good nick. All of his establishments are well maintained."

"Who is Romeo?" Lauren kept her voice light. She glanced at Trout but he seemed content to let her continue.

"Romeo Ingels. He's the guy who set up the place." Jazzer talked with the ease of long friendship. "You might have heard of him, Lauren. He went off grid a few years ago and wrote a book about it."

"Of course. That's where I've heard the name before! It became one those unexpected bestsellers."

"Yeah, he did well out of it. Allowed him to buy this place and set it up. There must be a dozen dwellings hidden in the scrub. He's made each one seem like the only one, so you've got peace and privacy if you want it and neighbours if you don't."

"What about this Moon-Fest then? Some sort of a festival? I don't recall hearing of it before now."

"Have to be in the know to hear about it. It's billed as the annual fundraiser to cover ongoing maintenance costs for this place." Jazzer tapped the tip of his nose. "Know what I mean?" At Lauren's nod, he continued. "It's open to the public. You'd be surprised at the crowd it attracts."

From outside V's voice sang out. "Tea's ready!"

"Thanks for showing us the inside. I've often wondered what one was like." Lauren stood for a moment in the doorway to allow her eyes adjust to the light. There was something unreal about the whole situation. She found herself saying a prayer that these people had been able to offer refuge to Hannah and her friends. She had a feeling they'd be a lot safer here than in the so-called civilized world at the bottom of the hill.

CHAPTER 10

As Lauren moved outside, a movement in the scrub on her left drew her eyes. A woman, long grey-brown dreadlocks half-covering the back of once-red dungarees, was disappearing into the trees.

"Jane brought bread and hard-boiled eggs. I have cheese and relish. We thought you might be hungry after your trek." V's husky tones drew Lauren towards the table.

"Thank you. Now that I see food it does seem a long time since we ate."

V hefted the teapot and began to pour the aromatic yellow-green liquid into the cups. A rustling at the tree line caused her to raise her head and arrested her mid-pour. Lauren followed her gaze.

A Jesus-like figure emerged and glided towards them. Lauren gasped, shook her head and looked again. This time the apparition took the shape of a man, in a pristine white grandfather shirt that hung down over a pair of well-worn, very clean jeans. He walked with a long, loose-limbed stride that brought him close to them in seconds. His dark hair was long and his equally dark beard was trimmed to the contours or his face but it was his eyes that drew all Lauren's attention. They were a deep, dark brown that made her think of a rich chocolate fondue that tempted you to dip your finger in just to feel the velvety, bitter-sweetness on your tongue.

Trout moved beside her and slipped a proprietary arm around her waist. The apparition smiled and Lauren found herself grinning back at him as if they shared a secret no one else could know.

"Good evening, all." His voice was low with perfect diction and without any particular accent that she could decipher. He turned to smile at V. "I've come to meet your friends, V?" The question mark at the end was subtle, but it was a question nonetheless.

"Of course, Romeo. And you will join us in a cup of tea." V resumed pouring, while Jazzer produced a cup from some hidden recess. "Lauren was the first person to welcome me to Knocknaclogga when I arrived there. Oh my God, nearly thirty years ago." She turned to Lauren. "Where has the time gone?" She didn't require an answer, simply turned back to Romeo. "We've been friends since. Her friend I only know to see, but his reputation is that of a good man. Sit – we'll have tea and Lauren will tell us about her godchild."

So, they sat and Lauren told them the whole story from Marina's arrival to the present moment. If Trout was restive at times, she ignored it. She was convinced that only the whole truth would benefit them in this situation.

As it turned out, her faith was justified.

There was a long beat of silence when she finished. Everyone looked at Romeo. He sat in the director's chair, with his eyes closed, taking an occasional sip from his cup of tea. At last, he sat up straight. "Thank you for trusting us with the truth." He enunciated his words clearly, like someone who seldom talked but when he did makes every word count. "The young people did arrive here. They were badly frightened but were reluctant to tell us why. We didn't press the issue. When someone comes to us for refuge we rarely question why. One of them in particular was terrified. Your godchild, I would think."

"Are they still here?" Lauren asked eagerly.

"No. They were anxious to move on."

"And where were they heading, do you know?"

"Yes, I do. To Waterford."

"Why Waterford?" Trout sounded surprised.

"Let me explain." Then Romeo paused, looked at Lauren and smiled. "She had a look, a cast to her features that, now I see you, was an echo of your loveliness."

Lauren returned the smile, wondering was this guy for real? Beside her she felt Trout stir. A quick glance caught the tightening of his lips. She bit the inside of her cheek to keep from laughing outright and dragged her attention back to the hypnotic voice Romeo Ingels used to such good effect.

"She called herself Louise but somehow the name did not trip off her tongue with ease, thus I doubted its veracity."

"It's her middle name," Lauren murmured. "She's entitled to use it but rarely does."

Romeo nodded.

She needed to ask him again where Hannah had gone but, before she could, he continued with his account.

"We gave them the use of the Bunk Bus. There was room for all three in it and Otti, one of our permanent residents, organized food. Later, when they felt safe, they told me a little of their story, which you have confirmed." He thought for a moment. "It was difficult. They weren't sure they could trust us, perhaps were even a little frightened by the nature of this place. The girl, Louise, told me she was anxious to get to Clare where she had family who would know what to do." Again, he directed a smile at Lauren. "She offered to pay. I asked her had she much money, she said not on her. She was embarrassed, not sure what else to say. I salute her that she didn't try to pull the rich-parents scenario. I suggested she return when all was well and tell us the complete story as a compensation for whatever food and lodging we could provide. She readily agreed."

"It sounds like Louise did all the talking?" Trout sounded as if he was thinking out loud.

"On the contrary, the young man did his share – the other girl, less so."

"Did they give names?"

"David and Isla. None offered surnames, nor did I press the issue." He reached forward and placed his cup on the table, allowing his eyes to linger on the rose pattern for a moment before raising his head and resting his gaze on Lauren. "I considered the problem and realized I could offer a little assistance." He paused, added delicately, "We have a regular delivery on a Sunday evening – one of the freight lorries drops off our supplies in the parkway at the start of the track. I usually contact him to arrange a meet time on a Sunday morning. I offered to ask him to take them with him as far as Waterford, in case someone was watching the station here. That was where he was going. And there they would find a hostel and have access to transport."

"Right," Trout said. "And is that what happened?"

"Oh yes. It all went without a hitch. They rested here for the night and most of Sunday and that afternoon I accompanied them to meet Gregor. He drives an eighteen-wheeler and has a sleeper cab. He has no problem with a few passengers, as long as they stay out of sight. And I was able to assure him that they wouldn't be a problem for him."

"And you trusted him not to harm them?" Lauren tried to keep the doubt from her voice but feared she didn't succeed.

"Absolutely. Gregor is as honest as any truck driver and he doesn't want any trouble when on the road."

Lauren wasn't sure that was settling her fears but knew she had to be content with it. She looked at Trout. He rose to his feet.

"Thank you for telling us. We'd want to be going. It's after nine o'clock and will be getting dark soon." As he spoke, he looked around. The clearing was still bright but the sun was low in the sky, denoting the July evening was closing in. Consequently, the scrubland was looking black and uninviting.

Lauren stood up. "And thank you for taking care of Hannah, I mean Louise and her friends. We'd like to –" About to offer some recompense, she saw V shake her head urgently at her and added with a slight blush, "We'll let you know what happened, when we have them safely home."

V was nodding like a wooden puppet, beaming a relieved smile all around.

Lauren turned to her. "Thank you so much for the food and everything. I'll see you when you're back in Knocknaclogga."

"Great. I want to hear the whole story myself."

"I will send Harry with you," said Romeo. "The track is getting dark and there are places where you could be torpedoed by roots and such like." He clicked his fingers and a tall, thin individual appeared on the periphery of the clearing. Romeo turned, took Lauren's hand and raised it to his lips. "I look forward already to our next meeting."

"Thank you again." Lauren was annoyed with herself that she sounded a little breathless and once more felt the inappropriate desire to laugh when she heard Trout curtly adding his thanks.

They followed the silent Harry as he led them through the gloom of the scrub. An occasional grunt signalled a place where extra care was needed. He stopped well back from the end and said in a rusty-sounding voice, "One hundred metres – the car park." He turned and disappeared back the way they had come.

Trout muttered sotto-voce into her ear, "They've seen us safely off the premises."

They continued on their way, returning to the silence that had prevailed on their trek. They were about to step out of the tree-line bordering the car park when the clatter of an old vehicle vibrated in the still air. It stopped with the screech of brakes, working off metal-on-metal. It seemed very close to where they stood, within discerning distance of the entrance/exit from the car park into the scrub. The ensuing quiet didn't last long. The purr of a more powerful car could be heard and the glow of side lights panned across the trees. Trout lay a hand on Lauren's arm and motioned her to move quietly. Together they crept nearer the opening. Just before they reached it, he stilled her and drew her off the path and further into the scrub. When she asked him afterwards why, he couldn't say – it was a feeling that he had, one that he had learned to respect during his time in the Force.

The clunk of a door closing was very loud in the quiet.

A nondescript voice said, "Hey, man, this is the place."

It was so close Lauren started and would have stumbled back only Trout held her steady.

"You're sure?" a cold, hard voice with a barely perceptible American inflexion queried.

Lauren remembered cold, shark eyes and shivered.

"Yeah, man – leads to the top of the hill and the bunch of tossers that live there. Think themselves too good for the likes of me."

They heard the grating sound of someone hawking spit.

"Watch where you're spitting." The cold voice held a note of disgust.

"Got you here, didn't I? You got the bread?"

There was a moment of silence.

"I'll double it if you take me to the top."

"No shagging way, man. I'm not welcome in that there ivory tower. You're better off on your own. You won't drop me in it, will you?"

"I'll do what's necessary to find the information I seek."

The distain must have stung because at once the other whined, "I kept my part of the bargain, showed you the only other way someone could have got away from the port, didn't I?"

There was no answer. Eventually a door clanged and an engine coughed, spluttered and groaned into life. The vehicle started away with a crunch of tyres and spraying of gravel.

"*Bloody hell!*" A light flashed. "I'm at the path to the hippie commune."

A pause. He was on his phone.

"How the hell should I know? The road and the railway have drawn a blank. I'm told it's the only other way out of the port."

A pause.

"No. It's not an exit, merely a bolt hole if you can find the path."

Pause.

"Oh, all right. I suppose I'll have to."

And on that ungracious note silence returned, but only temporarily. Lights flashed as a car was locked and footsteps crunched on gravel.

"*Fuck! Fuck! Fuck!*"

The bitter swearing was so close Lauren thought she could see a puff of breath as the man passed. The flash of the phone torch briefly illuminated the path. Lauren silently said a fervent thanks that it was far enough beyond where they stood not to illuminate them.

They waited, immobile, until the sound of the footsteps had faded into the distance. Then, moving quietly, they hurried out from the trees, into the car park and headed to where Trout had left his car.

CHAPTER 11

The car park was deserted and looked forlorn in the half-light that preceded full darkness when they stepped out from the path hiding among the trees. The outlines of big rigs and containers awaiting pick-up were barely discernable in the far distance, nearer to the entrance from the port itself. Here, where the path began, only a handful of vehicles waited, most of them old and had seen better days. Trout's dusty Lexus was parked between a '94 VW Camper and a decommissioned P&T van, the logo faintly discernable through the flaked paintwork. Trout breathed a sigh of relief when he saw that the Lexus wouldn't be noticeable unless one was looking for it. On the other hand, the black Jeep Grand Cherokee with tinted rear windows, parked to the right of the concealed path, stuck out like a sore thumb.

Trout looked at it for a long moment. "I'm tempted to disable it," he said, "but I don't want to draw attention to our presence. As long as we can stay under the radar, we have an advantage over the Shark. Bob's name for him is very fitting, by the way."

"So it was the guy from the station?" Lauren fretted as she turned towards the Lexus.

"Most likely." Trout flashed the keys and the car blinked in response. "Sit in. I'll take a photo and get a good shot of the number plate in case we can get someone to run it for us. Probably some sort of a hire-car but it'll be helpful to know the number anyway."

"Do you think they'll tell him what they told us?" Lauren climbed on board, grabbed the seatbelt and proceeded to click it into place.

"I'm inclined to say no. Not the people we talked to anyway, but we don't know who else is up there and the Shark seems to be flashing a fair wad of cash from what we heard."

"*Damn and blast!*"

"Hey, look at the positive – so far we're ahead." Trout started the car and reversed into the gravelled driveway that ran grid-like throughout the parking area. "Pull up Google Maps and check the directions to Waterford. I'm pretty sure I know the way but I don't want any mistake to slow us down."

"What can we do at this hour of the night?" As she spoke Lauren swiped open her phone. "*Holy cow!* Twenty missed calls from Marina and messages as well."

"You can ring her in a minute. Get us on the road first. By my reckoning Waterford about an hour away."

"Fifty-seven minutes according to Google. Head southeast and turn right on the main road." She flicked to Marina's messages. She listened to a couple. "Wouldn't you think she'd know we're too busy trying to find Hannah to ring her?" she muttered, half-vexed. "This one was sent ten minutes ago." She lowered the volume, put the phone on speaker, and swiped. Marina's voice, shrill with panic, filled the space between them. "*Where are you, Lauren? Why don't you ring me? Don't you know I'm worried sick? And Karl is cross. He can't get here until tomorrow but either himself or his secretary has been on to me God only*

*knows how many times. He's contacted the Irish police to check yourself
and Trout out. Lauren, for God's sake ring me!"*

"You'd better ring her."

"Ring her? And tell her what? When Marina's like this there's no
talking to her. I'll send her a text, say we're on the trail and tell her say
a prayer we find Hannah soon. No, I won't say that – she'd read it as
Hannah being in immediate danger. Only she is, in danger that is, isn't
she, Trout? What can I say?"

"Just say you can't ring at the moment, that we're following a lead
and you'll ring her as soon you can."

"Yeah, that'll do." Chewing on her bottom lip, Lauren typed the
message and pressed send. "Maybe when we get to Waterford I'll send
her another message. Or something."

"Now, while you're at it, give a quick look at what accommodation
is available in Waterford."

She glanced at him, looked out at the headlights cutting through
the encroaching darkness. "I suppose we'll have to wait until morning
before we continue our search."

"You suppose correct." Trout softened his tone. "There's nothing
we can realistically do until then and we need to sleep some bit
ourselves. Otherwise, we won't to be able to keep going."

"Yeah, I guess you're right." Lauren sighed, swiped her phone and
opened a search. "Well, there's lots of hotels anyway. How will I narrow
it down?" She scrolled some more. "Trout, there's a hostel listed, at
least I think it's one." She frowned as she read the details. "It welcomes
backpackers. That could be a place to check out."

"For us?" Trout laced his voice with a smile.

"We-l-l...no...they're full for tonight anyway – but maybe there's somewhere nearby and then we'll be ready to check it in the morning."

Trout nodded. "Yes, possibly at this hour our best bet is to find a place in the hostel area and go in and ask if they have rooms available. Can you get the address and directions and we'll try that."

"Well, Google has picked up that I'm interested in Waterford and is bombarding me with all sorts of irrelevant information." Lauren was muttering away to herself as she scrolled and swiped. "Ash Lane, that's what I need to – *Jesus Christ! Oh my God! Stop, stop the car, Trout, I'm going to be sick!*"

"What is it? What have you found? Talk to me!" Trout indicated, pulled onto the hard-shoulder, stopped the car and engaged the hazard lights.

Lauren fumbled with her seat belt, scrabbled to open the door, tumbled out and staggered to where a steel crash barrier divided the road from the dark fields beyond it. Trout rushed around the car and came to stand beside her. She had one hand on the barrier and was gulping air as if she was suffocating. Her right hand was tightly clenched around her phone.

Trout put his arms around her and turned her gently to face him. "It's OK. Whatever it is, we can deal with it. What was on the phone?"

Hand trembling, she held out the phone. "It's in recent news."

Trout looked at her, took the phone and tapped it awake. A local news site came to life on the screen, bold headlines proclaiming: **BACKPACKERS INJURED IN UNPROVOKED ATTACK.** The item continued in smaller print: "**Three young backpackers stopped to ask for directions to a local Youth Hostel in**

Waterford city, at approximately 19.30 on Sunday evening. A local who wishes not to be named gave them the information and had directed them towards Ash Lane when a gang of youths accosted them and in the ensuing skirmish one of the backpackers, a young girl, was injured. She was taken to University Hospital Waterford where her condition is described as critical. Gardaí are appealing to the public for anyone who may have witnessed the incident or seen the three young people over the course of the day, to come forward and help them with their enquiries. The injured girl is between fifteen and seventeen years of age, of slim build and was wearing a yellow shirt over a multicoloured T-shirt. Contact Waterford Garda Station if you have any information."

CHAPTER 12

"*Christ*!" Trout blew out a breath. "OK. Let's not run ahead of ourselves." He looked at Lauren, noted her pallor but was relieved to see her breathing was steadier and she was dashing away tears with an impatient hand. "We'll head straight to the hospital and find out for sure if it's Hannah."

Lauren closed her eyes, took a deep breath and took her phone from Trout. She marched to the car, sat in and buckled up.

"At least it's a local news site so it's unlikely Marina will have seen it," she said.

"Even if she did, it will mean nothing to her. She doesn't know the details we know." Trout started the car and pulled back into the traffic, which had become noticeably less busy. "It just goes to show that it was just as well you didn't get to ring her. We're less than a half an hour from the city, so just pull up the directions to hospital and we'll go straight there."

Lauren did as she was bid and left the map open in the background while she scrolled through the news feed to see if there was any update on the backpacker news story. "They said it happened Sunday evening, today's Tuesday." She sighed. "Imagine, it's still Tuesday. It's like days have passed since eight o'clock this morning."

"We've got a lot done. Roundabout coming up. Which exit?"

"Second exit. There's a few roundabouts coming up. I'd better concentrate on the map. We're not that far out, a bit less than ten kilometres."

"And the traffic isn't too heavy at this hour of the night."

Concentrating on the route helped to shorten the remaining drive to the hospital.

Trout followed the signs for the Accident and Emergency Department and found a parking spot close by. "This is probably our best option for getting in." He looked at his watch. "Eleven-ten. Yeah, I reckon the main entrance is well closed by now."

The lighting in the car park was adequate while the A&E shone like a beacon in the night. They stood for a moment, side by side as if for solidarity, after exiting the car.

Lauren clutched at Trout's arm. "I'm frightened."

Trout turned her towards him. "I know. The thing is, Lauren, what you imagine is always more frightening than the reality. With the reality, you know what you're dealing with." He spoke softly, keeping his eyes locked on hers all the time.

"You're right, of course you're right. It's just that Hannah is so precious. If anything has happened to her . . ."

Trout linked his fingers with hers. "Come on, we'll go and find out what we can."

The glass doors parted with a swish as they approached and funneled them into a brightly lit waiting room. Rows of green and cream plastic chairs, bolted together and to the ground were arranged in groupings of four or six. An array of people in various stages of distress had their eyes glued to the pictures on a muted television in one corner, played with mobile phones or simply slumped in a fug of fatigue. A few raised their eyes to view the newcomers and as quickly dismissed them as of no drama. A security guard gave them the once-over and decided to await developments.

Trout and Lauren went straight to the reception desk.

A middle-aged woman with impossibly black hair looked up at Trout through a glass screen. She indicated the speaking holes and said, "How can I help you?"

"We'd like to talk to someone about the young backpacker. We saw the story on the news and think we may have some information that might help."

The receptionist blinked at him. "I'm afraid you're in the wrong department, sir. This is Accident and Emergency."

"Yes, but it's also gives entry to hospital once the main doors are closed."

"Only if you're a relative that's been called in for a crisis situation. In that case I'd have your name on my list. Currently I have no list, therefore no names."

"The thing is," Trout was at his most persuasive, "we think we may be able to identify the victim. To do that we need to see her."

"I don't know anything about that. I'd have thought it's the police station you'd be needing, not the hospital."

"Except we don't know for sure. Could you ask the staff of the unit where the patient is if we could visit for a few minutes?"

"I don't know if I can do that. My job is to take the details of patients attending A&E."

"What's the problem here, folks?" The security man, a burly fellow with an overhanging gut, had moved to stand beside Trout and Lauren.

"Oh Andy, these people think they might have information about that poor little girl in Intensive Care."

"Do they now? Perhaps if you come over here to my desk, we can talk about it. You're holding up the queue at the moment."

Neither Trout nor Lauren had noticed the four people who now were standing stoically behind them.

"My apologies." Trout raised a hand as he moved to one side.

Curving his arm around Lauren, he drew her with him after the security guard. They moved to a high desk that commanded a view of the whole room and saw that it also housed a row of monitors that showed various angles of various corridors. A younger, fitter version of the security guard was ensconced in front of the monitors. The older man led them behind the desk, well away from where the bulk of the public waited.

"Now," he said, "what are you saying about the assault victim? And if you know something, why haven't you already gone to the Gardaí?"

Trout debated with himself for a moment. "Look," he said, "is there anywhere more private where we can talk. Some of the information I have is sensitive and I would prefer if the general public couldn't overhear it." He kept his voice low.

The younger of the two glanced at him suspiciously, while the older one rocked back and forth on his heels, studying him thoughtfully.

"You a cop?"

"Ex. I'm now a private investigator. Thomas Tegan. This is my colleague, Lauren O'Loughlin." Trout held out his hand in a classic shake gesture.

After a moment's hesitation, the security guard took it and said, "Andy Calhoun. This is Chris Talon. We're the regular night security here at the hospital." He was still scrutinizing Trout with an intensity that bordered on uncomfortable.

Trout returned stare for stare and waited.

"Tegan. You're the guy who was in the news a couple of months ago. Pulled the rug from under that Dublin gang?"

Trout nodded.

"Put it there. That was a great job you did." And Andy grasped his hand again and this time pumped it enthusiastically. "Chris, come and say hello. We read everything we could lay our hands on about that in the papers, didn't we?" He stepped back as the younger man stood, all suspicion gone, but suddenly shy.

"I applied to join the Guards when I read about you," he said, the awe in his voice unmistakable. "I got through the interviews and everything and I'm waiting for a date to start."

"Well done. The force needs all the good men it can get." Trout was generous in his praise and, catching Lauren's eye, added, "Women too. Lauren was part of the equation for our success. Indeed, I'd go so far as to say I couldn't have done it without her."

Lauren was now greeted with equal enthusiasm. She smiled before saying tartly, "If the mutual admiration society has finished business, could we please find out what we came for?"

"Of course. Come on into the office and we'll talk. I presume I can fill Chris in afterwards?"

"Definitely but I would appreciate if it goes no further. As I said, it's sensitive and there is a possibility that anyone who is deemed to know too much might be in danger."

"*Wow!*" Chris's eyes went wide with excitement. "If you want us to help?"

"You watch the waiting room and the corridors," said Andy. "That's the help you can give at this moment. Come on in, Mr Tegan, Ms O'Loughlin, and we'll see if we can be of any assistance to you."

CHAPTER 13

Andy ushered them behind the desk and into a small, cramped office. A table, piled with a telephone and an assortment of papers, a floor-to-ceiling arrangement of shelves and pigeon-holes stuffed with files, keys and other paraphernalia, and four chairs were barely contained in the space. They sat on the regulation plastic chairs and Trout told him a condensed version of their investigation.

Andy listened with folded arms and his chair tilted recklessly on two legs. Occasionally he pursed his lips and when Trout finished said, "The Gardaí found no identification on the young one and the two, another girl and a young man, disappeared while the paramedics attended their friend."

"If what we saw on the CCTV at the train station is valid, they're afraid for their lives and that is no exaggeration." Trout's voice was grim.

"Please, do you think we could see her?" Lauren pleaded. "The clothes described in the news item were what my godchild was wearing in the video."

"I'll see what I can do. Let me think." He plopped the chair back on its four legs. "Angela is the duty manager tonight. She's not the worst of them." He reached for the phone. "You realize you'll need to talk to the Guards?"

"We thought we'd do that in the morning. When we see who's here, we'll be in a better position to answer their questions."

"Well, if you don't know the score, Mr Tegan, nobody does." He turned his concentration to the phone clamped to his ear. "Angela? I've a couple of people here who think they might be able to identify the little girl in ICU. Thomas Tegan and Lauren O'Loughlin. Ms O'Loughlin thinks the girl may be a relation of hers. They were on their way from Rosslare when they saw the press release." He paused. "OK."

He dropped the phone back on its cradle and looked at Lauren's expectant face. "Angela will be here in a couple minutes. I'd say she'll let ye in but she'll want to know what the story is. Powerful nosy Angela is – we'll have to warn her to keep her trap shut." He gave a long-suffering sigh. "All I can say is good luck with that one."

It wasn't that long, although it felt longer in the cramped office, until the night manager arrived. She was a big-boned woman, with dark hair severely pinned back from her face. She had two rosy spots of aggravation mottling her cheekbones. They heard her mutter to Chris as she passed, "This place would drive anyone insane." Nonetheless as she marched into the office, she plastered a smile on her face and examined first Trout, then Lauren with a quizzical expression.

"You think you know who the young girl is," she said abruptly.

Both Trout and Lauren stood up.

Lauren answered. "We have reason to believe she is my cousin and godchild."

"What reason?"

85

"Perhaps you'd like to sit for a minute and we'll tell you," Trout intervened smoothly.

"I really don't have time for this. I haven't finished my rounds yet." Still, she moved further into the office and leaned against the wall. "I'll stand. If I sit down now, I might never get up again. Go on, I'm listening."

Trout gave an even more condensed version of events. Out of the corner of his eye he could see Andy nodding approvingly. "You understand our concern, given this unknown person who the youngsters seem to be mortally afraid of and our need to find them asap."

Angela's gaze had flickered between Trout and Lauren as she listened. When he finished, she remained silent for a couple of seconds, then with a suddenness that probably made her a good manager and a possible thorn in the side of her staff, made her decision. "Come on. I'll take you to ICU," she said.

She led them with a long loose-limbed stride out of A and E.

They hastily thanked Andy and hurried after her.

She led them past a bank of elevators, "Stupid things take all night, we'd be above while we're waiting for it," up the stairs, "ICU is on the second floor." All the while she passed comment on where they were, what they passed or life in general. She didn't seem to require an answer which was just as well as it took all of Trout and Lauren's breath to keep up with her.

She waited for them to catch up outside a double door of opaque glass, said a brusque "OK," pulled out an ID card on a long retractable string that was clipped to her tunic and swiped it across the keypad on the left of the door.

She led them into a long dimly lit room. Directly in front of them a curved nurse's station separated the patient area from the public entry. Five beds, well-spaced apart, lay beyond the desk, drapes half closed to give the illusion of privacy. Two small rooms completely separate from the main space at either end designated isolation areas. Two nurses worked at computers on the desk. Two more moved between the beds checking monitors, adjusting drips and writing notes.

Lauren took a deep breath and steadied herself. The distinct sound of an intensive unit, the hiss of oxygen, the rhythmic gurgling of ventilators and the intermittent beeping of machines designed to keep a person alive, hammered at her ears. Her nose tingled from the smell of disinfectant and, in spite of her careful breathing, her pulse went into overdrive. She braced herself for what she might find.

"These two want to have a look at the young one." Angela waved a hand in the general direction of Trout and Lauren. "How is she now?"

The nurse at the desk looked at them curiously but only said, "She's relatively stable. We unhooked her from the ventilator, as Dr Quinn ordered, about an hour ago and so far, so good. Kay will be able to give you a full account. She's with her tonight." She called quietly to her colleague on the floor. "Kay, these people are here to see your patient!"

A slim dark-haired girl looked around, nodded, pressed a button they saw was recording the patient's vital statistics and came to the end of the bed to meet them.

Angela again led the way. She lowered her voice to a husky whisper. "Outline the condition of your patient, nurse."

Keeping her voice low and even, Kay said, "A young girl, possibly late teens, brought in with trauma to the head on Sunday evening. Extensive brain swelling was discovered on CT. The admitting doctor ordered her to be placed into an induced coma for forty-eight hours and attached to life support for the duration. This evening's follow-up CT showed the swelling markedly decreased and the doctor recommended weaning her off the ventilator and monitoring her stats to ensure she remains stable. At this moment she's been breathing unassisted for an hour and we have begun the process of bringing her out of the comatose state."

Lauren was listening with her heart in her mouth as the nurse made her report. She was unable to see the girl properly because of the angle of the bed and the assortment of machines surrounding her.

Angela was saying softly, "This lady thinks she might be her cousin."

Kay looked at Lauren. "Come closer and see her."

Lauren nodded and followed Kay to the head of the bed.

The girl was almost transparent she was so pale with a red track from the corner of her mouth around her lower face from where the airway device had been secured. It looked livid against her white skin. Her dark hair was in a tangled cloud around her head. She seemed very small and vulnerable surrounded by the hissing, sighing, beeping machines.

Lauren reached forward and touched her hand. It felt warm and she found this reassuring. She turned to Kay with tears running down her cheeks.

"It's not my godchild. We were told this girl's name is Isla. Unfortunately, there was no mention of a surname but I'm sure once we give our information to the Gardaí they'll know where to look for it." She turned back to the bed and gently took the girl's hand between her own. Speaking softly, she said, "If you can hear me, Isla, I'm Lauren, Hannah's godmother. I can see you're a good friend of hers so I want you to know we're looking out for her and for David. You concentrate on getting better and we'll be back to see you soon." She held the small hand gently for another minute as she said a silent prayer that all would be well, before placing it back on the bed.

"Thank you," she said to Kay, who simply smiled and nodded.

She turned and picked her way back to where Trout and Angela waited.

"It's not Hannah. It's her friend. I told Kay we believe her name is Isla. Oh Trout," she reached out a trembling hand, "I feel so guilty about being relieved that it's not Hannah. That poor girl!"

Trout took her hand.

"At least you'll be able to point the Guards in the direction of who she is." Angela was brisk and businesslike. "I'll show you down and you can sort out the rest of it." She glanced at her watch and sighed. "I'd say later on today will be time enough."

Trout and Lauren spoke quietly, profuse in their thanks to Kay and made their way out the door after Angela.

CHAPTER 14

"We need somewhere to stay and something to eat." Trout pulled his phone from his pocket and opened a search. "There's a hotel that looks to be about ten minutes away. I'll give them a call."

Himself and Lauren were sitting in the car. They had left the hospital quickly after the visit to ICU, stopping briefly to update the two security men and thank them for their help.

Trout could see Lauren had expended all the energy that had kept her going throughout the day. He had supported her back to the car and now she slumped in the passenger seat, too spent to even talk.

In his ear he heard a female voice asking how she could help him.

He gave his name and explained that they were just leaving the hospital and needed a room for the remainder of the night, then requested some food when she said there was a room available.

"Thank you. We'll be with you in less than ten minutes," he said.

He closed the phone, placed it on the dash and started the car. "OK, Lauren. We'll eat and rest and cross tomorrow's bridges, or, should I say today's, when we've done that." He was pleased to see her attempt a smile, leaned over and kissed her. "We'll find them. Things will look better after some sleep."

"I wonder why Isla was wearing Hannah's shirt? Trout – I'm afraid – could it be a case of mistaken identity?"

He kissed her gently again. "Lauren, just rest now. Hopefully we'll find out more in the morning."

In spite of not getting to bed until after two, they were down for breakfast by eight. One of TLCI's or at least Trout's edicts was that they each keep a bag with basic overnight requirements in the office. He had slung them into the boot as a matter of form before they left and both of them were grateful for the chance to face the world looking and feeling somewhat refreshed.

They discussed their plans for the day over a full Irish and a gallon of coffee.

"The Garda station first. Hopefully whoever caught the case will be available and we can fill him," Trout caught Lauren's eye, "or her in, on what we know."

"Will they share anything with us?" Lauren was back to her optimistic self after a peaceful albeit short night's sleep.

"They might. It will depend on a few things and, of course, what they know as against what we can tell them." He smiled at her, a slow satisfied smile, and thought how calm and practical she was after the harrowing day they had yesterday.

"It's just that we seem to be back to square one, with even less of an idea as to where to go from here," she said.

"I wouldn't say that. We can find the hostel and check it out. They may have stayed there."

"Or they may not. Given that they were identified as backpackers and were asking for directions, they may have feared that it would be too obvious to anyone looking for them."

"True, but you know, Lauren, until we've talked to the Gardaí we haven't enough information to decide anything."

"Then what are we waiting for? I'm finished here, and it'll take all of two minutes to put our bags together. If you don't mind, I can do that while you settle the bill and we'll be out of here in next to no time."

"Right." Trout downed the last mouthful of coffee. "You do that, I'll do the other and we'll meet in the foyer in five minutes."

Lauren raised an eyebrow at him, laughed, and said, "You're on." She rose in one graceful movement and hurried out of the dining room.

She was waiting for him in the foyer when he arrived. "Four minutes and forty-five seconds. You thought I couldn't do it."

"Would I be guilty of such a thought?"

"Yes. But that's all right. I knew I could do it."

They laughed together and Trout snatched a quick kiss. "I'm glad you're with me, Lauren O'Loughlin. Let's go – we have a couple of teens to find." He picked up the bags.

"I promised Isla we would."

"Do you think she could hear you?"

"I don't know but I've read enough to believe that even when a person is unconscious there's a level where spirit, or consciousness or soul or whatever you want to call it, is alert and aware of its space."

They left the hotel and headed for the car.

CHAPTER 15

The Garda Station was exactly where Google said it would be. Trout found parking on a street nearby and together they climbed steps that gave access to the large modern building. The desk sergeant, his insignia designating him so, took their details.

"So, you think you have information that will help identify the young backpackers who were the subjects of the assault?" He was a good-looking young man, already showing signs of fatigue at the peculiarities of the human species.

"We know we have information that will help." Trout spoke with quiet authority.

The young man's gaze sharpened. "Are you the same Tegan who sorted out that problem in Dublin a couple of months back?"

"Possibly."

"My sister works in Dublin Castle. She says you're the real deal." He smiled and his face was transformed. "You can't always accept a woman's assessment – in case she's blinded by a pretty face." He grinned. "Of course, we males can be accused likewise." He sobered as fast. "If you just hold on for a minute, I'll get someone to talk to you." He ignored the telephone on the ledge in front of him and disappeared into a cubbyhole at the back of the desk. They could hear a rumble of talk as he consulted with someone out of sight.

Trout raised an eyebrow at Lauren, looked around and indicated a couple of seats by the wall. She shook her head and moved to read the notices stuck higgledy-piggledy on a cork board. Trout leaned against the desk. Where the sergeant had talked to them had a reinforced glass protector with speaker holes. He noted it only covered the immediate area around whoever was manning it – further along the desk was open albeit too high for an ordinary mortal to vault it easily. He eyed the noticeboard but Covid advice, the Garda hotline number or information about dog licences held no interest for him.

The sergeant was back in a couple of minutes. "If you go through the door there on the left, sir, Inspector Eacrett's office is the third door on the right."

"Thank you. Come on, Lauren."

The sergeant pressed a buzzer and the indicated door opened. He leaned across the unprotected part of the desk and said quietly, "Mr Tegan, Inspector Eacrett can be a bit – a bit hasty. We don't all agree with him."

Trout held his gaze for a long minute, nodded and followed Lauren through the door.

The third door on the right was halfway along an artificially lighted corridor. A big man was standing half in half out of it, watching them proceed towards him. He was more than regulation height but his girth was such that it made him look smaller. He examined them, unsmiling, with a look Trout found hard to identify. To the best of his knowledge, he had never met the man before.

As they drew level he spoke. "Well, if it isn't the great Tegan himself. Come to bring a bit of help to the country cousins, Tommy, or what's this they call you? Something fishy – Barracuda or Pollock or something like that." He smiled in as close a proximity to a sneer as made no difference.

Lauren faltered at the fake bonhomie in his voice, frowned and stopped just short of the threshold.

Trout studied his would-be intimidator and said softly, "I don't think we've met."

"We haven't but that doesn't stop me knowing you. You could say your reputation proceeds you – Saviour of the Force and all that."

"We have information we believe could be of assistance in a case I'm led to believe you're in charge of," said Trout. "If you're not interested, we won't take up your time."

"Who said I wasn't interested? Sensitive little soul, aren't you, that can't take a bit of ribbing?" The big man laughed. "I hear you think you're Sherlock Homes now, or would you be more the Mike Hammer type?"

"Come on, Lauren. I don't think our information is wanted here. "

"*Inspector Eacrett!*" a woman's voice called sharply from inside the room.

"Ah, feck it! I was only having a bit of fun." He bared his teeth in a conciliatory smile. "Come in and meet my sergeant – she's a fan anyway." He stood aside and pointedly waited for them to enter.

Trout waited a heartbeat, weighed up the possibility of an exchange of information, thought it unlikely but who knew, and guided Lauren into an unexpectedly tidy office. A large modern desk took up half the space, with files in orderly piles on either side. A neat woman in regulation pants and shirt stood beside it, with a look of acute embarrassment on her face. She was mid-to-late thirties and looked fit and healthy, apart from the two red spots of anger or shame that bloomed on her cheeks. She looked at Trout as if she would like to apologize but he understood she was constrained by having to work with the man.

The big man sauntered in after them, closed the door quietly behind them, went behind the desk, hitched his pants and sat down.

"No offence, Tegan," he said. "Just a little test of my own devising to see if a man's worthy of my attention. When all's said and done, you're after information, whatever way you disguise it." He looked at Trout, his eyes shrewd and calculating. "You're a private dick – whatever you know won't be the same as what we know."

Trout felt Lauren draw a deep, angry breath and laid a pacifying hand on her arm. She looked at him, her eyes stormy, hesitated and dropped her gaze.

Trout turned, with lazy indifference, to meet the inspector's gaze. "Well analyzed," he said. "Perhaps we should come to terms before we proceed if that's the case."

"That depends on what you have for me."

"I have nothing for you, Inspector, but I am willing to share my information if you share yours. That is, if what you have is worth sharing."

"I don't believe this," Lauren muttered under her breath.

"What are you offering?" the inspector asked.

"The names of the backpackers and a possible back-story." Trout was conscious of the sharp inhalation from the sergeant. "What have you?"

The inspector drummed fingers like giant sausages on the desk. He looked sideways at his sergeant. "CCTV footage from the incident."

"Done." Trout held out a hand.

The big man smirked and slapped down hard on it. "Seamus Eacrett." He pointed to himself, jerked a thumb at the woman. "Sergeant Pamela O'Leary. No pull with Ryan Air but a handy little sergeant all the same."

Sergeant O'Leary tightened her lips, gave a nod towards where Trout and Lauren were standing, swiped open a phone and sat with a stylus poised over it.

"Sit down, will ye, and don't be trying to intimidate me." Inspector Eacrett laughed again and pointed to the two chairs in front of the desk.

Trout pulled one back for Lauren before seating himself in the other. His thoughts were swirling in contrast to his measured movements. He'd like to see that CCTV but he'd have to be careful not to underestimate the inspector. His bulk might slow him physically but his mind would devise ways and means with a cunning that wasn't lost on Trout. He sat back and crossed a leg over a knee.

"It began for us yesterday morning," he said in his best storytelling voice and proceeded to give a limited-edition account of what had happened over the past twenty-four hours or so.

Eacrett watched Trout all the time he was talking and listened as if he was assessing the quality of the merchandise.

"Your people will be in a better position to check the passenger list for surnames for Isla and David and perhaps you'd have some facial recognition software to identify them and the man that seems to be following them."

"Facial recognition what-ware?" Eacrett guffawed. "Where do you think you are, the set of *CSI*?"

Sergeant O'Leary had been tapping away diligently on her phone. Now she looked up with a frown.

"Do you think this unknown man poses a serious threat to the youngsters?" she asked.

"Yes. Unfortunately, we do."

"Do you have any idea why?"

"No."

"Unless," Lauren spoke carefully, "it's something to do with Hannah's father."

"And who might he be?" Eacrett made no effort to sound pleasant.

"Karl Offenbach."

"Karl Offenbach? Of KOE international?" the inspector almost snarled. "Fecking hell, why didn't you say so in the first place?" He surged to his feet. "Come on, the incident room is upstairs."

CHAPTER 16

Trout and Lauren looked at each other and as one at Sergeant O'Leary.

She shook her head and asked quietly, "What is KOE International?"

"It's one of the most traded conglomerates in the world with billions of dollars in assets, and has a worldwide presence."

"He must have shares," she said dryly. "We'd better follow him."

"Really, Trout – 'I'll trade you if you trade me'? I didn't know you went in for ass-dealing." Lauren couldn't resist muttering in his ear as she stood up.

"Know your man and be with him," he shot back equally sotto-voce and grinned at her. "It worked, didn't it?"

For a big man Eacrett had a turn of speed worthy of an elite athlete. He was powering down the corridor when they exited the office. They followed him. Trout managed to catch the double-doors at the end before they hit him in the face. He held them open to allow Lauren and Pamela O'Leary through and they hurried up the polished concrete stairs after Eacrett. He led them like a homing pigeon along a corresponding corridor on the second floor and into a room at the end.

"Find Denny and Carew and get them in here asap!" he barked at the sergeant, with barely a hint of breathlessness in his voice.

Lauren had to admit to herself, as she breathed slowly and deeply to get her breath back, that she was impressed. She looked around and took in her surroundings. Her first impression was of a small classroom, a dozen chairs, somewhat less small tables all facing towards the wall at the end. A projector hung in front of it and, as she moved further in, she saw that half the wall was covered with some sort of pliable material, cork she thought. It had pictures stuck all over the upper half. She moved closer as if drawn by a magnetic force from outside herself and looked closely at the stills. That was what she thought they were, stills from closed circuit cameras, a lot of them grainy and poorly defined. Still, she could recognize the three young people from the video in Rosslare. They were shown walking on a street she didn't recognize, talking with a man pointing off to his left on a different street, and shockingly, one showed Isla lying still on the ground, Hannah kneeling beside her, the young man David in mid-swing of a backpack in an attempt to scatter a dozen youths that were frozen in snarling violence against the three.

"He tried to defend them." Trout was standing beside her. "If that's what they have they don't have much."

"That's what we have," Eacrett's heavy voice said from Lauren's other side. "And some dashcam footage of two backpackers hitching on the Newrath road, who may or may not be them. I'm hoping you can tell me that."

"Where does the Newrath road lead to?" Lauren was trying to picture a map of the southern part of Ireland in her head.

"Anywhere you might like. There's a roundabout with roads to the rest of Ireland off it, just beyond Newrath village."

"Would it bring you to Limerick or Clare?"

"Eventually but it wouldn't be my first-choice route for either. Limerick is too out of the way, but I suppose if you were taking a scenic route to Clare you'd get there eventually. I'll show you what we have."

Two men strolled in while he was talking. A neatly suited individual, sporting a well-trimmed red beard, and a scruffy party in a leather biker jacket, black hair greased into a cross between a mohawk and a quiff. They nodded at Eacrett and surveyed Trout and Lauren with open curiosity.

"Detectives Denny Woulfe and Lorcan Carew." Inspector Eacrett waved a hand at the two, without distinguishing which was which. "Seeing as the case has taken a sinister turn, I'm putting two of my best men on the job. Boys, this here is Thomas Tegan and his side-kick Lauren O'Loughlin. *Aha!* I see the boys recognize your name." He turned pointedly to Trout. "Told you they were good."

The men nodded a greeting.

The redhead, with a look at the inspector that Lauren couldn't decide was defiant or apologetic, said, "Denny Woulfe. It's an honour to meet you, Mr Tegan."

"A bit blinkered at times," Eacrett added sourly, "but good all the same. Find a pew and Pammy will set the video rolling."

Trout pulled out two chairs and himself and Lauren sat. The two newcomers perched on the edges of tables. Eacrett stayed standing.

Sergeant O'Leary fiddled with the controls of the projector and in a few seconds the wall beside the case board filled with a ghostly image of the three young people.

"Get the light, Lorcan, will you, please?" she said.

With the room in semi-darkness the image became clearer. The sergeant pressed the controls some more, the image sharpened and began to play.

"Here's where we picked them up on Watery Street," said the inspector.

Three young people were standing and, if not arguing, were at the least having an animated conversation. The features of all were blurred but Lauren could easily identify Hannah and recognize Isla, looking tiny but more robust than the wan creature she had seen in the hospital. She noticed that Hannah was carrying her shirt and that Isla was drooping and dejected-looking. As they watched she swung off her backpack, dropped it on the ground in front of her and rubbed her arms as if she was cold. Hannah held out her shirt. Isla shook her head. David watched them, his stance impatient. Hannah shook out the shirt and held it until Isla gave her a watery smile and pushed her arms into it. David picked up Isla's backpack and smiled at her. His face was transformed by a softness that said as loud as words "She's mine". Yet it somehow seemed to Lauren that David's look didn't show the possessiveness of a boyfriend. She stored the image away to think about later, murmuring, "I wondered why Isla was wearing Hannah's shirt." She watched, her heart hammering, as the silent pantomime was being played out.

Hannah said something to David. His face took on a mulish look but he shrugged. She turned and smiled at someone coming into the picture.

"The next we see is the do-gooder man by the name of O'Hare, giving them directions to the hostel. Don't know why they didn't use their phones, but it's a bitch of a place to find at the best of times. The next time a camera picks them up is here."

The three young people had stopped, the tiredness still in evidence, but they were looking warily at a bunch of teenagers, boys and girls around their own age, who had confronted them on the street.

"*Damn!*" Trout swore. "The mob smell their vulnerability. It was a wrong-time, wrong-place job."

The lad they knew as David moved in front of the girls and this appeared to set off a round of jeering, going by the faces of the gang accosting them. Isla had her arms wrapped around herself, hugging Hannah's shirt tightly to her body. The gang swaggered forward, crowding around the three. In a fast move David swung Isla's backpack in a circle around the mob, causing them to step back. A hand grasped at Isla who jumped, twirled around, caught her foot on a bicycle stand and fell with a thud that vibrated on the screen. She lay completely still. Hannah's mouth opened in a silent scream as she rushed to her friend and dropped on her knees beside her. David snarled and swung the backpack again. A blocky lad in the forefront of the gang, made a chopping motion with his hand and the whole lot of them turned and ran.

One girl hesitated, said something to David, who was now looking at Hannah and Isla with a dazed expression. She pulled out a mobile phone, dialled and spoke urgently into it.

Lauren's heart was pounding as if it would break out of her chest. She feared that she would burst into tears, the whole debacle was so heart-wrenching to watch.

"At least one of them had enough decency to try and help." Eacrett said heavily as the scene continued to unfold.

The girl with the phone said something more, turned and ran. David lifted his head and for the first time they had an almost clear look at a narrow intense face with the scraggy growth of a couple of days' beard.

Almost immediately an ambulance came rushing up the street and stopped beside them, its lights twirling on screen, and two paramedics joined the girls. They gestured to Hannah to move away and she stood. David still held Isla's backpack. He looked stricken but suddenly seemed to wake up.

"The ambulance was coming from an aborted call and was redeployed. They were there in less than a minute," Eacrett's heavy voice droned in the background.

On screen David pulled Hannah back from where the ambulance crew were working on Isla. He said something to her and she whirled to face him. A short swift argument ensued before he grabbed her arm and pulled her away from the scene. They faded out of the picture.

"They had enough savvy to keep the argument quiet. The paramedics didn't know they had gone until they turned to ask them a question."

There was a pause and a new scene came up.

"This is our next pick-up, dashcam, the following morning from a passing motorist."

Two backpackers trudged along the hard-shoulder of a wide road. They became clearer as the car came nearer to them, showing the back view a tall angular male and a smaller more shapely female, his frame distorted by the pack on his back, hers outlined by a smaller pack. The lad half-turned as the car approached and stuck out his thumb. They could see the shadow of a smaller pack he was carrying in his other hand. The car passed them quickly.

The screen went blank. One of the detectives turned on the lights. They all blinked for a moment.

Eacrett said, "We've no other reported sightings but that's only a matter of time. This is Ireland, people see things and sometimes they even tell us."

"What was that there in the distance?" Lauren asked suddenly. "It looked like a filling station."

"Yeah. A popular truck-stop. There's no sign of them on its CCTV nor has anyone come forward to say they picked them up." Eacrett turned to the detectives. "These two have given us potential identities for the three and reason to believe that they may be in danger. I want you to –"

The door had opened. The desk sergeant stuck his head in.

"*Yes, what it?*" Earcrett barked.

"Sir. There's a gent at the desk wants to talk to someone about a possible disappearance. Says he's head of security for something called KOE International, and that he's tracked the relevant party from Rosslare to Waterford."

CHAPTER 17

A beat of silence greeted his announcement. The sergeant glanced around, panning across each face in turn, lingering longest on the inspector.

"Well, well, well," said Eacrett. "This gets more and more interesting. Send him up, Sergeant."

Trout looked at Lauren, a perplexed frown drawing his brows together. "Surely Marina would have told us if Karl had put his own security people on to finding Hannah?"

"I'm ringing Marina," Lauren said. "There's no way Karl knew that Hannah was missing before she told him." She suited action to her words and pulled her phone from her bag. Still talking, she stood up. "Marina told him Sunday evening, that guy we saw was already in Rosslare Saturday. He couldn't be Karl's security chief. And why would Hannah have anything to fear from him?"

She moved to the far side of the room, swiping the phone as she went. Before it went to a second ring, Marina's voice was squawking in her ear.

"*Lauren? Where are you? Why didn't you ring me? The stupid text message you sent last night told me nothing. Where the hell are you?*

Karl is here. He was expecting to meet you. He wants to talk to yourself and Trout."

Marina was forced to take a breath. Lauren grabbed the chance.

"Calm down, Marina. Did Karl set his security people to looking for Hannah?"

"What? What security people?"

"That's what I'm asking you. Did Karl send his head of security to look for Hannah?"

"How would I know. *Oh!*"

A smooth mid-Atlantic accent filled her ear. "Lauren. Karl here."

"Oh! Hello, Karl."

"What's going on? Have you found Hannah?"

"Not yet but we have some leads. Karl, did you send your head of security after Hannah?"

"My head of security?" Karl enunciated each word using his precise CEO voice, as if he was pondering the question, before adding crisply, "What name?"

"Don't know his name yet. On the off-chance that it's the same character we've already come across, I'll say medium height, broad shoulders, Clark Gable moustache."

"That sounds like Larry Caligula. He is head of security in our British office but he's the last person I'd send after Hannah. If I had sent anyone, which I didn't."

"Why?"

"Why?"

"Why wouldn't you send him after Hannah?"

"The question is moot. I didn't send him. Hannah abhors him, says he gives her the creeps." His voice sharpened. "Why are you asking about him?"

"Some guy has arrived here to Waterford Garda Station, saying he is representing the head of KOE International – that's you, isn't it?" On Karl's affirmative she continued, "He says he's looking into a potential disappearance. That he's tracked the party from Rosslare to Waterford. We're waiting to hear who he is and what he has to say. He's on his way upstairs to where we are."

"What are you doing in Waterford Garda station?"

"We were interested in seeing some CCTV we heard they had, showing some backpackers. Look, Karl, I have to go. I'll ring you back."

"We'll come to Waterford. Who do I look for at the Garda Station?"

"Are you sure that's the best thing to do?"

"We can't stay here twiddling our thumbs. At least if we're in the vicinity we might be able to do something. Who do I ask for?"

"Inspector Seamus Eacrett. I really have to go." She swiped the phone to disengage. "Karl knows nothing about him," she said directly to Eacrett.

He nodded. "Sit there and be quiet. Pamela, cover the board and make sure the projector is off. We'll have a little look-see as to what this gent is all about."

CHAPTER 18

Lauren had barely composed herself when the door opened and the desk sergeant ushered the shark-eyed guy from Rosslare train station into the room. Medium height or a bit along with it, round head sitting on broad shoulders and a Clarke Gable moustache. Exactly as Lauren remembered him from Rosslare. He marched into the room like a soldier on parade.

Trout nodded at Eacrett, who beamed an expansive smile at the newcomer. "Welcome to Waterford, Mr –?"

"Caligula. Larry Caligula. I'm the head of security with KOE International, based in London"

Lauren wondered if he had a military background, given the stance and the clipped way he barked the information.

"Imagine that now. London, you say." Eacrett examined him, with his head on one side. "That's powerful like an American accent you're sporting."

"That's because I am American," Larry's cold eyes scanned the insignia on Eacrett's shirt, and correctly added, "Inspector –?"

"Eacrett. Seamus Eacrett." The inspector made no move to introduce the rest of the people in the room. "London. Big change from US of A. Are you settling in all right?"

"I've been in London five years, Inspector. I'm well settled in." Caligula was starting to sound impatient.

"And now you're here. Whereabouts are you from? I've a brother in New York, Queens. You might have heard of it?"

"I'm a New Yorker myself, Inspector, but it's a city of nine million people, give or take. We can't know everyone there."

"Sure, how could you? We don't know everyone in our own little island and its only half that amount of people." Eacrett settled himself on the edge of a desk. It creaked ominously but held firm. He beamed benignly at Caligula. "And how might we be of assistance to you, Larry? I may call you Larry, I presume?"

"Of course."

"Would you have a little bit of an ID now, Larry, so we could be sure you are who you say you are? It's not that we doubt you, but you can't be too careful with all the different people that rock up here these days."

Lauren raised an eyebrow at Trout. Eacrett was hamming it to such a degree that Caligula would surely become suspicious. Trout shrugged. Caligula seemed to take it as normal.

"It's in my wallet. I need to reach into my inside pocket to get it."

"Work away. This isn't a movie and this isn't US of A so we don't expect you to produce a gun." The inspector was at his expansive best.

Caligula hesitated, made a grimace that could be a smile. "Of course not," he said.

Lauren blinked and quickly averted her head, He has a gun, she thought, and although they were in an Irish Garda Station she immediately felt a hum of low-level apprehension. Karl's assertion that Hannah abhorred Caligula bothered her. Her godchild had good instincts and, if she didn't trust the KOE security chief, Lauren was willing to back her any day.

The man in question had handed over a laminated card with an embossed security logo that caught the light and shone a rainbow of colours that Lauren had no difficulty seeing from where she was sitting.

"Very nice." Eacrett turned it round and round, his big paws almost engulfing it. He handed it to Sergeant O'Leary. "Make a copy of that, Sergeant," adding a belated "please," as she took it. "Take a seat, Larry, and tell us what we can do for you."

"Perhaps we can be mutually helpful." Caligula eyed the big man and reluctantly sat down. He waited but when nobody said anything, added, "We have reason to believe that Hannah Offenbach, daughter of Karl Offenbach, CEO and owner of KOE International, is in Ireland, possibly the victim of a scam or, in a worst-case scenario, a kidnap."

"Who are 'we', might I ask?"

"The security team at head office in London."

"That being yourself?"

"Well, yes. I am head of that team."

"A kidnap is serious now. Have you had a ransom note or what is it that makes you think she's kidnapped? What age is she anyway?"

"She's fifteen, still a minor in the eyes of the law. I don't know for definite that she's kidnapped but I've reason to believe that she travelled to Ireland in the company of a young man."

"Did she now? Maybe she's gone off on a little skite of her own? Fifteen-year-olds nowadays!" Eacrett shook his head. "Sure, they think they're all grown-up and they as wet as a new-born puppy behind the ears."

Lauren caught the rapidly concealed irritation that crossed Caligula's face and wondered again if Eacrett was laying it on too thick.

"I believe Hannah is a bit of a handful," said Caligula, "but at the same time I don't think she's the type to do anything too out of the way."

"And what does her father say? And her mother too? I presume she has a mother?"

"Naturally she has a mother. She is, I believe, currently somewhere in Europe. Her father is busy and I don't want to disturb him unnecessarily."

Lauren stirred restively. Trout lay a placating hand on her arm. She looked at it and gradually allowed herself to relax.

"Modern parents!" Eacrett shook his head, a lugubrious expression giving him more prominent jowls. "Still, you sound like you know the girl well, Larry. A friend of the family, are you?"

"No, not as such but Hannah has visited the offices with her father over the years and I have got to know her fairly well. She was, is gregarious and friendly, and I guess when she was younger she was something of a pet of everyone."

"So, what makes you think she's been coerced into coming to Ireland? If she is in Ireland, that is."

"A week, certainly not more than two weeks ago Hannah came to my office and, after asking me could I guarantee that it wasn't bugged, proceeded to spin the most ridiculous yarn, or at least I thought it was at the time." He paused, seemed to choose his words carefully.

"She claimed that she had overheard some employees of the company plotting to kidnap her and use that to force her father to withdraw from the International Currency Regulation talks for which he is the neutral liaison. All the parties involved trust him." Caligula couldn't fully hide his sneer. "The talks are currently at a sensitive stage and it is well known that it's Karl Offenbach's reputation for integrity that has brought the talks to this advanced stage." He hesitated. "I have heard that some elements were looking at ways to encourage Mr Offenbach to withdraw. I believe his daughter was mentioned as his, shall we say, Achilles' heel."

"Is that a fact? You surely have your ear to ground to get that barrow-load of information." Eacrett shook his head as if such a feat was beyond comprehension. He seemed to commune with someplace deep inside himself. "Now why would anyone want to dismantle such beneficial talks, I wonder?"

"Money is big business, Inspector, and not everyone makes it honestly. The International Currency reforms would make it more difficult for criminals, drug barons, you name it, to launder money. And, because it's an international project, every country in the world was expressing an interest in signing up to it. Especially . . ." this time Caligula made no effort to hide his disdain, "as the regulations would give governments the power to take a substantial cut of the ill-gotten gains."

"And you're saying the young one got wind of a plot to derail the talks by kidnapping her in order to force her father out of the equation?"

"That's more or less what she said."

"Would it have worked? If they had managed to get at Karl Offenbach, would the whole shebang have fallen asunder?"

"Most likely. His was the voice of reason. His straight talking had got the diverse groups as far as discussing a prototype. One that, across the spectrum of governments, financial institutions and monetary commissions, was considered worthy of consideration. It appeared that these diverse entities were willing to get behind it and, by all accounts, agree to trialling it."

"Commendable." Eacrett looked like one of those nodding Buddhas one saw in Chinese Medicine Clinics. "So, what did you do about the information, Larry?"

"What could I do?" Larry spread his hands, impatience lacing his voice. "She had no details, no names. To be quite honest with you, it all sounded OTT to me." He paused, made a grimace. "I thought she was looking for attention."

"Why would you think that? It's a big jump from her fearing she was going to be kidnapped and you thinking she was looking for attention."

"You must understand that Hannah is a precocious young lady. A couple of months ago, she thought she had discovered a fraud ring within the company. It turned out to be some low-level trading that a couple of secretaries were involved in – nothing exactly illegal, you understand, but they were using knowledge from the company contacts to gain some money on the side for themselves. Peanuts, really, but they'd been doing it for years and it had accrued a goodly sum. It still wasn't worth making a public denouncement about. They were reprimanded and almost immediately removed. Hannah's father made out he was very impressed with how she picked up what was going on and made a bit of a fuss over her."

"Proper order, don't you think?"

"Well, yes, but Karl told me he didn't want her getting a reputation for carrying tales and that he'd warned her not to go sticking her oar into things that could be dangerous." Caligula sounded terse. He stopped, added abruptly, "She could be a right little minx when it suited her."

"In what way?"

"She'd get an idea in her head and no way would she let it go until the whole place was in uproar. Then her father would have to step in and soothe everything down."

"What did her father say when you went to him with her latest story?"

"I didn't go to him."

"His daughter fears she's going to be kidnapped and you didn't tell the man?"

For the first time Lauren felt Eacrett's outrage was genuine.

"Mr Offenbach has been pretty busy recently, between the international money business and a major company restructuring project he is undertaking in the States. I didn't want to bother him without some kind of evidence, something more concrete than gossip from the ladies' locker room."

"When did you change your mind?"

"Change my mind?"

"About taking her seriously?"

"When I couldn't find her on Friday."

Lauren had to stifle a gasp. Why was Larry Caligula looking for Hannah on Friday? Two days before anyone knew she was missing.

"More likely Saturday." Caligula tightened his lips, suddenly sounding more cautious. "I set enquiries in motion when I heard her mother was away and there was no reliable information as to where Hannah was. One of my contacts told me a girl answering Hannah's description took the ferry from Fishguard to Rosslare on Saturday in the company of a young man who was unknown to me. When I realized what had possibly gone down, I used the company jet to fly to Dublin and made my way to Rosslare. Unfortunately, I missed them at the port and only heard incidentally that they may have hitched a lift on a container truck heading to Waterford. So, " Caligula attempted an ingratiating smile, "here I am, hoping the Irish police force will be able to offer me some guidance as to where I might go next."

"You've timed it well, Larry. I was just about to deploy my people to various chores around the town." Inspector Eacrett raised his eyes and looked at each person in the room. "You've heard the story. I want you all to concentrate on finding the little girl." He turned back to Caligula. "Would you happen to have a picture of her?"

"I have one on my phone."

"Send it there to Pamela. She'll send it to the lads. Pamela, give him the number. Go on, get going, the rest of ye! Larry and myself will just go over the finer details so that we'll leave no stone unturned in our effort to find the little girl. Hannah, wasn't it, you said?"

Lauren noticed that the look on Caligula's face suggested he was not best pleased at the turn of events.

CHAPTER 19

Thus dismissed, Trout and Lauren wasted no time in leaving the Garda Station. Trout had paused at the entry and given his phone number and Lauren's to the sergeant, asking him to pass them on to Pamela O'Leary and Inspector Eacrett. By mutual consent they made no mention of anything until they were back in the car, their seat belts on and Trout was pulling out into the late-morning traffic.

"What do you think?" Trout had great respect for Lauren's insights and now felt she would have an interesting summing-up of their morning.

"Well," she drew out the word thoughtfully, "the sheriff seems to have everything under control. At least from his point of view."

"The sheriff?" Trout suppressed his laugh and waited to hear more.

"Did you not think the inspector is a very – cut your hair or get out of town – type of personality? Behind all his blustering he didn't let Caligula away with a thing."

This time he did laugh. "Now that you mention it, I can see where you're coming from." He sobered. "He did give us a chance to hear what Caligula had to say."

"True. Did you get what he said about looking for Hannah on Friday? If we hadn't known Marina's story it might have passed over us. But in light of what we do know, as in, nobody was aware she was missing until Sunday, it puts a very sinister twist in the tale." Lauren frowned at the windscreen. "Nor did he seem to know about Isla. I wonder how she came to be there?"

"From the video, David seemed concerned about her."

"Yet he persuaded Hannah to leave and took Isla's rucksack, presumably so she won't be identified too soon."

"We've got more questions now than we ever had. Did you notice Caligula didn't elaborate on why he was looking for Hannah. I thought Eacrett might pick him up on it but he let it pass." He concentrated on the flow of traffic for a moment. "Whip out your googleizer there and see where the Newrath road is."

Lauren did as she was bid. "It's not that far. We need to cross the river. Let me see, we're here, stay on this road for one kilometre, bear right at the junction and that will bring us onto Rice Bridge and across the Suir. Newrath doesn't seem any great distance from there."

"OK, you're navigating."

"We need to talk to Marina and Karl. They might have some ideas about Caligula's involvement."

"And it would be interesting to know if Hannah said anything about the possible kidnapping to either of them. Let's concentrate now on getting out of town. Then you can ring them."

"Good idea. *Wow! Some bridge!* I didn't realize the Suir was that wide!"

"You have to remember by now the Three Sisters have all joined together and Waterford is the estuary from where they reach the sea."

"The Barrow, the Nore and the Suir. The Three Sisters. We learned them off by heart at school. If I remember correctly the Barrow is the longest of the three – still none of them measure up to our own river, the Shannon."

"Do I hear a touch of smugness there?"

"Not at all, just stating facts. Left coming up."

"There doesn't seem to be much here."

They drove along a stretch of road, without houses or any sign of people. Off it, left and more or less under it were some industrial type buildings. Ahead the logo for a well-known petrol brand dominated the skyline. Off to the right a wide opening showed in a wall that curved out of sight. Behind the wall and towering over it was a high beech hedge. A glimpse here and there of a series of lawns, flower beds and eventually, a row of long low buildings was all that could be seen from the road.

Lauren was looking around, trying to pinpoint anything that might give them an idea as to where Hannah and David went. "Hang on. What's that place? Can you pull in a minute? I'm going to check it out. You go on up to the filling station and I'll be up after you."

He stopped and Lauren hopped out of the car.

"Is this one of your gut instincts?" he asked.

"Something like that," she said, walked behind the car, waited for a gap in the traffic and ran across the road.

Trout watched for a minute and saw her disappear behind the high hedge. He pulled back into the traffic and drove the five hundred metres to the filling station. He might as well check out any CCTV they might have while he was there.

Lauren rounded the tall hedge and got a better look at what she had caught a glimpse of – a series of single-storey dwellings that looked like the type of sheltered accommodation they had in the local town at home. There were manicured green spaces and lots of raised beds, with flowers of every type and hue adding colour and gaiety to the place. In the distance she could see a glasshouse and guessed that a vegetable garden lay beyond it. A minibus was parked at the end building to her right. From the entrance she meandered towards it on tarred paths where the air was peaceful and calm. Birds twittered among the bushes and the drone of insects was soothing. She took a deep breath and wondered what she expected to find here. Whatever it was, she needed this bit of time out to allow her mind and spirit regroup. The thought had no sooner crossed her mind when a group of chattering girls erupted from a door to her left and surrounded her.

"Hello!"

"What's your name?"

"Have you come to visit us?"

"My name is Maria."

"I'm Sophie."

"Are you coming to the seaside with us?"

Soft hands reached out to touch her and beaming smiles accompanied the questions and comments. Lauren smiled and touched the hands held out to her.

"My name is Lauren and I just came in to see your beautiful garden."

"I sowed the daisies!"

"And I pruned the roses! Lily showed me how to do it without getting a thorn."

"Look, these are nasturtiums. You can eat the leaves but they're very hot."

"I don't like them. I prefer the lettuce."

"That's in the back garden."

"Do you want to come and see it?"

"Girls, girls, give the woman some air! Anyway, we haven't time to show her the garden now. We're going to the seaside. Remember?"

A soft "She could come with us," led to a chorus of:

"Come with us!"

"It's lovely at the seaside!"

"We've a picnic!"

"You can tell us a story like the other lady!"

"Enough chatter, girls. You all need to get on the bus or it will be too late to go." The woman, compact and competent-looking, clapped her hands, made a shooing motion and turned to Lauren. "They don't mean any harm. They're just excited to see a new face." The woman had a soft face and kind eyes. "Did you just wander in or were you looking for someone?" For all her softness there was a hint of steel in her tone.

"A little bit of both." Lauren decided to be completely frank. "We were passing and I noticed this looked like a care facility. I took a chance on coming in."

"*We?*" the woman interrupted sharply. She looked at Lauren with narrowed eyes. "I don't see anyone else, nor any car."

"I told my friend to go on to the filling station and wait for me. I thought two of us might be too much if my idea was correct." She saw the woman make a movement to demand an explanation and added quickly, "I know a bit about special needs and didn't want to cause so much excitement you'd have difficulty settling the young people."

"That was thoughtful of you." She turned to where the girls were still hesitating. "Onto the bus, girls, seatbelts on! Annie is coming out with the picnic baskets in a minute. We have to get ready to go."

There was an immediate clamour to get on board. The woman turned back to Lauren.

"So you were looking for someone, you said?"

"Yes. I'm searching for my godchild. Her name is Hannah but she may be using her second name which is Louise. I have reason to believe she came this way on Monday with a friend of hers called David. I was wondering if you or any of the girls saw her?"

The woman studied her for a long moment. "You say she's your godchild. Is there more to the story?"

"Yes. My cousin, Marina, came to me, oh my God, was it only yesterday morning? She said Hannah was missing and she thought she had come to Ireland."

"From where?"

"London." Lauren looked at her, wondering if she knew something. When the woman said no more, she continued. "My friend Thomas, he's a private investigator – he came with me to look for her and we've traced her to a sighting on this road. It seems Hannah and her friend were trying to thumb a lift. I believe she may have been trying to get to me and that due to a series of events has been set off on a roundabout route to get to Clare, where I live." She grimaced, hesitated. "There is someone else looking her also but I'm afraid he means her harm."

There was a couple of minutes' silence. Lauren was conscious of the girls crowding around the bus windows, watching them avidly. She was aware on the periphery of her vision of another woman, moving back and forth between the building and the bus, carrying hampers and boxes.

At last, the woman sighed. "Hannah and her friend were here. She had already told the girls her name was Hannah when I arrived on the scene. Possibly she had answered them automatically when they were so excited to see her. David waited outside. We got to know his name later on." She stopped, seemed to weigh what she wanted to say. "Will any of this have consequences for us?"

Lauren shook her head. "From our point of view this is a private investigation and, although we have informed the authorities that we're looking for her, we've moved on now and will be following our own course. I can guarantee you that anything you tell me won't go any further than my colleague."

"I'll trust your word. You understand my first responsibility is to protect my girls and I don't want them upset in any way."

Lauren nodded and waited in silence.

"Hannah and her friend David came to Tramore with us on Monday." She took a deep breath. "Let me tell you what happened."

CHAPTER 20

Lauren waved the bus off and stood for a minute, contemplating her next step. She could see the filling station in the distance but her phone map showed it was a seven-minute walk.

She swiped Trout's number and said when he answered, "Will you pick me up if you're finished up there?"

"Two minutes, they're just finishing a couple of cappuccinos for us."

"Thanks."

She sat on the outside wall and thought about all she had learned. The woman had introduced herself as Bernadette, the house manager of the Holly unit. All their houses were called after trees growing in the grounds, she had explained. There were eight girls in the Holly unit but this week two of them were on holiday with their families and she and Annie, the other carer, had decided to make it a holiday week for the remaining six as well. They had gone to the seaside early on Monday but today they were leaving later as they had done a cooking session with the girls to prepare their lunch. All the girls took turns at cooking as part of their independent-living learning. On Monday one of the girls, Sophie, generally the most gregarious of then, had noticed the two backpackers at the entrance. Before anyone could stop her, she'd run over and invited them in. The girl, Hannah, had laughed and come in. The boy was more reluctant but eventually had followed, although at first he stayed in the background.

"These are teenage girls," Bernadette had said, "and the prospect of being in the company of a young man was very exciting for them."

By the time she'd come on the scene, they were all laughing and talking together and she reckoned it was no harm to give the newcomers a lift to Tramore with them. They were both really good with the girls and the young man, David, told her that they volunteered in a shelter in London where meals were provided for the homeless and vulnerable.

"They stayed on with us at the beach for a while and had lunch with us," Bernadette had said, adding, "It meant a lot to the girls."

Hannah promised the girls she would call in on the way back and tell them about her travels but had warned them that it could be a good while before she returned.

"She was aware of their lack of time perception and then told them that a 'good while' meant many days. She even held up her two hands several times, so they could see her ten fingers repeatedly, conveying the idea of 'many days'. The girls are still talking about it. Do you think there's any chance she will come back?" Bernadette had sounded wistful.

"If Hannah said she'd call back, she fully intends to," Lauren had told her. "All going well, she will. And if there's a problem, I will personally let you know."

"Thank you. I got the impression that she would but I'm well aware that life has a habit of interfering with one's plans."

"I wonder . . ." Lauren had paused, about to ask a delicate question. Caligula had implied that David was intimidating or coercing Hannah and Lauren wanted to know what this astute woman thought of that. "What would you say was the relationship between Hannah and David?"

Bernadette had laughed. "Nothing untoward anyway. The girls asked them if they were boyfriend-girlfriend and they both said no – best friends they said."

"Could he have been coercing her in any way?"

"Good Lord, no! There wasn't a sign of anything like that. Once they relaxed with us, they were just two young people off on an adventure together."

"Thank you. I'm relieved to hear that. Now, do you have any idea where they went after leaving ye?"

"Yes, I do – they talked about cycling the Greenway and I know they hired bikes, because we all went with them to wave them off."

"That's brilliant to know! Thank you so much."

"Will we have to tell the Gardaí?"

"I don't think so. I'd say the quieter we keep it, the safer it is for them."

"Safer?"

Lauren realized she had spoken her thoughts aloud and had hurried to reassure the woman. "It's a complicated story, Bernadette, and I am going to add my promise that when Hannah is safely home, we'll both come and have a party with you and tell you what we can."

"Thank you, we'd all appreciate that."

"Also, we'll be going on to Tramore now ourselves. Is there an ice-cream parlour or a bakery near the beach where we can get some treats to add to your picnic?"

"There is indeed and the girls would love that."

"Then we'll call on you as we're passing through."

"You're very thoughtful. Thank you."

"It's only a small token of how thankful I am to you, for talking to me and for your kindness to Hannah and her friend. Where exactly will we find you?"

"Oh, you can't miss us. Just walk along the beach. It's five kilometres long, you know," she laughed at Lauren's expression, "but, never fear, we won't be too far from the town!"

"See you there!"

Bernadette had hurried away at that and the bus had pulled out immediately, the girls waving madly.

Lauren heard the car stop and hurried to where Trout had pulled into the kerb. "I'm guessing you had no luck at the filling station."

"Not a dicky-bird. Nothing on camera, nobody saw them or if they did they're not telling." Trout idled the car, waiting to hear what Lauren had to say.

"They didn't see them. They never made it as far as the filling station – instead they went to the seaside with the girls from here. Our next stop is Tramore."

And as Trout pulled out into the traffic, made a U-turn and took the road to Tramore, Lauren proceeded to fill him in on all she had learned.

"So, we're going to Tramore," she concluded, "to buy treats for the girls' picnic and find somewhere that supplies bikes for the Greenway."

Tramore proved to be only twenty minutes away. They found the Old Tramore Road and followed it all the way to the promenade.

"*Wow!* What a fabulous view!" Lauren exclaimed.

The sparkling blue water, tipped with an edge of white, mingled with a paler blue sky on the far horizon. She hopped out, stretched and took a deep breath, filling her lungs with the unmistakable briny sea smell that held just a hint of seaweed. She moved to the railing and saw the beach, almost white in the sun. It curved into the distance as far as the eye could see. There were people dotted here and there in groups, lying on colourful towels, swimming languidly in the sun-dappled sea, and further out paddling gently or swaying rhythmically on paddle boards.

"Isn't that an amazing beach? This is my first time in Tramore." She turned to Trout, her face alive with the delight of a child at the seaside, but sobered as quickly. "It's just a pity we can't be here for fun."

"When we come back to visit the girls, we'll come here for fun."

"I'd like that. Now to find some treats and then Bernadette and the girls."

"Well, I'd say the treats are sorted. Look across the road – a bakery-café – and that huge 'ninety-nine' suggests they sell ice cream as well."

They crossed the road, bought two boxes of mixed pastries and arranged for the girls and their minders to have any type of ice cream they fancied on their way home.

"Bernadette said we couldn't miss them – that they'll be a little way along the beach." Lauren squinted along the promenade. "There's a mini-bus along there – probably them. I certainly can't see any other bus."

They set off, carrying a box each. The clear air seemed to renew Lauren's energy and raise her spirits.

"Bernadette will be able to tell us exactly where they got the bikes."

"That was some hunch you had. I had almost forgotten the sharpness of your instincts."

"No more than yours with the commune."

"And, of course, as good investigators do we followed up rather than dismissed our ideas. One of the cornerstones of investigation, Lauren. Leave no stone unturned."

"There, it's even given you an opportunity to teach your apprentice." Lauren smiled at him.

He returned the smile full force. "You're a natural. Best apprentice I've ever had."

"Seems to me I'm the *only* apprentice you've ever had. Look! That's the bus alright. They'll be somewhere nearby."

"Let's get onto the sand – there are some steps coming up."

On the sand, Lauren kicked off her flip-flops and picked them up, being careful not to overbalance the box. She wriggled her toes into the warm sand, felt the yield and pull of each step and welcomed the burn in her calves as she went forward.

They hadn't gone far when they heard a shout and a gaggle of girls in brightly hued swimsuits ran to meet them. They surrounded Lauren with cries of welcome, but moved back shyly from Trout.

"This is my friend Thomas. He came along to help me carry the buns for your picnic."

This set up another round of excited chattering that carried them all along to where Bernadette, Annie and the driver, who was introduced as Ken, were sitting on deckchairs, surrounded by the picnic paraphernalia. Lauren put the box onto the picnic-rug in the shade of one of the baskets and indicated that Trout should do the same.

"There should be enough for everyone." She smiled, pleased at the excitement generated by a couple of boxes of buns.

"Thank you for coming. You see, I hadn't told the girls just in case . . ." Bernadette looked uncomfortable. "Not everyone realizes how important it is to keep one's word," she finally murmured.

"Not to worry. And before I forget . . ." Lauren handed Bernadette the receipt for the ice cream. "Ice cream for everyone on the way home."

This set up another round of excited chattering.

"Now I insist you share our picnic with us," said Bernadette. Lauren began to protest but Bernadette held up a hand. "No, I insist."

Lauren looked at Trout. He turned to Bernadette. "Thank you. We're delighted to accept."

The picnic was a happy half-hour and when Lauren and Trout rose to go, they were given an exuberant send-off and clear directions to the bicycle shop where the girls had left Hannah and David.

CHAPTER 21

McTeggert's Cycles was only a short walk from where Trout had parked the car. It was a long narrow shop with everything and anything one might need for a bicycle or a camping trip. The far end opened into a workshop where two lads, hands black from grease or handling tyres, or both, worked on unheeding of who was there. The smell of rubber and oil, while not unpleasant in itself, lay heavy on the air and tended to overpower the nose in the narrow confines of the shop.

The cherubic proprietor sat on a high stool behind a glass-fronted counter and surveyed the town's coming and goings through a large street-front window, full of cycle paraphernalia. He looked more like a laughing Buddha than a committed cyclist, but was a mine of information, mostly about the Greenway of which, he informed them with the proprietorial delight of one who was involved in putting it in place, he was a long-time supporter. He had no qualms about telling them anything they wanted to know – indeed he did rent bikes to two young people as described and as they weren't at an access point in Tramore he gave them a lift in the old mini-van to Kiloteran. Sure, it was only up the road and anyway it was part of the service to encourage visitors to explore the Greenway. Were they interested in cycling it themselves? No? Some other time, he'd do them a good deal.

The youngsters? Well, it was late enough when they got started so he recommended they try for Kilmacthomas that day, a short run, only sixteen kilometres, easy enough for a couple of young ones, even ones like the young fellow who hadn't, by the gip of him, much experience on a bike. He was game though and, as he told them, they couldn't get lost and there was no danger from traffic so they'd get a good run at settling into the cycle. What? How far did they say they were going? They paid to the end of the line, two days. He'd told them to do it over two days with lots of breaks and they'd be grand. He'd told them to drop the bikes at the Rent-a-Bike at the end of the Greenway line. They'd be returned to him from there.

Trout eventually managed to halt the flow, thanked McTeggert for his help and he and Lauren escaped to the sea-laden air of the prom.

"*Phew!* His capacity for breathing while talking was amazing." He shook his head. "Or not breathing in that air. Imagine what his lungs must look like? Did you get all that?" At Lauren's nod, he continued. "We'll head for Dungarvan. If they've cycled there, even if it's over two days, they'll probably need a rest and we might catch up with them."

"That would be truly great. Especially as I think friend McTeggert would give exactly the same information to anyone else who asked, just as easily as he gave it to us."

"There is that," said Trout, "but who else knows that Hannah and David were going to cycle the Greenway?"

"They haven't exactly been keeping themselves under the radar, have they?"

"It's possible they're feeling confident that they've shaken off Caligula and Co. You have to hand it to them – cycling the Greenway gets them off the main thoroughfare and presumably in the direction they want to go."

"Surely if they're aiming for Knocknaclogga they'd take a more direct route?" Lauren said. "From here they'll nearly have to go to Cork to get a train or bus."

"Whatever they're doing, our most likely next stop is Dungarvan." Trout consulted his phone. "It's a fairly straightforward run and, according to this, less than an hour away. We'll actually go through Kilmacthomas. We can make enquiries there if we think we need to." He started the car. "Tramore seems like a nice place – we'll definitely come back and take a proper walk along that beach."

"I'm sure that would be nice but all I can think of now is Hannah and where we might find her. Maybe if we just go straight to Dungarvan we can work our way back if we don't find them there. How big a place is it anyway?"

"Haven't a clue. I don't think I was ever there."

"I'll have a look." Lauren rooted for her phone, swiped it open and entered Dungarvan in the search box. "A coastal town on the Waterford-Cork road, it's the third largest town in the county with a population of ten thousand plus. That's big enough."

"You'd better check where exactly the Greenway ends. McTeggert told them to drop the bikes off there."

"I have the brochure for the Greenway here. I picked it up while I was listening to ye talk. Let me see." She put the phone on her lap and scanned the brochure. I wonder . . ." The phone beeped, vibrating against her thighs. "A message." She opened it, frowned. "It's from Sergeant O'Leary." She read it, reread it, started to tap urgently at the phone, muttering, "Pamela O'Leary says we need to have a look at what Larry Caligula has posted on Instagram and elsewhere. *Oh my God!*"

Trout glanced at her. She was scrolling through her phone, her face suffused with fury.

"*Bastard!* Well, this proves he means Hannah no good. *Fuck, fuck fuck!*"

"What is it? Lauren talk to me."

Lauren took a deep breath. "Listen to this: '*REWARD €10,000 offered for information as to whereabouts of pictured girl. She is believed to be travelling in the company of a young man and may be suffering from delusions of persecution. She is considered vulnerable, please do not approach. Contact immediately through this medium.*' For fuck's sake, Trout, it's only up an hour and it has six hundred hits already and – I can hardly believe it – two hundred messages."

Trout blew out a breath. "Are any of the responses valid?"

"I'm scanning them at the moment but, Trout, he's put it out on Instagram, Twitter, Facebook and who knows what other platforms I have no access to."

"We're still ahead of him, so that is something we can work with and, now that we know, we can monitor the responses ourselves."

"There's hundreds of them. *Oh shit!* Just now: '*A girl looking like pic stayed near Kilmacthomas last night. For further information contact.*' We're up against private messages as well as everything else. What will we do?"

"We won't panic for starters. OK, we need someone to monitor social media. Otherwise, it will waste too much of our time."

"It's something that can be done from anywhere, preferably by someone who is tech savvy. I'll ring Brendan." Lauren was already pulling up his number.

"Lauren?"

"Brendan, I have a job for you."

"For TLCI?"

"Yes. I want you to monitor social-media sites that are offering a €10,000 reward for information about a young girl, picture provided. Look at Instagram first."

"Hang on. Give me a minute."

Lauren waited.

"Got it, I think. *She is believed to be travelling in the company of a young man and may be suffering from delusions of persecution*?"

"That's one of them. It's on Twitter and Facebook too."

"I can see it's on another bunch of sites I have access to as well."

"Hey, don't do anything too illegal."

"Wouldn't dream of it."

"Why don't I believe you? Well, if any information as to her whereabouts pops, I need you to let me know asap."

"Will do."

"Thanks, Brendan."

"Stay safe."

She disengaged.

"That young man is way ahead of us. He says he has access to a bunch of other sites besides the usual." She closed her phone. "I wonder how he was able to access so many sites almost simultaneously and faster than I could talk."

"We'll leave it with him. Anyway, we're nearly –" His phone buzzed. He fished it from his pocket and handed it to Lauren. "Get that, will you, in case it's important."

"Hello?"

"Mr McTeggert, Bruce."

Lauren looked at Trout and pressed the icon for the speaker. "I've put you on speaker, Bruce, so we can both hear what you have to say."

"That's a good idea. My lads have brought to my attention a story doing the rounds, offering a reward for that little girl you were asking about. Now I know people and there's no way that young one was delusional. She was as up front and natural as you could ask for, so I said to myself there must be a story there and I'd better check with yourselves before I let the lads do anything foolish."

Trout and Lauren exchanged a glance.

"Mr McTeggert, Thomas Tegan here."

"Bruce."

"Right. Bruce, we're grateful for your call. As you say there is a story and we are convinced the man who posted the reward intends to hurt Hannah, the girl in the picture. That's why we're trying to find her first."

"Well, he won't be hearing anything from me or mine. I'll even get the lads to put a note online to say the whole thing's a scam."

"I never thought of that," said Lauren. "Thank you." She didn't try to hide the relief in her voice.

Bruce McTeggert was still talking. "I've a granddaughter around the same age. I'd do a lot to protect her. Ye have my number there, let me know how it goes."

"We will," said Trout.

Lauren added a profound "Thank you" before disengaging.

"Well, that's one for the books!" said Trout.

"Lucky you gave him your card." Lauren shook her head. "Fair dues to him."

"I wouldn't have expected it but you never know what people will do in a situation. There's the sign for Dungarvan. Does the brochure say where the cycle shop is?"

CHAPTER 22

They found the Rent-a-Bike easily, at the end of the Greenway, not far from the big roundabout just across the river. Inside two young people were in the process of returning bikes. They were talking excitedly about things they had seen and done along the Greenway while the attendant half-listened. There was a nervousness about their chatter that caught Lauren's attention. She looked at them curiously – two teenagers, healthy and windblown after a day cycling. They each carried day packs with water bottles stuffed into the side pockets. Boyfriend, girlfriend, she thought indulgently.

Then she heard, "That's everything. The bikes are fine. Glad your trip went well." The attendant looked at the slip of paper, smiled mechanically. "David, Louise, enjoy the rest of your holiday."

Lauren felt a slam of unease and looked at the two more closely. She didn't recognize them in any shape or form. David and Louise were in no way unusual names, but still she was disconcerted. The two looked at each other, giggled and headed out. She looked around for Trout but he was engrossed, examining a bike with the biggest tyres, Lauren had ever seen. She chewed her lip for a second, then hurried after the young people. They had paused beyond the row of bikes and were high-fiving each other.

They made to set off along the footpath as Lauren called, "*Excuse me, could I have a word?*"

They turned expectant faces towards her and she moved nearer, suddenly anxious that they might get spooked and she would lose them. "My name is Lauren O'Loughlin," she said quickly. "And I'm a private investigator."

"For real?" The young man's interest picked up a notch while the girl's eyes became wary.

Lauren smiled. "Yes." She fished one of the TLCI cards from her bag. "This is my card. I work with a colleague, Thomas Tegan. I couldn't help overhear you returning the bikes and I wonder if you can help me?"

The girl was staring at her with wide apprehensive eyes, while the boy grinned confidently. "Sure, if we can."

"Is there anywhere nearby where we can get a coffee or ice cream. It would be more comfortable than standing here on the footpath."

"We really should go, Ken." The girl was definitely nervous now.

"We can give the lady a few minutes. We were going to have an ice cream anyway." He glanced at the card he held in his hand. "Look, it says *TLC Investigations*. I've never met a real PI before."

"Then I'd better introduce you to my partner," Lauren said. "He's the real deal. I'm still learning."

"Wow! Can you learn to be a PI?"

"Sure you can. You have to, if you want to get a licence." Out of the corner of her eye Lauren saw Trout coming up beside her. She gestured toward him. "This is my partner, Thomas Tegan, nicknamed Trout."

"Cool," said the boy.

"Trout, I've just told these young people we'd buy them an ice cream and I could do with a cup of coffee myself."

"Good call." Trout cocked an enquiring look at the boy.

"Ken Cahill. This is my friend Zoe Long."

"Ken and Zoe," Lauren murmured. "I could have sworn the shop assistant called you Louise and David." Beside her she felt Trout's interest quicken.

"*Oh crap!*" Ken looked taken aback.

"Now you've blown it!" Zoe accused him angrily.

"You haven't, you know," Lauren said. "If you show us where we can get the drinks, I'll explain and maybe we can help each other out."

The girl, Zoe, looked very young and miserable. Ken held a hand towards her. "Come on, Zoe, the least we can do is listen to what they have to say."

"We promised."

"Well, Louise did tell us if we found someone, someone we could trust, we could decide whether to tell them or not."

Louise! They'd met Hannah! Lauren could barely restrain herself from grabbing the boy and demanding answers.

Slowly the girl put her hand in Ken's. "I suppose."

"And, look, she's got red hair."

Zoe raised her eyes to examine Lauren's hair more closely. "Is it real?"

"Yes. I don't think they've managed to get this colour out of a bottle yet."

"Louise had red hair," Ken said. "She joked about it, said you could always trust a foxy redhead." He waved a hand towards the river. "Best we cross over to the other side. A café there has good ice cream. You have a car?"

"Follow me," said Trout.

The café was in a small square ringed with artisan shops and the back entrances to larger stores. Two more alleys exited in different directions. The sunshine bathed the space in a warm glow. A couple of small metal tables with matching chairs stood empty, invitingly placed under the awning outside the bubble-gum-coloured ice-cream shop.

"Why don't we sit here and the boys can get us the ice creams?" Lauren suggested to Zoe, as she dropped onto one of the chairs. She studied the array of concoctions advertised on the window. "Oh my God! They've got knickerbocker glories! How retro is that? That's me done." Lauren gave her order to Trout.

Zoe looked at her with wondering eyes, took a deep breath. "I'd like a triple fudge sundae, please?" She held her breath as if waiting for a telling-off.

Trout simply said, "Knickerbocker glory, triple fudge sundae – come on, Ken, we'll pick ours inside." He led the way into the shop.

Zoe dropped onto the seat beside Lauren. "Louise said some bad people were after her. You don't feel like a bad person."

"Thank you. I'm not the bad person who is after her. I'm her godmother and her cousin – hence the red hair."

"You said you're a PI."

"I'm that too. Let's wait until the boys come back and we can exchange stories. Do you live around here?"

"A bit outside the town. Ken's my boyfriend. We were walking the section from Durrow to Dungarvan. My mum dropped us over this morning."

Zoe traced the pattern on the iron tabletop with a slender finger. Lauren noted her nails were trimmed and buffed but not varnished.

"Are we in trouble?" Zoe asked.

"No. Actually, far from it. You'll see when we've talked."

Trout and Ken came out just then, carrying the ice creams. They placed them on the table and sat. It was a bit crowded with the four of them but they all seemed to be of a mind to keep close together and block out the rest of the world as they talked.

For a couple of minutes, the whole concentration was on the treats. Trout had opted for a bowl of plain vanilla with a couple of wafers stuck in it. Lauren dug into hers, bringing a mix of fruit, nuts and ice-cream to her mouth in each spoonful, which she savoured with a dreamy look on her face.

Eventually, keeping her eyes on her glass, she said, "Why don't you tell us how you came to bring back Louise and David's bicycles?"

Zoe and Ken looked at each other. His double scoop was melting over a warm chocolate brownie. He shovelled a large spoonful into his mouth, chewed, swallowed and said, "We were walking the section from Durrow back to here, today. We've being doing a section each week when we've got a day off from our summer jobs."

"Why walking?" Trout asked.

Ken reddened, said simply, "We could have the whole day together that way."

Trout nodded. "Good call."

"Zoe's mum dropped us to the access point in Durrow this morning. It's only ten k and we had lunch and everything with us." He stopped to eat another mouthful of his sweet. "We were about halfway when we came up on Louise and David. They had a puncture. You should have seen the look on his face – he hadn't a clue what to do. They were walking the bikes and making a poor hand of it when we caught up with them. We reckoned they were having a right old argy-bargy so we sort-of offered to help. So, I just said, casual-like 'Want a hand with the puncture?' He looked at me like I had two heads and said sort of snooty-like 'Unless you're able to mend it, no thanks'." Ken had changed his Waterford accent to a precise English enunciation.

Lauren immediately added a voice to the picture of David in her head.

"'As it happens, I can,' I said and he thawed out a bit. He didn't even know he had a little repair kit attached to the saddle. He was all right though when we got started and, between the two of us, we repaired the puncture. Zoe and Louise got chatting and when we were done with the wheel, we shared our lunches."

"Louise was really upset." Zoe joined in the conversation. "She told me they had been attacked by some scumbag types and their friend was in hospital and they couldn't find out how she was because they were afraid, if they turned on their phones, some guy who's after them would be able to trace where they were. I thought she was joking at first." Zoe raised wide apprehensive eyes and locked them on Lauren. "Then she said she had overheard this man and his girlfriend plotting to kidnap her and force her father to vote against some big deal he was involved in. The bad guy told his girlfriend – Louise said her name was

Shyrl and she was really nice and she couldn't believe she was part of something so horrible – but the bad guy said there was ten million in it for them if they pulled it off. I sort of laughed and said 'Who's got ten million?' but when I saw Louise's face I could see she was dead serious." Zoe played her spoon around her dish. "I sort of said I didn't think the Greenway was a great hiding place but she said that they were on it by accident and at the time it seemed as good a place as any."

"They walked along with us and we tossed a few ideas that might help them out," said Ken. "We'd come along the Viaduct. Zoe and myself were going to spend a bit of time on Clonlea Strand and I was saying to David and Louise that Dungarvan was only a few k's away and they'd have to take back the bikes and they were right miserable, like, about it." Ken concentrated on scraping out his bowl for a minute. "I said straight out 'Me and Zoe can take back the bikes if you like. If someone is watching for you, they won't expect you to go straight to the bus stop. If you don't leave back the bikes, they won't know you've arrived. I told them to get a bus in the opposite direction from where whoever's after them would come." He stopped, raised his head. "It might have been a bit of a stupid idea but it was all I could think of, that might give them a chance. And that's what we did. And I'd do it again like, if we had to."

CHAPTER 23

Lauren's phone rang as Trout finished giving a severely edited version of where they were coming from in their efforts at finding Hannah. Or Louise as they stuck with, as Ken and Zoe knew her as that. He warned them to keep all their information off social media and to ignore the post about rewards or anything pertaining to it, as it would only make trouble for everyone.

"Brendan," Lauren said as she swiped the icon to answer the call. "Are you sure?" She surged out of her chair. "Brendan says he's accessed a post that has tagged Hannah as being in Dungarvan and that someone has eyes on her at this moment and is directing the Shark to her. Thanks, Brendan. I'll call you back."

"Where's the place ye told them to get the bus?" Trout had his keys out and was leading them out of the square. "Is it far? Can you show us?"

"Davitt's Quay, it's back across the river and down the road from the Rent-a-Bike, only a couple of minutes."

Trout began to jog and the others ran after him.

When they reached the car, Trout said, "Hop in but for God's sake if I tell you keep down, hit the floor and stay there."

Lauren dived into the passenger seat and the others climbed in, Ken quivering with excitement, Zoe tense with apprehension.

Back across the river, Ken directed Trout to drive down the road past the Rent-a-Bike. Ken was breathing fast even as he tried for a cool tone.

"The bus stop is up the other end just beyond the new roundabout."

"Did Brendan say where Caligula was coming from?"

"Kilmacthomas." Lauren sounded terse.

"There's the bus stop," Ken said excitedly. "There's a bus there."

Trout chanced a look, saw the bus, engine running as evidenced by the blue-grey smoke pulsing from its exhaust.

"And there's the fucking Cherokee coming up behind us!" Lauren heard the hysteria in her voice but couldn't do anything about it.

Trout floored the accelerator and swung right around the roundabout. "Hold on to yeer hats," he said grimly. The Lexus surged forward, dodged around a slower-moving vehicle and straight into the path of the black Jeep Cherokee, also moving at speed.

The crunch of metal meeting metal echoed and vibrated through the car. Trout threw off his seatbelt and lunged out the door. "Get out the far door and go home – we'll be in contact!" he threw over his shoulder to the two in the back seat.

The stunned young couple stumbled from the car and left, hand in hand.

"Attack is the best form of defense," Trout growled. "Lauren, contact Eacrett and tell him we need a friend in Dungarvan." He stormed over the where a furious Larry Caligula was jumping from the jeep. "*What the fuck do you think you're doing running into me like that?*" He stood directly in front of Caligula and, when the no-longer suave-looking man snarled something unintelligible and made to go around him, stepped with him and blocked him.

"*I need to get that bus!*" Caligula grabbed Trout and tried to push him aside.

"*You need to stay and face the damage you've done!*" Trout grunted, swinging the man around to face him.

"*Fuck you!*" Caligula shouted and took a swing at Trout.

Trout ducked and went in for a body grasp. Caligula writhed like a snake, his fists flaying at Trout's chest, and almost got away. Trout tightened his hold. Around them the traffic from both sides was building up and horns blared, doors slammed as people got out of cars to see what was going on. Caligula went still and Trout raised his head, just in time to take a vicious uppercut to the chin. Loosening his hold, he reeled backwards. Caligula turned and let fly with a string of expletives as he saw the bus pulling away, picking up speed and turning out of sight. He turned back and aimed a kick at Trout who was staggering to stay upright but Lauren launched herself onto his back, screeching like a banshee. Caligula roared and attempted to shake her off but she clung on like a mussel that has glued itself to a rock.

Into the melee thundered a Garda car, siren wailing, lights flashing. It screeched to a stop, and two burly Gardaí exited, leaving the lights twirling, after silencing the siren.

"*What's going on here?*"

One of them plucked Lauren from Caligula's back while the other restrained him as, freed from his burden, he made another lunge for Trout.

"I'm going to let you go now," Lauren's Garda said. "Stay where you are, OK?"

Lauren gave a breathless "Yes," and the Garda released her and went to help his colleague.

"*Quit that!*" The Garda holding Caligula gave him a shake.

"*Arrest that man!*" Caligula shook a furious finger at Trout. "*He deliberately ran into me!*"

Trout made his shaky way to Lauren. "Are you OK?"

She nodded, still breathless, and laid a trembling hand on his arm.

Trout indicated the cars, wincing at the sight of the jeep embedded in the front wing of the Lexus. "I'd say if you look at the cars, Officer, that statement is far from correct."

"*He attacked me!*" Caligula growled.

"No, sir, that he did not!" One of the onlookers was offering his tuppence worth. "You attempted to flee the scene and when the gentleman went to stop you, you took a swing at him."

Caligula glared at him.

The man shrugged. "It is what it is," he said.

"Like hell it is!" Caligula tried, unsuccessfully, to shake off the Garda's hold. He looked straight at Trout for the first time, narrowed his eyes. "I've seen you before. You were in Eacrett's office this morning. Why the fuck did you run into me?"

"Did I?" Trout gave him back stare for stare. "In my head I was quietly crossing the junction when your jeep ploughed into me."

The two Gardas' heads went back and forth between the two as if they were watching a ping-pong match. Then one of them tilted his head as if listening. "Reinforcements," he said with what sounded like relief.

A few moments later a second police car had pulled in behind the first. Inspector Eacrett hauled himself out of the passenger seat while Sergeant O'Leary exited from the driver side.

"Can ye not stay out of trouble for an hour while I get on with a bit of police work?" he rumbled as he stomped towards the fracas at the junction. "You – Doherty, isn't it?"

The Garda who had dealt with Lauren straightened himself and said, "Yes, sir."

"Clear this junction. Get the people gone, out of the way."

"Sir!" He turned towards the crowd of avid spectators. "OK, folks, show's over. If we need any of you to make a statement we'll advertise. Keep an ear to the news." And, talking as he approached the crowd, he began to herd people back into their cars, and waved a hand to disperse the pedestrians.

"*You*." Eacrett pointed to the Garda who still had a hold on Caligula. "Name?"

"Moloney, sir."

"What's with the death-grip on your man?"

"He was attacking the other gentleman, sir, and I needed to restrain him."

"I have my doubts if either of them are gentlemen," Eacrett grunted, "but you can let him go now. He won't be going anywhere without my say-so. Isn't that right, Larry?"

Caligula glared at him. Reluctantly, in the face of the beaming smile Eacrett was bestowing on him, he nodded but added. "They were on that bus and this bungling idiot has caused me to lose them."

"Larry, Larry, no name calling! I'm a mite precious about my people and I wouldn't like to fall out with you." Eacrett turned back to Garda Moloney, who was standing to attention, awaiting instruction. "Clear the junction. Direct the traffic around the crash. We'll have a better idea of what needs doing when we can see the situation clearly."

By now Garda Doherty had the pedestrians moving. He went to the opposite side of the junction and, between the two Gardai, the snarl of traffic was successfully cleared.

Eacrett waited in silence and perforce the others also remained silent, although Caligula's surly glares said more than words what he'd like to do to Trout.

"Now, lads, we'll see if these here vehicles are drivable. Note I didn't say roadworthy, but if they're drivable we'll escort ye to the station and try and clear up this fine mess ye've caused me." He waved a hand at the two guards. "Hold the traffic for a minute until these two *bastoons* get moving" He beckoned Lauren to one side as he waited for Trout and Caligula to get into their respective vehicles. "I'd advise you to get along to the garage on the upper quay and hire a good car – tell them I sent you. You can join us at the station afterwards to give your statement." He guffawed. "Or whatever."

CHAPTER 24

Eacrett was in full flow when Lauren arrived at the station. The duty sergeant had her name, cautioned her to be very quiet, led her along a short corridor, opened a door at the end, pointed to a strategically placed chair and left as quietly as he'd brought her there. The Inspector made the room look small as he paced, over and back, over and back, in front of where Trout and Caligula sat, beside and either end of a battered-looking wooden table. Lauren thought of her reception at the garage and wondered at the power of the man. She had arrived breathless after hurrying the length of the quay only to realize she had left her bag in Trout's car. A quick check of the phone she still held in her hand showed her emergency VISA card tucked into the cover. She would have to bluff her way through with it, she thought. But there was no need. Once Eacrett's name was mentioned, there was no problem getting whatever she wanted and, with the added security of her card, she was soon fixed up with a Golf GTi, taxed, insured and ready to roll. It wouldn't normally be her choice of car but, as she manoeuvred it through the traffic and felt the latent power waiting to be unleashed, she reckoned Trout would enjoy letting it loose on the motorway.

She pulled her focus back to the room and Eacrett. His ire seemed to be directed at Larry Caligula but he managed to get in an odd sideways swipe at Trout.

"How do you think I felt, Larry, when I found out you'd fed me peckle of lies? I'll tell you here and now I don't like being made feel like an *amadán*. Especially in front of a gentleman, note this time a real gentleman, like Karl Offenbach."

Lauren noticed the way Caligula stiffened when Eacrett said Karl's name. He worked his mouth as if to say something, only to have the Inspector's beefy finger wagged in his face.

"So, you went looking for the little girl on Friday, did you? A full two days before anyone knew she was missing. The why of that was one of the little details you left out when you elicited the help of my department."

Caligula stirred but was again quashed by the sheer force of Eacrett's voice.

"As for you, private dick – playing on my good nature, were you, and you leaving the girleen's mother fretting in the dark?"

Lauren saw the wink he gave Trout as he turned for another bout of pacing and wondered what he was playing at.

"What are you saying about a private investigator?" This time Caligula would not be silenced. "Who ordered a PI? I'm the security chief with KOE, security is my business and I certainly didn't sanction any investigation. It's imperative Hannah's disappearance is not made public. There are too many enemies out there that would use the information against KOE."

"So, the rumours I'm hearing that you've reached out to The O'Carthy for help in locating her couldn't possibly be true. Not if you want to keep the whole shebang on the Q-T," Eacrett rumbled over him, like the stirring of a mountain before an avalanche started.

Lauren saw Trout's shoulders tense when he heard the name O'Carthy and she wondered who he was and where he fitted into the situation.

"Buddy McCarthy and myself were in the army together." Caligula's voice had hardened.

"Which army would that be now? The US of A or that little schemozzle he was involved in down South America way?"

Caligula's suave urbanity cracked a little more. "Buddy was one of the bravest men I've ever fought beside. Surely even this hick force can understand a man contacting his friends?"

"Be careful, me buck, who you call hick." Eacrett cast a thoughtful eye over Caligula. "I've heard he was a reckless bastard all right. And you were right there beside him. I wonder now does Mr Offenbach know that little bit of history?"

"I had the courtesy to inform the Irish law enforcement of my reason for being here, and all I've got to date is hindrance." Caligula made an effort to sound civil but his eyes were hot.

"What exactly would you call hindrance now?" Eacrett's voice was suspiciously soft.

"You held me up while you let this PI loose, your officers have dragged me here after the same PI accosted me which allowed the bus I believe the girl was on to go on its way and now you're wasting my time and yours with this ridiculous kangaroo court."

"Hold it right there before I throw you in a cell for perverting the course of an investigation."

"I will not hold it. I'll have you know you'll answer to Karl Offenbach if anything happens to his daughter and I'll guarantee you I won't hold back when I tell him about your bungling inefficiency when I give him my report."

"Isn't it lucky so that he'll be arriving in fifteen minutes or so and he expressed a desire to meet you too."

"I've had enough of your bluster and obstruction. Mr Offenbach is in Mumbai."

The room went still. Lauren felt herself holding her breath.

Inspector Eacrett straightened himself. "Are you calling me a liar, Larry?"

Perhaps it was the quiet tone, perhaps the glint in Eacrett's eye, whatever it was Caligula refrained from answering, simply shrugged his shoulders and dropped his eyes.

Eacrett brooded over him for a long minute before turning and stomping back to the table. "I've told Karl Offenbach you'll be here when he arrives, and here you'll stay until then," he said sourly. "The rest of ye get the hell out of my sight. Quick now before I change my mind."

As fast as he said it Trout was on his feet and gesturing to Lauren come with him and the two of them left without a backward glance. She felt herself hustled down the corridor, saw Trout sketch a salute to the desk sergeant and was propelled out into the street.

"What sort of a car did you get us?" He spoke over his shoulder as he led the way into a yard beside the station where the Lexus was parked.

"Grab whatever you need, we'll have to leave the car here. The sooner we're on our way the better."

Lauren retrieved her bag from beside the passenger seat while Trout extracted their overnight bags from the boot. Her phone pinged a message as she turned to see what Trout was doing.

"Brendan." She opened it, frowned, went to read it out, only to have Trout hold up his hand and stop her. "We'll wait until we get in the car – where is it?"

Lauren fished a key out of her pocket and handed it to Trout. "It's there, just outside the gate."

Trout eyed the Golf that flashed in answer to his press of the key-fob.

"I asked for the most powerful car they had available." Lauren remembered the feeling of curbed power she got while manoeuvring the car through the streets and raised her chin defensively. "That's what they gave me, and I'd say it'll do whatever you want and more." Lauren was determined to give as good as she got if Trout made any adverse comment.

"Did I say anything?"

"You looked it."

"Looks can be deceptive. Climb aboard. I happen to like Golfs – had one years ago and I look forward to showing you how she moves."

"Of all the cars going I doubt a Golf could be considered female."

"Why not?" Trout sounded genuinely surprised. The car started with a growl and Trout gave a satisfied grunt.

"It has neither the shape nor the form of a female." Lauren clicked her belt into place and turned impatiently towards him. "Can we quit this stupid conversation so I can tell you what Brendan says."

Trout indicated and pulled into the traffic. "Work away. I just thought it was better be somewhere we couldn't be overheard."

"I know. I understand and it's just as well because Brendan says he's intercepted a message that says the 'package' is on the bus to Cork and a reply that stated it will be picked up at the other end. He says there's no signature. Package – Hannah."

"*Damn it!*" He indicated, changed lanes. "Cork for us so. It fits in with the O'Carthy angle, but by God I'd be better pleased if it were anyone else."

"That was where the four-o'clock bus was scheduled for. I checked the time-table as I was passing the stop on the way to the garage. What's the story with O'Carthy?"

"The O'Carthy. Nothing good if he's who I think he is. When we're on the dual carriageway I'll get you to give Mac a ring and he'll give us a rundown on the whole lot of them."

"Mac?" Lauren frowned. Mac was Trout's mentor from his days in the Gardaí and was one of his staunchest friends and allies. He was a sergeant in Dublin, an unapologetic policeman to his core and a died-in-the-wool Corkman. "What can he do? He's in Dublin and didn't you tell me he's on desk duty as his retirement is so near?"

"Yeah. But he still keeps his ear to the ground, especially for all things to do with Cork."

"OK. That will give me time to ring Marina and talk to Karl before they arrive at the station."

"Good idea. Prepare them for Caligula."

"And, you know the way Zoe said Hannah mentioned someone called Shyrl. I guess she must be working for KOE – how else would Hannah know her?"

"Correct. And it will be one more piece of information for Karl before he tackles Caligula."

Lauren opened her contacts and accessed Marina's number. Before she swiped it, she looked at Trout, "Do you think we should be worried about Brendan's ability to hack into people's accounts."

"Not today anyway, but I suppose I'd better have a chat with him when we get back."

"He says he's put an alert on the number and when the next communication comes, he'll let us know. We need the information but I don't want him getting into trouble."

"I hear you."

Lauren had swiped the call. She held up a hand. "We'd better talk to Karl. He'll need all the information he can get to deal with that slippery customer Caligula."

CHAPTER 25

The phone was answered on the first ring. A picture of an angry Marina, phone clasped in a sweaty hand, swamped Lauren's mind. A barrage of cackling issued from the phone.

"Hang on, Marina, I need to put you on speaker."

She jabbed the icon and immediately Marina's voice filled the car, high-pitched and in full-flow.

"Nobody's answering their phones and I'm left here not knowing what's going on. I'm worried out of my mind," she snatched a breath, *"I can't take much more of it, I'm* – what is it, Karl? I'm talking to Lauren."

"It's more like haranguing her from what I can hear." Karls calm tone overrode Marina's. "Give me the phone." There was no doubting the authority in his voice. "Lauren, Karl here."

"Actually, I wanted to talk to you." And in the spirit of diplomacy Lauren added a belated "As well."

"What progress have you and your colleague made? I may add that I have checked and the Irish police force are very complimentary about your investigative skills, Mr Tegan, but I have yet to see what you can accomplish."

"I believe you've been in contact with Inspector Eacrett and are on your way to Dungarvan the moment?"

"Yes. Our ETA is ten minutes, according to our driver."

Lauren kept her voice smooth and professional. "We've just left there. The Inspector has detained Larry Caligula so you can talk with him. There's a couple of things you might need to know before you meet him."

"Like what?"

"You told me earlier that Hannah didn't like the security chief – besides that, have you any reason not to trust him?"

"Larry Caligula has headed the London office for at least five years and, in that time, he has given me no reason to distrust him. Why?"

"We've talked to some young people who befriended Hannah and her friend David and she told the girl that she had overheard Caligula planning with someone called Shyrl to kidnap her and use her as leverage against you."

"*Damnation!*"

"Does the name Shyrl ring a bell?"

"My PA's secretary is a woman called Shyrl Baker. I'd have to ask Angela if she knows of any association between her and Caligula. What did they want from me? Or do you know?"

"Caligula told Inspector Eacrett that some unnamed someone wanted you to pull out of whatever negotiations you're undertaking for the International Monetary Commission. According to our source, Caligula told this Shyrl it was worth ten million to them to scupper your plans."

In all the years Lauren had known Karl Offenbach, she had never heard him swear beyond an exasperated *Damn*. If pushed she would have said he didn't know any words that could be constituted as swear words. Now she stared at the phone in amazement as the airways turned blue with an exotic vocabulary of swears, some of which were new to her.

"We thought you'd need to know that before you tackled him," she said quietly when he finished.

"Where is Hannah now?"

"She's on a bus to Cork. Thomas and myself are heading there this minute but we've lost more than an hour and the bus, I believe, takes a little over an hour to make the journey."

"Is she safe?"

Lauren hesitated. "We don't know. It seems Caligula has friends in Cork who may be alerted to intercept her."

"*Bloody hell!* We'll be pulling up outside Dungarvan Police Station shortly. I'm grateful for the information. When I've torn strips off Caligula, I'll let you know the most likely place you'll find our girl."

Lauren stared at the now blank phone-screen in her hand.

"He's gone. Do you think he'll actually find out where Hannah is?"

"Realistically?" Trout glanced at her before pushing his speed another ten kilometres over the limit. "Not a snowball's hope in hell. Use my phone and call Mac."

"How's the boyo?" Mac answered with his usual exuberance.

"Hi, Mac, Lauren here. I've got you on speaker, so the boyo can hear you too."

"My favourite sleuth! How's she cuttin', Lauren?"

"How are you, Mac?" Trout joined in the usual Mac banter.

"Pulling the devil by the tail and I'll risk a swipe from Old Nick himself and venture this is not a social call."

"Right as usual, Mac."

In a few short sentences Trout filled Mac in on their investigation and the information he needed about Cork and the O'Carthy.

"Leave it with me for half an hour and I'll be back to you, with what you think you need, and what I think you need." And with his rich chuckle Mac disconnected.

Lauren had barely left the phone down when her own rang. She frowned. The number was unknown to her. She accepted the call.

"Lauren, Pamela O'Leary here. Mr Tegan's phone is engaged."

Hearing the panic in the sergeant's voice, Lauren hit speaker.

"Caligula is gone and I thought you needed to know it asap."

"Gone?"

"How the fuck?"

"Eacrett's on his way to the hospital." Pamela sounded close to tears. "Caligula broke some sort of a glass vial and released a gas that caused the Inspector to have an asthma attack. We found the broken glass and are trying to identify what could have been in it. Whatever the gas was, it has affected him badly. He's in critical condition. *Oh shit!* Offenbach's here. I have to go."

"Jesus Christ!" said Trout. "All we need now is –"

Lauren held up a hand. "It's Brendan," she said, and accessed the message. It was a forwarded WhatsApp. She read it aloud: "'*Package secured. Awaiting your arrival for handover.*' He's added his own message. *Just came through.*'"

"*Shit!*" Trout beat a tattoo on the steering wheel.

Lauren said nothing, chewed on her lip for a moment, told herself not to panic and said, "We're still ahead of him, aren't we?"

"Yeah. We're less than thirty minutes from Cork but we don't know where they're holding them. Caligula does, or if he doesn't he has the connections to find out."

"Well, we have Mac. And I'm not going to give up that easily. I'll tear Cork city apart if I have to until I find Hannah." Lauren injected a resolve she was far from feeling into her voice, repeating to herself that words have energy. She was keeping hers positive, come what may. Still, she couldn't help the tremor that ran through her. "Mac said half an hour. And he doesn't say things if he doesn't mean them."

CHAPTER 26

Silence prevailed in the car as the outskirts of the city were reached. Trout swore another pithy "*Shit!*" as they hit the evening traffic.

Lauren kept her own council, deeming it wiser to say nothing. She almost jumped out of her skin when Trout's phone rang in her lap where she'd dropped it when Pamela O'Leary's call came through on her phone.

She swiped to answer and hit speaker.

"Well, now, me old segotia, I hear you haven't lost the knack of ruffling some seriously dangerous feathers. Not that I'd hold it against you but the O'Carthy is one vicious bastard and that was even before he honed his skills in the army. He has tricks up his sleeve that we wouldn't be able to imagine. Are you sure you want to tangle with him?"

"We have to, Mac. Now he's got Lauren's godchild and the young man who's helping her."

"*God Almighty!* If that be the case, listen closely and I'll tell you what I know and what I've found out." Mac took a deep breath and exhaled loudly. "The O'Carthy, one Benjamin Séan O'Carthy, known to his few and very select friends as Buddy. Born in Ireland of Irish-American parents and moved to the US when he was a child. Brought up in Pittsburg, did a stint in the army, which by all accounts couldn't hack his antics and he left before anyone could fire him or whatever they do in an army. The next few years are a bit blurred but it's generally accepted that he led a band of mercenaries to fight for whoever paid the top dollar, mostly South America but there was some talk of Europe and Russia along the way." Mac paused. "This you understand is a seriously potted history and I'm only setting the scene for his return to our little island."

"No harm to know where he's coming from, Mac. Keep going and if you have any advice for getting through Cork at rush hour, you can throw it in for good measure."

"Ye've arrived, have ye? I'd say find a spot and pull in – that way if I'm giving ye directions ye'll be starting from where ye are if you get my gist."

Trout looked at Lauren and raised his eyebrows. "Go on with your story. I'll look for a place to pull in."

"I only wish it was a story but I'll go on anyway. As you can imagine, the buck got notions on his travels and learned to like the trappings of high living. Not earning them, mind you, but anything that made an easy buck was grist to his mill. He discovered the ins and outs of the drug trade doing a bit of business in Columbia, remembered he came from a little island on the edge of the world and thought coming home and setting up a trading post would be an idea. He thought to give himself status, he'd resurrect the old title, not you understand that the O'Carthys were ever entitled to one – that would be the Macs, as in the McCarthys – but then there wasn't anyone going to take him on given that his reputation preceded him home. He acquired a block of the old warehouses along the docks and set up business about ten years ago and you might say he has gone from strength to strength since."

Trout inched his way through the Dunkettle Interchange and finally reached the roundabout. He made a hard left, onto the docklands, pulled into a space facing the water and stopped the car.

"Anyone try to stop him?" Trout reached for his phone but kept it angled towards Lauren so they were both still listening together.

"One or two but between accidents, revenue audits, mysterious fires, merchandise going missing, people got the message and left him well enough alone."

"He doesn't sound like someone I'd like to see taking Hannah." Lauren tried but couldn't keep the fear from her voice.

"I'm with you there." Mac sounded grave. "There was a murmur this evening that he was expecting a visit from an old pal and that orders were all stops were to be pulled out to give him whatever he wanted."

"We got a message ourselves that we believe means that O'Carthy has apprehended Hannah and her friend and is holding them for his pal whom we have identified as one Larry Caligula, the security chief with KOE, Hannah's father's business."

"Holy smoke! That's one for the books."

"And to make matters worse the same Caligula released some sort of a gas that has sent Waterford Inspector Eacrett to hospital with a life-threatening asthma attack."

"Seamus Eacrett. I know him, a bit of a bully if he could get away with it but sound behind it. It's not like him to get caught."

"An underhand trick. Caligula broke a vial of whatever he had in his pocket on the desk in front of Eacrett and skedaddled out of the room. Lucky enough his sergeant returned fairly quick and was able to pull him out of the fumes but the immediate damage was done."

"I'm sorry to hear that. I wouldn't wish it on the man."

"Nor would I. He's been an enormous asset to us, in spite of his dodgy attitude." Trout thought for a second. "Would you have any suggestion as to where O'Carthy would stash the youngsters? We have a bit of a lead on Caligula and should try to find them before he arrives."

"By all accounts the bulk of his disreputable work is carried out in the second block of warehouses."

"Second block?"

"Did I forget to mention that he has a legitimate freight business that services the need to hide excess cash? Where are you?"

"I pulled into the docks beyond the Dunkettle Roundabout."

"You couldn't be better placed. If you go straight along almost to the other end, you'll come some fairly derelict-looking warehouses. Old stone ones. Don't be fooled by them – they're as solid as the day they were built only the insides of a couple of them wouldn't be up to much. The farthest over one has his shipping offices and word on the ground has it that at least one of the others, probably a derelict one, is used by young ones on their uppers and customers that want easy access to his products."

"A likely holding-place by the sounds of things."

"You've said it. There's a sort of a quadrangle at the back where you can get into them without too much bother as long as you can by-pass whatever security he might have in place."

"Would there be much do you think?"

"Less than you'd expect, I'd say. There's an alleyway to the street at the upper side, where the young ones come and go – pedestrian only but it might be a good place to suss out and have as a bolt passage."

"It's going on for seven o'clock so we have around two good hours of daylight left but we'd want to move now rather than later. I'll look around this minute and get a move on it before Caligula arrives and throws a spanner in the works. Thanks, Mac, I owe you a big one."

"You mind yourself and let me know how you get on."

Trout disengaged and looked hard at Lauren. "Showtime," he said.

CHAPTER 27

Trout drove cautiously along the docks. In the distance he could see ships of all sizes from pleasure crafts to freight monsters.

Lauren was frowning at the water. "I didn't realize that big ships still come right in so close to Cork city."

"For the moment. They have a huge regeneration programme ongoing. Eventually all this will be fancy apartments and restaurants. Those look like the warehouses Mac was talking about. Take a good look at them as I pass."

"Oh!"

"What's the 'Oh' for?"

"They're like a cliché, old and dark and dangerous-looking." Lauren shuddered. "There's a darkness around them even on this lovely evening."

"Ideal then if you want a place away from prying eyes. The more sinister a place looks, the less ordinary people want anything to do with it."

"I suppose. I hate to think that Hannah might be incarcerated in such a brooding, unpredictable place."

"Unpredictable?"

"Can't you see it?" Lauren's voice held a note of fear. "It's a place of dark deeds and nothing about it asks for forgiveness."

"It's an old, almost derelict warehouse, Lauren." Trout took his bearings, passed the warehouses, pulled onto a wide street and kept left. "Try not to let your imagination imbue it with any more evil than it already has." He circled the block, headed back towards the water, passed once in front of the warehouses and began another circuit.

Lauren shuddered again but said nothing.

"That must be the alleyway." He pointed to a narrow opening between two tall old buildings. A little further on the Cork port sign could be seen and beside it a large P to designate public parking. Trout indicated and pulled into the first space, right beside the opening.

"Right. Time to reconnoitre."

"I'm coming with you."

Trout went to say something, saw the set of her lips. "OK, but when we've seen what's what you'll have to do exactly what I say."

"Right." Lauren opened her belt, hopped out, hitched her bag across her shoulder and waited for Trout to lead the way.

He caught her hand in passing. "We're just out for a stroll in the evening sunlight." Together they wandered back the way they came and, as they came level with the alleyway, turned casually into it as if it was the most natural thing in the world. The alley was blocked to traffic by an iron bollard set into cobbles. It ran along the side of a cut-stone building to an adjoining one of older stone and on into a roughly cobbled courtyard. The warehouses that made up the sides and the ones opposite were older and more decrepit than they looked from the road. Nonetheless they seemed, to all intent and purposes, intact. Trout halted Lauren in the shadow of the alley opening, poked his head into the opening itself and surveyed the area. To his left he could make out another wider opening with tall spike-topped iron gates Through it the gleam of water showed where they had passed along the docks on their way around the warehouses. The square was litter-strewn but otherwise looked deserted. His eyes tracked up the buildings. They showed three rows of windows. Whether the internal three storeys were intact remained to be seen. Blank, barred windows were obvious on the ground level and, as he craned upwards, he fancied he could see the glint of glass in higher windows. Directly opposite, big double doors were set into the wall, an enormous iron running-bolt keeping them closed. He cautiously leaned further out, looked to the left and right and pulled back with a satisfied expression.

Trout leaned close to Lauren's ear. "I'm going in. I want you to keep watch. Text me if anyone comes. I'll put my phone on silent but I'll feel the vibration." He indicated right. "There's an alcove just there, where you'll be out of sight unless someone stands directly in front of you, where you'll be able to see anyone who comes or goes from any direction." He caught her in a fierce hug. "Get into place before I move and put your phone on silent." He went to say something more, gave her another quick squeeze. "Mind yourself."

"Back at you, Trout. Be as careful as you can." Lauren took a deep breath, flattened herself against the wall, slunk around the opening, melded into the alcove Trout had indicated and was out of sight in the blink of an eye.

Trout waited to make sure Lauren was settled, shrugged the tension out of his shoulders and thinking '*Nothing ventured, nothing gained*' quickly crossed the quadrangle and silently approached the door. Up close it was an iron-clad structure that once had boasted a royal-blue colour, going by the remnants of paint hanging on it. Now it was mostly rust. Nonetheless it gave every appearance of a solid barrier. The big bolt was old, heavy and black with oil. It was pulled back and a large new padlock hung from its latch. He grasped the handle and gave a cautious pull. The door slid silently open, with an ease that had Trout straining to keep it from opening too wide. All he could see was pitch-black inside. He stepped softly over the threshold, pulled the door back into place and stood still, trying to penetrate the darkness around him.

For almost thirty seconds he thought the darkness was complete. He fingered the phone in his pocket, debated using its torch app and decided against it. He needed to know what he was dealing with before venturing to announce his presence. Instead, he closed his eyes and counted one-one-thousand, two-one-thousand, all the way to twenty. When he opened them again the darkness didn't seem as dense. Still, he stood absorbing the space. A musty, musky smell permeated the air, like old mushrooms on a damp evening. Mould, he thought, reminding himself to breathe through his nose in case of spores. He extended his arms in front of him – nothing – widened them out until he felt his left hand connect with a dank, rough surface. Wall to the left, he thought, already knowing the door was on his right. His eyes were growing more accustomed to the lack of light and he could discern outlines, shadows of deeper grey in the gloom. He turned his head. A row of tall barred windows, dull with years of accumulated dirt, ranged sightless along the wall, further to his right and beyond the door. Directly in front of him, looming like the set of a haunted ruin, he made out a line of arched openings that fronted a deeper darkness. They vanished upwards, drawing his eye to a railed walkway that appeared to float in the murky gloom. He moved cautiously forward, his feet shuffling through dust and debris. Somewhere a floorboard creaked. Trout stilled. His ears strained with the effort of pin-pointing the source of the sound. A faint click, as of a door closing, echoed high in the vaulted ceiling. The air settled and the silence again became complete.

Trout hurried now and quickly reached the arches. Up close the brickwork was damp and crumbling but the arches themselves seemed intact. He inched around the first pillar, saw that it hid a wooden stairway and tracked it with his eyes, as it curved upwards to the first-floor walkway. The steps were sagging and part of the safety rail was missing. He listened intently. The silence pressed around him. He stood for a moment, his foot raised towards the bottom step, took a breath and surged upwards quickly, light-footed, using only the inside edge of each stair. He was breathing fast when he reached the top and stood to ground himself, quieten his breathing and listen some more. His eyes had fully adapted to the gloom and he could see fairly well albeit in a surreal, grey-light sort of way. It occurred to him he would find the whole escapade funny if it wasn't so serious. He shook himself. This was no time for levity. He was on a mission and the sooner he completed it, the sooner he could leave this crumbling fortress whose very walls gave off decay and despair. He looked around. Solid wooden planks formed the floor and iron railings, once white, now rust-covered, prevented anyone from inadvertently walking over the edge. He grabbed the nearest rail, found it solid and felt a moment of relief that he wouldn't have to worry too much about falling into the abyss below. Patches of paleness against the dark dotted the wall that ran along the walkway, opposite where he stood. Doorways, he thought, at regular intervals, and further over darker shadows showed where some were most likely closed and he presumed intact.

Here goes, he thought, time to see what stood behind them and inside them, even if it was nothing.

CHAPTER 28

Trout cat-footed forward, listening intently. Cautiously he approached the first tall rectangle of pale grey superimposed on the dark background, peered around the jamb of a doorless opening and saw what appeared to be a makeshift kitchen. A long, narrow window, nearly the length of the wall but almost at ceiling level, lightened the dark to some extent. A gas can with a two-ring top lurked in one corner, flanked by a small camping stove and a large Kettle barbeque. Sagging shelves held a small array of tinned foodstuff and a three-legged table with a pile of magazines providing a makeshift fourth leg, were ghostly silhouettes in the gloom and completed the furnishing. It looked relatively clean as if someone had made an effort to bring a semblance of order to a no-win situation. He moved on. Communal sitting room, he thought, eying the ancient sofa with its stuffing spilling out, a couple of wonky chairs, a tatty, rattan chaise lounge and a moth-eaten rug. So far as squats went, he had seen worse.

The next opening told a more graphic story. Here was a rougher feel and piles of newspaper and cardboard boxes, in pointedly territorial heaps, told a less hopeful story. The next three rooms had closed doors. He hesitated at the first one then tentatively turned the knob and peered in. Somebody was trying to make a sanctuary for themselves, he thought, a tight feeling in his chest as he noted a rolled-up sleeping bag on a shelf with a battery tent-heater nestled against it. A steel coat hanger was hooked over the edge of the same shelf and bulged downwards under the weight of a pair of jeans, a check shirt and a faded yellow jumper. Perched beneath it in an attempt to get what little light the high window offered was a once-elegant armchair, faded and torn, and leaning drunkenly against it was an orange crate of books. A pang of sadness went through Trout and he backed out of the room and quietly closed the door.

A snuffling sound distracted him as he opened the next door and quickly looked inside. A bleary-eyed individual untangled himself from a blanket on the floor and glared at him.

"You OK, mate?" Trout said quietly.

A mumbled "Fuck off," answered him and a louder "*Get the bloody hell out of my room!*" had Trout scurrying away in case someone came to investigate. The last room had a door but it was stuck half-closed, half open. Here the real business of the warehouse was most in evidence. The newspaper and cardboard boxes were there but also half-melted candles stuck onto various surfaces, blackened spoons, discarded syringes and balled up tin-foil. Trout made a grimace – poor sods. He moved on.

Just past the last room another stairway swayed to the top level. It felt decidedly unstable but as Trout had seen no sign of those he sought, he continued his quest, more soft-footed than before. Here the walkway felt very close to the sturdy wooden trusses crisscrossing the roof. Only two rooms appeared to have doors and they were solidly closed. The others he passed displayed cramped, rubbish-strewn interiors, half-bricked up windows and skittering, gnawing, rustling sounds that proclaimed rodents as the primary occupants.

Trout stood outside the first closed door and listened intently. There was no sound. Slowly he extracted his phone and flashed the light on the door. It was old, a stout wooden structure, oak he thought and as solid and impenetrable as the day it was installed. An old-fashioned iron latch allowed entry and a shiny new stainless-steel bolt, fully engaged, ensured that currently anyone inside couldn't leave. He edged towards the second door, also solidly closed. As he came opposite it, he heard the rattle of a latch, about to be raised. Quickly he spun around and in a fluid movement whirled inside the next opening and flattened himself against the wall.

A harsh voice, enunciated clearly, "I'll get us some food. You stay here and keep an eye on things."

A mumble of words issued from further away.

"The local inhabitants have nothing to do with this level," said the first voice. "They'll keep away. They know it's out of bounds and their continuing to stay here depends on them doing just that."

Again, a mutter, more querulous this time.

"You've some nerve to question me." The tone was quieter this time, cold with a dangerous edge to it. "Our guests are our priority. And, remember, they're not to be harmed." The voice iced even further. "It's me you'll answer to if you fuck this up and don't think friendship will interfere with what I'll do. Bolt the door when I leave – you'll hear my key and can let me in when I come back."

The door was pulled to with a decisive click. Silence reigned. Trout held his breath. He heard the smooth grate of a well-oiled bolt. More silence, this time pregnant with the anticipation of any wayward sound. After what seemed an infinite minute, he heard the soft tread of the erstwhile speaker moving towards the stairway. An occasional, barely perceptible creak allowed him track the unknown's descent. He waited, allowing him time to reach the ground floor, cross the warehouse and finally heard the soft thud of the outer door. Still, he remained motionless, allowed the old building settle back into its own definition of quiet before he padded back onto the walkway. Flashing the phone light, he saw the door in front of him was fitted with a Yale lock and understood the instruction about hearing a key. Knocking on this door would serve no useful purpose.

Trout considered his options. He moved to stand before the first door. Was it possible Hannah and David were being held in this room while their goaler remained next door? He eyed the structure, wondered would there be a corresponding bolt on the inside. Only one way to find out. With infinite care, he manoeuvred the bolt open, saying a silent prayer of thanks for whoever had oiled it so efficiently. He shrugged the tension from his shoulders, an old habit that had served him well at times during his career, and took a deep breath. Slowly, slowly he lifted the latch. It too had been oiled recently and he felt the skim of oil transferred to his fingers. No time to worry about fingerprints although he doubted such things would be on the minds of whoever had taken the youngsters. The next bit was even more tricky. He hoped the wielder of the oil can had thought to do the hinges as well. Carefully, he pushed the door, opened it incrementally and thankfully without as much as a creak of the wood.

Once the gap was wide enough, Trout moved partially inside. He kept one hand on the door and allowed his eyes, now fully acclimatised to the gloom, to roam the space. Immediately he saw them. The boy was slumped on a wooden chair, his arms pinned behind its back and his legs tied in front. His head lolled on his chest and he gave no indication that he was aware of his surroundings. The girl was held upright by the rope wrapped around her body. Her head was up, her closed eyes dark smudges against the ghostly white of her face. For a terrible moment Trout feared she wasn't breathing until she pulled in a shuddering breath and her chest jiggled against the rope.

Trout glided fully inside. The room was empty except for the two. An archway opened into the adjoining room and the faint glow of a lamp looked eerily yellow in the dullness. Trout could discern the end of a table through the opening and heard a creak as if someone had rocked a chair back on two legs. He closed the door but didn't bolt it. The heavy oak held it in place. He stood, muscles loose and ready to react in an instant, and studied the position of the chairs. They were in full view of the opening and presumably of whoever remained on watch. There was nowhere to hide. He needed to figure out a way to neutralize the guard and get two traumatised youngsters out of the warehouse before the second guard came back. *No pressure, Trout*, he told himself, *but get a move on*. Time wasn't on his side.

CHAPTER 29

Lauren shrank into the alcove, acutely conscious of her light-coloured summer clothes. Her silvery-grey linen-blend culottes and oversize lilac top weren't especially bright but she had no doubt would glow like a beacon if someone was taking a close look along the old-grey walls. All she could hope for was that in the dullness of the courtyard she would appear as just another shadow. She reminded herself that if anyone appeared she should turn her face away. It was harder to dismiss the form of a face than the shape of a person, which tended to blend better with its surroundings. At least, that's what her reading of crime-related novels would suggest. And what about hair, a voice in her head questioned. Yours is red, not the easiest colour to camouflage. She gave a vexed shake to her shoulders. How would she know? She had never put any of her crime-based reading to the test before. You need a hat. Well, tough! She hadn't one with her and would just have to trust that by staying completely still she would remain unseen.

The next issue that her mind brought to her attention was her complete lack of a means of defending herself. Now was not a good time to raise that issue, she argued with the voice in her head. Her alter ego, or whoever was in there, argued back, urging her to at least try and think of something. Anything, or any means that could be used to protect herself, buy time to get away or disable a thug. Like what, her mind countered. There must be something in that bag of yours? It's big enough and you keep stuffing things into it. Maybe a handy little derringer, or a flick knife, even a bottle of pepper spray? Her alter ego was nothing if not imaginative.

The everyday Lauren's voice was aware of the absurdity of her internal conversation. Her more adventurous alter ego was tut-tutting at how little she had prepared for the role of an investigator. Investigators may be faced with dangerous, challenging situations, normal Lauren admitted. Alter Ego snorted and would have turned her nose up in the air except that she was determined that Lauren find something. Some little thing that could at least be held in her hand, so she could pretend to be prepared for an encounter.

She ran through the possibilities. Phone, Alter Ego suggested. Need it to warn Trout, her head countered. Anyway, it wouldn't stop a snowflake let alone a determined thug. Have a root in the bag, Alter Ego commanded, there must be something we've overlooked.

The tendency to argue with herself in her thoughts was a long-held habit of Lauren's. She generally used it successfully to tease out decisions that needed a for-and-against approach. At this moment, she wasn't sure where she was going with it but she admitted that she was using it as a distraction. Her eyes were roaming the quadrangle, she could feel the tension mounting with every circuit. She drew a ragged breath. She knew she needed to be calm and alert and ready to react decisively. In the meantime, rooting in her bag would keep her hands busy.

She hefted the bag, feeling its weight as she did so and recalled the way David swung the rucksack to deter the gang from coming any nearer to him and his friends. It had potential but probably wouldn't stop anyone determined to get her. She doubted the soft-leather olive-green tote would stop a bullet or a knife. It might slow them down. If it came to it. She'd prefer if it didn't come to it. Her fingers scrabbled at the pocket flaps. The first pocket yielded her keys. OK. Definite potential there. Mrs Dillon, her old schoolteacher, had taught all the children some basic self-defence, including how to hold a fistful of keys with one protruding between the two first fingers, if one needed to take a swing at an attacker. Then she had proceeded to threaten immediate and terrible retribution on anyone she found using such a low strike without their life being in immediate danger.

The second pocket held a notebook and pen. She shuddered. She really didn't think she had the stomach to stick a biro into someone's eye or any other soft-tissue area an attacker might offer. If she was desperate enough, Alter Ego prodded. *No.* She shuddered. She'd want to be very, very desperate and, even then, she didn't think she could do it.

She stilled. Was that a car at the gate? Her gaze skittered to it, saw the car pull up, watched for a moment, saw the glisten of water through the bars and realized the car had seized a break in traffic and passed onto the street. She blew out a breath and allowed her eyes to roam once more around the space enclosed by the warehouses. The greyness of the old stone was looking more oppressive the more she looked at it. The moss and ivy clinging to the walls added a layer of darkness to the already lengthening shadows. Almost convulsively she dug her hand into the main pocket of the bag and resumed her search. Tissues, wallet, her old and faithful Swiss-army penknife. She remembered MacGyver. She used to love that television programme. He could just about do anything with his self-same penknife and that was pre-digital so the chances were he really could do it. Still, she didn't think she'd be channelling MacGyver any time soon. Her questing fingers dug deeper and closed around her newly bought bottle of Provocative Woman. She snatched a breath and lifted it out. It was a full-sized bottle and it felt substantial in her hand. She flicked the lid back into her bag and placed a finger on the atomizer. It might not be pepper-spray but she'd bet it would fairly sting if someone got it in the face. Needs must, she decided, and held it lightly in her right hand. It felt surprisingly reassuring.

A dull thud had her eyes swivelling to the big double doors through which Trout had disappeared. A thick-set man in a muscle tee and cargo pants exited, banging the doors together, careless of whatever noise they made. His shaved head gleamed in the dimming light and he moved purposefully towards the gate and left through a pedestrian gate hidden one side of the stone posts. Lauren pressed herself back against the wall and held herself completely still until he was out of sight. The courtyard became still and silent again. Lauren waited, her mind now reciting with as much bravado as she could summon: *They also serve who only stand and wait.*

CHAPTER 30

Trout slunk along the wall, keeping his hands to his back and using them to mark his progress around the room. As he came opposite Hannah, some instinct caused her to straighten her head. Her eyes snapped open, widened, her lips parted. Trout urgently tapped a finger to his lips. She drew in a sharp breath, barely nodded and attempted to straighten herself as best she could within the constraints of the ropes. Trout held up one finger. She gave an almost imperceptible nod. He inched around until he was almost at the opening, still in Hannah's sightline but out of sight of anyone who would approach her from the other room. He flattened himself against the wall, as if he would meld into the grey plaster.

"*Call him,*" he mouthed at her.

Hannah frowned, went to shake her head, then realizing what he was getting at, gave another nod. "*Hey, you!*" she croaked, cleared her throat and said more loudly, "*You in there! Come in here – I want to talk to you!*"

David's head shot up. "Are you crazy?" he hissed, saw Trout and gurgled a strangled sound that he changed to a groan as he registered Trout's frantic signals to stay quiet.

The thud of a chair landing back on its four legs was followed by a crude laugh. "Want to negotiate with me, honey-pot?" A thin wiry individual with a narrow weaselly face appeared in the archway. "What could you offer me now, that might persuade me to be nice to you?" He licked his lips and took another step towards Hannah.

David struggled against his ties. "Don't, Hannah," he whispered. "Don't lower yourself to the level of that filth."

"Who you calling filth? You're the one tied up here and you'd want to remember!" He moved towards David, his eyes glittering, his arm upraised to deliver a punch.

His words were cut off as Trout's arm circled his neck from behind, while his thumb exerted the right amount of pressure to render him unconscious.

Trout let him fall none too gently onto the floor and turned his attention to Hannah. His trusty Swiss army knife made short work of one part of the rope and he quickly unwound the rest, coiling it as he went. He hauled her to her feet. "Stamp around there get some circulation going." He handed her the open penknife. "Release David while I tie up this specimen."

Hannah gave him a startled glance, did a quick dance-shuffle, and turned to cut through the cable ties that bound David's hands and feet. He in turn stood and tried to get his circulation going. Trout tied the unconscious man's hands behind his back, bent his knees and brought the rope down from his wrists and repeated the action, tying his ankles together. The man was well trussed and releasing him would slow down his gang-mate when he returned.

"We need to get out of here, fast," Trout said. "Can ye walk?"

"We'll run if we have to." David caught Hannah's hand. "Lead the way."

Trout nodded, ushered them out the door, paused to engage the bolt and directed them down the two flights of stairs. They had reached the ground-floor when the outside door opened. Trout said a soft, pithy, "*Shit,*" indicated they hide behind an arch and motioned them to stand completely still. They did so, backs against the crumbling surface. A big broad-shouldered shadow crossed the warehouse, carrying a paper bag in one hand and a tray of take-away cups in the other. He ascended the first flight of stairs, and turned towards the end to access other stairs. Trout edged the two around the arch so they remained out of sight, indicated the far wall and when he heard the creak as the man stepped off the top step onto the walkway, led them silently and hurriedly in the shadow of the wall, to the outside door. He eased it open and cautiously poked his head out. The alley had grown considerably greyer while he was inside the warehouse but it was still far from dark. It seemed quiet, deserted. A ripple of movement across the square attracted his attention. Right in the middle of their bolt-alley.

"*What the hell! Damnation!* I'd forgotten the residents."

A ragged group of people – young men and a scattering of girls – came clattering into the courtyard from the alley through which himself and Lauren had entered. They carried bottles and cans and at least one of them had a bag that clinked, suggesting more bottles. They were, en-masse, heading for the doorway where he stood with Hannah and David. His eyes probed the gloom further and he made out the lighter shadow in the alcove that assured him Lauren was still in situ.

"Look as normal as possible and head for the alleyway those people just came through," he said over his shoulder, pushed the doors wide open and stepped out. He stood to one side and allowed the two rescues to go before him. A further clatter at the gate attracted his attention. A black Jeep Cherokee with a dented front grill waited with the engine revving as an unknown individual unlocked the gate. Trout studied the newcomer through the bars of the gate. He was tall, his head almost level with the original top of the gate, which now sported a row of lethal-looking spikes, to deter would-be climbers. He pushed the gates inwards with a force that showed impatience and a contained strength that belied his narrow frame. They were barely open when the jeep jerked through and roared into the yard.

Above the din, Trout heard a bellow from high in the warehouse. *"Run!"* he yelled.

Hannah and David ran.

The arriving residents looked at them curiously but made no move to stop them, only turned as one to stare at the black vehicle. It ground to a stop almost on top of the gaggle of youngsters. The driver, whom Trout saw was Caligula, stared through the windscreen and surveyed the group with barely concealed contempt. For a second, Trout wondered where the man who opened the gate was. He spotted him on the far side of the jeep, watching the crowd with hooded eyes and a contemptuous twist of his lips.

A young man in ragged jeans and a shirt flapping open to reveal a bare, bony chest reached out and caressed the shiny black surface of the Jeep. "Nice," he said in a dreamy voice. "Come and feel it, guys."

Muscle Man erupted through the doors, roaring, "*Where are they?*" He looked wildly around, ploughed his way through the residents surging around the Jeep and sprinted for the alleyway.

Caligula slammed open the jeep door, jumped down and made to go after him. Trout launched himself at him in a rugby tackle and the two of them went rolling over the cobbles, locked in an unrelenting embrace.

Lauren stepped out of her alcove into the path of Muscle Man and sprayed a continuous mist of perfume straight into his face. He clawed at his face, roared, "*You've blinded me, you bitch!*" and lunged at her. She screamed and threw the perfume bottle at him. It connected with his nose with an audible crunch and blood spouted like a cascading fountain. Muscle Man covered his face with his hands, crashed into the wall and as he staggered back, dazed, Lauren stuck out her foot. The big man tripped over it and fell heavily to the ground. His head bounced off the cobbles and he lay still. She went to run around him, caught sight of Caligula straddling Trout with his fist raised to land a finishing blow. She screamed at the top of her lungs, grabbed the strap of her bag and, swinging it in the air, ran at Caligula. The bag caught him full in the face and sent him sprawling. Lauren's momentum carried her with it and she landed on top of him, jerked upright, grabbed her bag in both hands and set to battering him around the head, face and shoulders with it, screaming at the top of her lungs the whole time.

Trout raised his head and slowly pulled himself to his feet. He looked around him. The black jeep was still there, the ragged bunch of residents leaning against it, watching the fray with all the signs of enjoyment. A couple were swigging from bottles and one or two were inhaling crisps with their eyes glued to something. Trout followed their gaze to see Lauren astride Caligula, pounding him with what looked like her bag. He became aware that most of the clamour in his head was her screaming, "*You've killed him, you've killed him!*"

He staggered over to them and, with a surge of strength he didn't know he possessed, lifted her off Caligula. "We need to get out of here!"

She turned startled eyes towards him, flung herself into his arms and burst into tears. "I thought you were dead!"

"I'm not but we need to go. *Now.*" He turned her towards the alleyway and caught the eye of the man standing on the far side of the jeep. The man who had opened the gate. He was watching them, an odd, grudging appreciation in his look. He made no move to stop them. Behind him, Caligula groaned and stirred.

Trout propelled Lauren into the alley and hurried her away without once looking back.

CHAPTER 31

It took Trout a minute to realize that the car that was responding to his key wasn't his Lexus. He swore softly. The Lexus was in the Garda yard in Dungarvan. He needed to get it to a garage but so far other things were taking precedent.

They settled into the low seats of the Golf. He looked at Lauren. "Where are they?"

"Hannah and David?" She threw him a startled look. "I don't know. They ran through the alley and that's all I saw of them."

He started the car. "They can't have gone far. I'll drive around and we'll find them."

The traffic had lightened but the road was still busy. Trout manoeuvred the Golf into the flow and glanced at Lauren. "Thanks for rescuing me."

"Any time." She smiled at his profile. "By the way, you owe me a bottle of Provocative Woman."

"I didn't know you got your attitude from a bottle. Does that mean if you get too much for me, I can stopper the bottle and tone you down?"

Lauren laughed outright. "It's my perfume and a brand-new bottle at that."

"Perfume? I didn't think perfume would be high on your list of necessities in the middle of our efforts?"

"Normally it wouldn't but, as I used my new bottle to such good effect on Muscle Man, I want a replacement to put in my bag."

"You took on that thug with a bottle of perfume?" Trout didn't know whether to be impressed or horrified at the risk she had taken.

"Well, it was the nearest thing to pepper spray I had."

"Pepper spray is illegal."

"So is attacking defenceless women, or if it isn't it should be."

"At the rate you were going at Caligula with your handbag, I'd hardly call you defenceless. Where did you learn to fight dirty?"

"Mrs Dillon."

"Mrs Dillon? Our old schoolteacher?" The car wobbled as Trout turned completely to look at her.

"Watch the road. Yes. She always gave the sixth-class girls a lesson in self-defence. She said it was important for every girl to feel safe wherever she was and that having a couple of little tricks up one's sleeve was helpful."

"What sort of tricks? Or dare I ask?"

"Mostly a sort of . . . you know that scene in *Miss Congeniality* where she tells the audience to remember to sing? An understated version of that."

"Remind me." Trout was already grimacing as he said it.

"She advised us to use whatever was unhampered – elbow, feet, hands, head – and aim for the solar plexus, instep, nose and groin."

"*Ouch!* But effective. I always knew she was ahead of her time." Trout changed lanes and circled around in such a way that brought them back by the warehouses. He noted the gates were closed and the black jeep nowhere in sight.

"That she was. Can you imagine she actually showed us how to fist a bunch of keys for maximum effect but warned us it was only to be used in a life-or-death situation. And that was back in the last century!" Lauren scanned the sidewalks probing for a sight of her godchild. "Where could they be?"

"We weren't that long behind them." Trout began a wider circuit of the area.

"Could the others have picked them up again?" Lauren couldn't stop the tremble in her voice. Reaction was setting in and she was afraid she would let the side down by bursting into tears. Again.

"I doubt it. We were out before the jeep and, as far as I'm aware, all the people involved in holding them were in the warehouse."

"But we can't be sure." The tiredness in Lauren's voice was more pronounced. She slumped in her seat. Somewhere at her feet a phone rang. Wearily she reached for her bag, hauled it up and stared at the mess of it. The soft leather was smeared with blood and snot and one of the front pocket flaps was torn and hanging on by a thread.

"It wasn't designed to be a weapon," Trout said quietly, "but you have to admit it was effective."

Lauren attempted a smile. "I guess."

The phone continued its demands to be heard. Using the tips of her fingers Lauren eased open the main pocket, fished in its depths and pulled out her phone. "Marina," she sighed, accepted the call and pressed speaker.

Marina's breathless voice filled the space between Trout and Lauren. "*Where are you, Lauren? Have you got Hannah? We're here at the Eleysium. Karl managed to get the penthouse so we've three bedrooms, loads of room for everyone. You must come straight here. I can't wait.*"

"*Marina, back up!*" Lauren sounded sharper than she intended. There was a beat of silence. "We don't have Hannah."

"*What?*" Marina's voice rose a couple of octaves. "I thought you were gone to Cork to get her."

Lauren rolled her eyes at Trout. "*To 'get her'?* Jesus, Marina, did you think it would be as easy as that?" She took a deep breath to calm herself. "We tried. The only consolation is, the other crowd doesn't have her or her friend either."

"*What do mean? Where are they? What happened? No, Karl, I won't give you the phone. I want Lauren to tell me what's going on!*"

There was the sounds of a scuffle and Karl's deeper tone replaced Marina's shrill voice. She could be heard in the background using language that Lauren knew she had learned from Matt Gardiner back when they were children in Knocknaclogga and would nowadays rarely admit to even knowing.

"Lauren. Karl here. What happened? I gather you've run into a difficulty and in the process failed to find Hannah?"

"We found her and her friend David, even got them out safely from where they were being held – but as we were leaving, Caligula and a guy, probably his contact here in Cork, appeared and one of thugs who had been guarding Hannah and David erupted out of the building. Thomas shouted at Hannah and David to run while we dealt with them. Afterwards," her voice wobbled, "we weren't able to find them. We –"

Karl cut in. "Is there anything more, realistically, you can do tonight?"

Lauren saw Trout shake his head. "No."

"Then come on here. As Marina said we have the rooms. I'm arranging food and you can tell what's happening."

"We'll do that, only Karl – it might be better if you warn the doorman to expect us." She looked down at her torn, dirty clothes. "We're not exactly looking like the cliental the Eleysium usually caters for."

"Therein lies a tale, I'm sure. Actually, Lauren, there's no need. There are parking spaces reserved for the penthouse. You'll find them on the second floor of the underground car park with a lift that takes you directly to the penthouse. I'll let security know to expect you."

CHAPTER 32

When Lauren googled the address Karl had given her, she found they were only ten minutes from the apartment block.

As they approached it, Trout nodded. "I remember now. That was one of the Celtic Tiger white elephants that has since come good."

Lauren allowed her eyes to drift upwards. "*Wow!* It must be one of the tallest buildings in Ireland."

"It was when it was built, now it's down to second. It's some structure. The tower is seventeen storeys tall. The view of the city must be magnificent."

"We'll find out shortly. No doubt the penthouse is somewhere up there in the clouds."

Something in her tone had Trout casting an enquiring glance at her. "Do you mind?"

"Mind what?"

"Marina? This? Money and glamour, a jet-set lifestyle wasn't it you called it?"

"Good God, no!" Lauren was silent for a long minute. "Marina can be full of shit at times but behind it all she's OK. It helped that she spent a lot of her childhood in Knocknaclogga where she was just my cousin and nobody gave a damn who she was after that. It gave her a foundation she might not have if she was brought up only in London. The entry to the car park is around the back."

"Thanks." Trout was already turning for the entrance.

"This business with Hannah has really thrown her. Part of it is that my godchild is a very determined, independent young woman and Marina wants to keep her a child for – maybe not forever – but for as long as she can. And Hannah is having none of it." Lauren sighed. "She could have told either one of them what was going on. Heck, she could have told me but she preferred to go off on this harebrained jaunt that has actually put her in danger." She gave a wry half-smile. "In a lot of ways, she's a regular chip off the old block."

"Meaning?"

"The scrapes Marina got us into would make the hair stand on your head. My consoling thought at this stage is that we survived and I've a feeling Hannah will too."

"Well, I'm a great believer in your thoughts." He lowered the window as a security guard approached. "Thomas Tegan and Lauren O'Loughlin to see the Offenbachs."

The guard grinned. "Mr Offenbach said you might look a bit rough but I don't think he realized just how rough is rough. I trust the other party is similarly distressed."

"He's worse," Trout said simply.

The guard laughed. "Right down to the end. The lift to the penthouse will be directly in front of you."

"Thanks." Trout saluted the guard and drove to where he indicated.

The mirrored interior of the lift caused Lauren to recoil in horror. She stared at her torn clothes, the streaks of mud and tears on her face, her hair sticking out in all directions. "Why didn't you tell me how bad I look?"

Trout examined her. "I didn't notice."

"*What?*" she shrieked. "*How could you not have noticed?*"

He indicated his own dishevelment, the large bruise on his cheek, his blackening eye, the cut along his chin. "I didn't think I was in any position to comment." He held both their bags in one hand and gingerly probed his eye. "I'm pretty sure I can see OK but I hate to think what it will look like tomorrow."

"Maybe we could get some arnica, or comfrey or something. They'd help with the bruising."

"Nine o'clock at night, I doubt it."

"You obviously haven't seen Karl in action. God, I hope there's a bath in the place. I need to soak away some of the stiffness in my muscles. Otherwise, I may not be able to walk at all tomorrow." She stole a covert look at herself. "And that Marina has some clothes I can borrow." She paused. "Trout, what will we tell them?"

"The truth. Or as much of it as seems fitting." Trout grimaced. "We can't exactly hide that we've been in a fight, can we?"

The lift opened onto a plush lobby with an elaborate pair of double-doors directly across from it. It had no sooner pinged than the doors were pulled apart and Marina rushed towards them, only to stop short and stare with wide incredulous eyes.

"Oh my God, what happened? Lauren, are you OK? Trout, your face!"

She went to pull Lauren into a hug but Lauren put up her hands and stopped her.

"Don't, Marina. I need to clean up."

"But Hannah!" Marina gasped. "Oh my God! Is Hannah hurt?"

"No, no," Lauren said hastily. "She wasn't there at that point. She and David had run off, as I told Karl."

"Thank God for that. But come in, come in. Karl has ordered food. You'll have time to get cleaned up before it arrives. Karl, they're here!"

She ushered them into an airy room, all sleek lines and modern furniture. It was decorated in muted tones of grey, white and silver and was dominated by a wall of glass that was open onto a patio that gave a bird's-eye view over Cork city.

Lauren stopped abruptly. "Well, I certainly can't sit anywhere here without getting cleaned up. I'd ruin the upholstery."

A tall silver-fox of a man hurried through the patio doors. He had the toned look of a regular gym user and moved with a contained power that suggested he was the dominant force in the room. He made straight for Lauren. Again, she held up her hands. "No, Karl, the dirt of the warehouse is still on me. I need to get cleaned up."

"We both do," Trout said beside her. "Then we can be properly introduced and talk."

"Of course. Marina, take Lauren and run a bath for her, and show Thomas where he can clean up, perhaps even find some clothes for him." He cast an assessing eye over Trout. "We're not too dissimilar in size."

Trout noted that the smooth mid-Atlantic accent was more compelling and potent in reality than when heard over the phone.

"I have food ordered and it will be ready when you are," Karl said.

"Come on." Marina led them up a short flight of steps, along a carpeted corridor and pushed open the first door on her left. "Bathroom," she said. "For you, Lauren, there's a fabulous bath. I'll just run it and then I'll sort out some clothes for you." She pointed. "Main guest room, last door on the left. There's a full ensuite and a good shower, Trout. I'll have Karl leave in some clothes for you."

She led Lauren into a good-sized bathroom with a deep full-sized bath tucked in behind the door. Lauren almost whimpered in anticipation when she saw it. Marina set both taps flowing and upended half a jar of bath salts under the flow, releasing the heavenly scent of neroli into the air. "Keep an eye on the heat." She indicated a fluffy white bathrobe hanging on the door. "Wrap up in that and come down to me when you're ready. The master bedroom is the second door on the right. I'll be waiting for you there." She went to close the door, turned back and said in a wobbly voice, "I've underestimated you again, haven't I? You're the only one I know for sure won't let me down." She pulled the door out after her as she said, "Take as long as you need, I'll wait."

CHAPTER 33

It was amazing the way feeling clean and wearing fresh clothes could perk one up, Lauren thought as she made her way to the main part of the apartment. Admittedly she could feel the aches and pains in her muscles like a whisper of what was in store for her tomorrow when she'd have actually rested them. Perhaps she could persuade Trout to engage in a bit of exercise that would knock the kinks out a bit more. She smiled as she thought about the ways and means she could use but dimmed it almost immediately when she realized she had reached the living room and needed to compose herself for the onslaught of questions Marina and Karl would surely throw at them. At least the simple, green-linen shift dress Marina had left out for her was both comfortable and made her look good, and for that bit of confidence-boosting she was grateful. She took a deep breath, turned the knob and walked in.

Trout was already there, looking spruce and handsome in slim-fit black jeans and a white polo-shirt. The two men were talking animatedly, and Lauren paused to admire the picture they made against the background of Cork city at night. Trout's eye didn't look so livid, now that he was cleaned up. She wondered if he had put something on it and what it could be. Her meandering thoughts didn't last long. Marina rushed at her, caught her in a tight hug, pulled her towards the men, plucked a glass of wine from somewhere and pushed it into her hand. Lauren blinked as it was all coming at her so fast but dutifully took a sip from the glass and felt the smooth liquid warm and aromatic on her tongue.

"Food's here, we'll eat while it's hot." Marina's desperate attempt at normality served only to highlight the unbearable tension.

"We can talk while we eat," Karl said.

His quiet authority seemed to settle Marina. She stopped fussing and led the way to an archway that separated the dining area from the seating area. For the first time Lauren realized the whole room was an open-plan space with the dining and kitchen area cleverly hidden in plain sight. The table was set for four and a tagine sat over a single flame, pulsing aromatic scents around the kitchen.

Trout's eyes lit with pleasure when he saw the bottle of wine standing open on the counter. "A Rioja Ontanon – 2015 Reserva. I tasted it at the Bodega a couple of years ago, before they put it down for the final maturation. It promised to be superb. I look forward to tasting it."

"Unfortunately, I have no proper means of decanting it but I spoke with the sommelier in the Wine Buff and he recommended it. I see Marina has already provided Lauren with a glass."

Lauren tipped her glass in a salute. "It's delicious."

"Good to hear. I asked him to send on a case." Karl picked up the bottle, poured a small offering into a glass and handed it to Trout. "I haven't tasted it myself but I'm familiar with other wines from the Sierra Yerga Mountains and find them more than satisfactory."

Trout twirled the wine in his glass, inhaled deeply, held it up to the light, took a sip and closed his eyes all the better to savour the taste. "Amazing." He held out the glass for a fill.

Lauren threw her eyes up to heaven, sat down at the table, lifted the lid of the tagine and in a parody of Trout inhaled deeply. "Oh my God, this smells divine. Have you a serving spoon, Marina? I need food."

"Wait until you taste the wine with it." Trout sat down beside her. "I've no doubt they will complement each other perfectly."

They ate in dedicated silence until the initial hunger was abated.

When Karl topped up the glasses, Trout took a sip of wine and said, "I'm sure you're both anxious to hear what's been happening. And I have to add and I think I speak for Lauren as well, that I'm more than grateful that you've been patient while we got ourselves together after the happenings of the past few days."

Marina gripped her fork so tightly that the tremble in her hand was visible around the table. "So you say Hannah is OK?"

"Judging by her speed as she ran from the warehouse, I'd say she's fine." Lauren kept her voice light.

"Warehouse?" Marina stared at her. "You talked about the dirt of the warehouse when you came in. For God's sake, tell us!"

Karl placed a hand on her arm. "Relax, my dear. Thomas and Lauren are going to tell us all."

"We are," said Trout.

He proceeded to recount most of the happenings of the last two days.

"Sergeant O'Leary told us about Hannah's friend Isla and her accident," Karl told them then. "We went to see her in the hospital and made sure that no expense was to be spared in treating her. Marina rang them this evening. She has regained consciousness and her mother has arrived." He pursed his lips. "I fear there is a rather ugly home situation. Her full name is Isla Slocombe. David Gilson is her half-brother." He indicated that Marina should continue.

"We had a long chat." Marina's eyes filled with tears. "It's terrible. Helen, Isla's mother, has discovered that her husband has been grooming Isla, his own daughter. I can't get my head around such evil. He threw David out over a year ago when David intervened in some row between Isla and him. David is five years older than her and has adored her since she was a baby. Helen didn't specify what the row was about but words were spoken that her husband claimed were beyond forgiving. Now she regrets not trying harder to find out what it was about. She thinks David's been living rough for the past few months. She was banned from contacting him and, God help her, she thought she was right to support her husband. It seems Isla has kept in contact with David and she reached out to him when she overheard her father telling someone she was ready and would more than neutralize any debt he owed. She was terrified when she realized the implications of what he said. David had promised to take her away and keep her safe until they could figure out what to do. He stopped her on her way to school on Friday and said he had to accompany a friend of his to Ireland and the only thing he could think of was to take her with them."

Karl reached and took her hand when he saw her getting more upset. Bringing it to his lips, he kissed it gently. "It's OK, my darling. Isla and Helen are safe now." He turned his gaze on Lauren. "We arranged accommodation for Helen near the hospital and she is hopeful that Isla will be well enough for discharge in a few days."

"They're coming to us then until everything is sorted out and Hannah and David are safely back with us." Marina turned her hand into Karl's and held on tight.

"I'm so glad!" Lauren's heart-felt exclamation elicited smiles all round. "I was worried that we could do so little for her."

"She was so worried about her brother and his friend that it was interfering with her recovery. When we assured her that they were safe, she was more content and hasn't looked back since."

"She didn't need to know we both had our fingers crossed out of sight," Marina said ruefully.

"You knew your cousin was on the job," said Karl, "and you believed and still believe she and Thomas will return Hannah to us. Isn't that so?"

"Yes, it is. And, Lauren, Isla says she had a dream where Hannah's godmother told her to concentrate on getting well, that she was looking out for Hannah and David."

Lauren felt her own eyes fill up. "I'm glad. I hope it helped her."

"Only now they've gone missing again." Marina's spirits plummeted again.

"And tomorrow we'll pick up the scent where we left off this evening. Possibly literally, if the remains of Lauren's perfume bottle is still around!" Trout attempted to bring a little levity to the table.

"What of Caligula? Is it possible that he has abandoned the scheme? My PA tells me that Shyrl Baker didn't turn up for work today. She had taken an arranged few days' holiday and was due back. Nobody seems to know where she is. Angela knew she was friends with Caligula but Shyrl had begged her not to say anything as we have a non-fraternizing policy in the company. Not always easy to implement but saves a lot of upset in the long run."

"Has anyone checked where she lives?"

"I've asked Angela to do so and get back to me." Karl frowned. "I was expecting a call before now but she will let me know whenever she has the details herself."

"Tell them about our visit to Seamus Eacrett." A thread of amusement laced Marina's words.

"Ah, yes – Seamus." Karl gave a small reminiscent smile. "An old friend."

Lauren turned startled eyes on Karl. "Really? You're friends? This I have to hear."

Trout's phone rang. He looked at the screen. "Mac. Could you give me a minute? I need to take this call." He swiped the screen. "Mac."

Mac's Cork accent boomed in his ear. "How's the boyo! You must be doing something right when you managed to impress The O'Carthy. Piss him off goodoh but impress him none-the-less! Word on the street is that he'd like you on his team – failing that he's asking what your price is. The boy's a bit old-fashioned – he believes everyone has a price. Mind you, that little girl of yours has been mentioned and I, for one, wouldn't like anything to happen to her. I like Lauren. Hell! If you were out of the way I'd have a go for her myself. Just thought I'd warn you, give you the old Boy Scout's heads-up. Be prepared. That said, the young ones seem to have vanished. It appears Buddy and his pal had words about his lack of dependable help but, whatever is between them, they're still in each other's pockets and the children are on the wind. They're not sure but think it's unlikely you've got them. If I hear anything else I'll let you know." He hung up.

Trout stared at the phone. "What the fuck are you involved in, Karl, that has all these people riled up?"

There was a beat of stunned silence.

"Sorry. That was out of line." Trout took a deep breath. "The good news is neither The O'Carthy nor Caligula has Hannah. They're looking for her, think maybe we have her and are currently pulling out all the stops to find us." He figured that was a judicial enough rendering of Mac's news. He could elaborate on it later for Lauren. If need be. He tightened his lips. Come what may, his priority was to keep her safe, above anything else. "What are you working on that would net Caligula and his pals ten million of any currency?"

Karl sighed. "Ten million is probably the tip of the iceberg. The international commission which I am guiding is a world-wide initiative to give governments a means of confiscating money and goods illegally made in their respective countries. That includes drug money, the proceeds of crime, money laundered from abroad, gambling – you name it, we're putting laws in place that will close nearly every loophole that a criminal can use to hide money. I believe the drug lords alone have put aside one hundred million dollars to fund a means of stopping us." He turned the wine glass in his hand round and round, watching the play of light in the depth of the wine. "Unfortunately, it's seen in some quarters that I am the force to be reckoned with and that if I can be neutralized the commission will simply fizzle out."

"In that case, no offence, Karl," Lauren looked him straight in the eye, "but why don't they just assassinate you and cut the crap?"

"*Lauren!*" Marina gasped.

Trout hid a smile. Trust Lauren to cut to the chase.

Karl smiled. "Because then I would be a hero and every government in the world would be forced to rally to the call for regulations."

"I see." Her phone pinged a message. "It's from Brendan." She read it, drew a sharp breath. "He says the reward for information, any information, has just doubled. Caligula, well, he calls him the Shark, is now offering twenty-thousand euro to anyone who has seen Hannah since seven o'clock this evening."

CHAPTER 34

Trout and Lauren were up early but not as early as Karl. He was sitting at the kitchen table, a carafe of coffee in front of him, staring pensively into the cup he held in his hand.

"Good morning," Lauren said tentatively while at the same time Trout said, "Coffee smells good."

"Help yourself." Karl indicated the pot.

Trout rounded the dividing counter and found two ceramic mugs in one of the overhead presses. He grabbed a carton of milk from the fridge, plonked the lot on the table and poured two cups of coffee. He pushed one towards Lauren and handed her the milk.

"I'm going to make toast," she said. "Anyone want some?"

"Yeah, I'll have some," Trout said at the same time as Karl said, "No, thank you."

Karl was still brooding over his coffee cup. Finally, he raised his eyes. "There's been a development overnight. I don't know how it will affect your search for Hannah but it's possible it will make it more difficult. Or, at the very least, make Caligula more desperate." He slammed a hand on the table. "To think I entrusted the security of my business to a man like that!" As quickly as he erupted, he became despondent again. "I seem to have a much better track record with stocks and shares than I do with people."

"What's happened?" Trout asked sharply.

"Angela contacted me this morning. The reason she didn't get back to me yesterday was because she was involved with the police until late. When she went to Shyrl Baker's apartment, after multiple attempts to get in touch with her had failed, she persuaded the manager to come with her and open the door. They found her dead."

"*Oh no!*" Lauren gasped.

"Is it considered suspicious?" Trout asked.

"Yes. Although until the post-mortem results are in, the police cannot be sure. But they are questioning the staging of the body."

"Staging? What staging?"

"I don't have the details."

"OK. Where does Caligula fit in?"

"The manager says he spoke with Caligula as he arrived at the apartments on Thursday night. He stayed the night as, apparently, he regularly does. At the very least he's the last person known to have seen her alive."

"That raises a few interesting questions."

"Like what?" Lauren finished her coffee.

Trout poured the last of the coffee into his cup and rose to put on a new pot. He was teasing out the implications in his mind. "You'd think if Caligula and Shyrl were in cahoots that they'd stick together until the money was secured. But she might have been getting cold feet. Caligula might have told her he planned on taking Hannah the next day and she balked. That would make her a threat to his plans." He put coffee beans into the top of a serious-looking machine, added a jug of water to the reservoir, pushed the pot into place, pulsed the beans and set the lot to drip. "Nice machine."

"You have one, you don't need another," Lauren reminded him.

"It's not as fancy as this but I take your point."

Lauren carried a plate of toast and a pound of butter to the table. "See if you can find some marmalade," she said over her shoulder. She saw Karl's eyes going between them with what could be construed as envy or perhaps regret. Not her business, she decided. Marina and Karl always had a volatile relationship but, in reality, theirs was more permanent than most of the people in their circle. It wouldn't be her cup of tea but it seemed to work for them. At some level anyway.

Trout slid onto his seat and placed a jar of artisan marmalade beside Lauren. "If he is involved in her death, he's burned his bridges and that will make him more determined to have his payday. We need to get started. Once the news breaks and the Gardaí alert the Met that he's in Ireland, he'll want to get his business here over and done with so he can disappear."

"What can we do at seven in the morning?"

"I'm thinking we start where we left off. We'll go back to the car park, see what cameras they might have around the place. We can decide then if we need to get on to the port authorities,"

"No doubt The O'Carthy will think of that too." Lauren dropped the piece a toast she was eating. Her appetite had deserted her.

"It's a possibility but it's what we have at the moment."

Karl stirred. "Would a counter reward serve any useful purpose? Heck, if I thought it would get Caligula off Hannah's trail, I'd give him the ten million and be done with it."

"Except at this stage I think it's gone beyond money," said Trout. "The man nearly murdered a Garda in a station full of Gardaí."

"You never did tell us how you know Inspector Eacrett." Lauren had it said before it occurred to her it mightn't be the most appropriate time to ask.

There was a beat of silence. "I dated his sister once upon a time." Karl half-smiled. "It was many, many years ago. I was in London, starting out, and was just about making the rent. I saw a deal I felt it had the potential to go big. Ciara asked her brother, her twin, for his savings. I remember it was a hundred pounds and he handed it over just because she asked him. He was saving for a car, so it was a big deal. When we made good, he took back the hundred pounds and told me invest his profit in something I thought would be suitable for him. I went back to the States soon after that but myself and Seamus kept in contact. Sporadically, if I'm in Ireland we try and meet up He's still one of my investors, one of the few I know by name. I have great respect for Seamus Eacrett. It grieves me to think that a man like him faced death because of me."

"From what I know of the man he's the last person to make you responsible for what Caligula did."

"That's the thing, Thomas. It wouldn't even occur to him to blame me. I think I can safely say he's one of the straightest men I've ever dealt with. I won't deny he can be abrasive but once he decides you're a friend he'd go through fire for you."

"He's recovering so that's something. Now, I think we'd better get going. If it's OK with you we'll leave our bags here. We can return here later, it's fairly central. And that way we'll all be in the loop."

"That's perfectly OK. I have the apartment for as long as I need it." Karl gave a rueful smile. "I think the letting agents are relieved to have a tenant, for the moment anyway." He considered Trout for a moment. "You think they're still here? In the city?"

"That's what we mean to find out." Trout stood up. "Do you need to get anything, Lauren?"

She looked down at her borrowed duds. This time a khaki cropped pants, matching vest, a loose cotton blouse in complementary silvery-sage and silver Sketchers. "I'd better go and tell Marina we're going and thank her for the clothes." She smiled and stopped Karl as he went to make a comment. "I know there's no need but Marina will appreciate it and she needs reassurance." She reached back and plucked a mug from a mug-tree on the counter. She had only noticed it when she sat down and Trout had already rummaged in the presses and found the others. "I'll take a coffee in to her. It will be as good an excuse as any. And I'll get my bag. *Ugh!* No. I'll have to borrow a bag off her. Mine is still covered in gore. I intended to put it in the bin last night but in view of the service it has given me I wondered if I could salvage it." As she spoke Lauren poured coffee, went to add a dash of milk, remembered Marina liked it black and finally left carrying her offering to her cousin. "I won't be long."

Karl looked at Trout. "I can't thank you both enough for what you've done and are doing."

"No need for thanks until we have Hannah safely home."

"Even to have someone who will say that and believe it is possible is something I am thankful for. Is there anything I can personally do that might help?"

"I can't think of anything at the moment but when I do, I'll let you know."

"And, Thomas, keep in mind that money is no object. It's the one thing I have that I can freely supply."

Trout nodded. "Will do. And I think when this is over there's a couple of worthy causes we'll be calling on you to support."

"Consider it done."

CHAPTER 35

They went back to the port car park. As Trout had thought, there were cameras. One at the entrance with a lens overlooking the parking area and another facing the street. He parked and together they walked to the hut where a security guard sat on a high stool and watched over the comings and goings.

"Good morning, folks. What can I do for you this beautiful morning?"

"Good morning," Lauren said.

Trout and Lauren had discussed how they might approach whoever was working and had decided to play it by ear.

"Are you the night security?" Trout asked.

"Yep. Got it in one. Shift ends at eight. Another half an hour. I can almost smell the breakfast that's got my name on it, at the Long Dock."

"Did you hear about the fracas here last night?"

The man eyed them curiously, his gaze lingering on Trout's discoloured eye. "Yeah. Stan was full of it when I came on at twelve. Seems The O'Carthy himself was on hand to be inconvenienced." His look sharpened and he studied them with shrew, accessing eyes. "Which party would you belong to now?"

Trout examined him back. He was short and wiry, mid to late fifties. He didn't have the look of a Garda but he had some training. He looked like he was a man who kept himself fit and presented himself with his boots polished.

Trout leaned against the door-jamb and asked, "You an army man?"

The security guard nodded and straightened himself some more.

"I'm an ex-Garda, doing a spot of private work. So, I guess I'm the party opposite O'Carthy, if that makes sense."

"And this isn't a social call? Stan told me he had a hell of a job with some git who wanted to see the CCTV footage."

"Did Stan know what went down?"

"*Naw.* Your man was a dickhead. Wouldn't tell him nothing but wanted to see what was on camera at the same time. Not saying anything now, but he gave Stan a monkey to step outside and have a smoke while he had a look at the screens."

"Did he do any damage?"

"No. No damage. Stan reckoned he didn't see much either. Didn't know what he was looking for, if you ask me."

"And if I was to ask you to let us have a look, what would you say?"

"*Glaine ár gcroí, neart ár ngéag, agus beart de réir ár mbriathar.*" The ex-soldier straightened himself some more.

"*The Fianna!*" Trout smiled. "Great motto. I always thought they were some special force!"

Beside him Lauren murmured, "*Clean of heart, strong of limbs and a word once given, our bond.*"

"I have my code. It has never stood me wrong. And I don't know you from Adam."

"I'm Thomas Tegan and this is Lauren O'Loughlin. We're private investigators, trying to find Lauren's goddaughter. We might have a better idea of what to look for in the video, Mr –?"

"Douglas McMillan. Dougie, I'm known as."

"McMillan from Cork. Any relation of Con's?"

"Big guy, without an ounce of BS in him?"

"That's Mac."

"Our fathers were first cousins."

Trout laughed and held out his hand. "Put it there! Any relation of Mac's is the real thing as far as I'm concerned."

"You're very trusting for a copper." Nonetheless Douglas shook the hand offered him.

"I'll tell you how trusting I am. Mac told me only last night that The O'Carthy thinks everyone has a price."

"The O'Carthy thinks a lot of quare things."

"I thought as much. So, here's what I'll offer, Dougie. I'll tell you exactly what happened last evening, and why it happened, the condensed version due to time constraints, and if you decide the story merits your help, we'll take it. If not, we'll go on our way without another word."

Dougie sized them up for a minute. "Maybe the young lady would like to sit down while you're telling the story?"

"I'd appreciate that, Dougie." Lauren moved into the hut, took the chair indicated, the only other piece of furniture besides the stool, and sank into it. Trout too moved inside the door and, leaning more comfortably against the jamb, gave Dougie a quick version of events over the past couple of days.

Dougie stayed quiet and attentive until Trout finished.

"I see," he said then. "There's more, I'm sure, but time is against us. If you step fully inside, I'll show you the relevant recordings from the CCTV."

"Recordings? Is there more than one?"

"Like I said, your man didn't know what he was looking for and he told Stan a gaggle of lies, thinking he was a bit of a fool. Well, I'm telling you here and now, whatever he looks like, Stan's no fool. He showed him exactly what he asked to see – but, if he had been any way civil, Stan might have explained what he *should* have been looking for." As he spoke, Dougie lined up a recording of the street that took in the alleyway. "Always busy that time of the evening, people are coming home from work, going out for the night, that sort of thing. It being a fine evening and all that, there was even more about. As big a crowd as usual anyway, yesterday evening." He paused the swirling picture, and set it to play at a normal speed.

They watched the gaggle of residents, as Trout identified them, disappear into the mouth of the alley. They saw a steady throng of people passing by without as much as looking into the opening, but saw no sign of the two youngsters emerging.

Trout looked perplexed. "Where did they go? I saw them run into the alley." He looked at Lauren. "You were practically beside them when they went in." He turned back and stared at a frame Dougie had stilled. "We came into the courtyard ourselves through it. It was a straight run, nothing off it. Nowhere to go."

"Well now, look here, very, very carefully – see that shadow on the wall. You'd think it was the darkness of the alley but there's a greyness over it and if you watch you'll see it getting lower and lower. And look here, a few of the people move as if they're going around an obstacle." He placed a stubby finger on the frame. "I think someone crouched down at the mouth of the alley and crawled into the middle of the crowd!"

"I see it." Laure sounded breathless.

"And follow along here . . ." Dougie moved the picture frame by frame and by the fourth one the backs of two extra heads were discernable, bobbing along among the throng and keeping pace with the shadow of a large woman laden with shopping bags. "Clever eh?" He stood back and studied the still. "I'm not saying it's the young ones, just pointing it out as a possibility."

The woman crossed at the junction, her shadows in the middle of the crowd still with her. They stayed almost out of sight on the far side of her as the traffic whizzed past, adding another layer of distance to camouflage the youngsters. A large once-white pick-up pulled level and gave them cover for a short distance until the camera range ran out.

"*Bloody hell!* Have we any way of tracking them from there?" Trout was leaning towards the monitor as if he could will it to show him more.

"I'll admit I was a mite curious. And when I was doing my rounds I called over to a mate of mine in the Bond Co-Op. I knew his camera would cover the next section over." He pulled a hi-spec phone from his pocket and accessed the gallery. "I took a video."

The same pick-up was stopped at the traffic lights they had seen coming up but there wasn't any sight of the two young people.

"Where did they go?" Lauren's voice wobbled.

"Well now, the way I see it . . ." Dougie turned back to his own screen and maximized the picture of the pick-up. "Look at the back of the truck. You see, a couple of crates and a good-sized pile of jute sacks, probably had potatoes in them." He jigged his phone back to life and expanded the picture of the pick-up at the lights. "I reckon that pile of sacks got higher from one picture to the other. What do you think?"

"Oh my God! You're right!" Lauren gasped.

"I'd say, if I was a betting man, that those young ones took advantage of the blind spot between the cameras and hid under the sacks. The crates would have hidden their heads nicely."

"It makes sense. Can you send those pictures to me?" At Dougie's nod, Trout called out his number. "Pity we can't see the number plate. Any idea who owns the pick-up?"

"'Fraid not, but that sticker on the back window says English Market. It's one of those stickers that allows a merchant or supplier to park, to drop off products. I'll bet someone there will be able to tell you. Ask the organic vegetable stalls who delivers their produce."

"Now you're really spooking me." Lauren gave a shaky laugh. "How do you know they were organic?"

"That amount of jute sacks in that truck, they had to be organic."

Trout laughed, sobered, and said, "Dougie McMillan, I'm saying thanks and I hope you know that I mean it and I give you my word we'll be back to tell you the whole story, and make sure you get a hell of a lot more than a monkey for your help."

"And we'll bring Mac along for the party," Lauren added.

CHAPTER 36

Neither Trout nor Lauren said anything as they headed back to the car. A flutter of movement caught Trout's eye. He shouted and broke into a run.

A decrepit individual rose from where he was squatting beside the Golf and started to back away with his hands in the air. "Ain't doing no harm. Just having a look-see." He turned and ran, surprisingly agile for someone who looked as if he was on his last legs.

Trout circled the car suspiciously but saw no undue signs of interference. The wheels were hard, the doors and boot still locked although it looked like someone had tried to open the boot with a blade of some type, going by the scratches around the lock.

"We disturbed him before he could get it open." Trout shook his head. "Not that there's anything in it." He flicked the key and they climbed aboard. "Any idea what time the English Market opens?"

Lauren had her phone out before Trout had the key in the ignition. "It says here eight o'clock."

"Perfect. Fancy having breakfast there??"

"'*The Farmgate café serves fresh local produce, sourced in the market downstairs*'," Lauren read off the website. "Sounds good to me. Make that a yes."

They surveyed the market from the Farmgate balcony as they tucked into the freshly cooked food. Lauren opted for the French toast with fruit compote while Trout went the whole hog and had the cooked breakfast with everything. The coffee was good and while it wasn't on tap there was no demur about bringing them refills. It was already busy but not yet overly crowded.

"It's a fabulous space, isn't it?" Lauren took a mouthful of her toast and fruit and closed her eyes the better to savour it, as the flavours burst on her tongue. "It's a pity we won't have time to explore it properly."

"We'll come back another time." Trout was surveying the crowd with a slight frown.

"What's up?" Lauren turned to look but couldn't pinpoint anything out of the way.

"I don't know. I keep seeing a couple of men circling but then they may just be trying to make up their minds as to what they'd like for dinner." His tone wasn't fully convincing.

Lauren took another piece of toast. "Was it the tramp? Did he spook you?"

"Maybe. There was something not quite right about him. Can you recall what he looked like?"

"My first impression was how shabby he looked, dirty, torn old coat, tied with a piece of string. Scraggy beard, battered hat." She paused, stared at the glistening mixed berries awaiting consumption. "But his shoes – they were top range Reebocks, navy with really white soles. I thought they stood out under the dark pants he was wearing. The pants didn't seem as decrepit as the jacket."

"That's it. I knew something jarred. A hasty, makeshift disguise. We didn't get near enough to see if the beard was fake but the rest was good enough if we weren't paying attention. I think we'll have to assume we've been rumbled and act accordingly."

"How?"

"We're having breakfast like any ordinary tourist who comes to Cork and we'll have a look around the market when we're finished. Buy a few things, talk to the stallholders."

"How do you think they found us? Watched the carpark to see if we'd return?"

"Most likely. After all, Caligula or one of his cohorts had the same idea. It's only luck really that they got the guy, Stan's back-up, and he showed them the CCTV recording but didn't make any effort to talk them through it."

"I suppose it's possible he didn't notice anything on it. After all, Dougie admitted it was curiosity and a bit of boredom that got him studying the recordings more closely than he normally would."

"True. And it would make sense that anyone who didn't see them on that recording would presume they had gone in the opposite direction. Dougie was pretty shrewd to examine the scene so closely that he saw them pop up."

"We are sure it's them, aren't we? In a way there was nothing to say one way or the other."

"Except the way they came into the picture, or at least the tops of their heads did and the way they stayed more or less hidden by the crowd. They kept out of sight as people shifted this way and that. It has to mean they did it deliberately. It's our best bet at the moment. All we can do is see it through."

"Where will we start?"

"I've been getting the layout in my head from here. We'll wander, not too slowly, mind, and make our way to the vegetable aisle. I can see buying a few vegetables in our future – just make sure you pick the non-perishable kind."

"I have to pick them? Why? Because buying vegetables is a woman's job?"

"So, *we'll* pick them!"

And, bickering good-naturedly, they quickly finished their breakfast and started to look around the market.

The range of produce was incredible. In easy stages, trying to look as if they had all the time in the world, they made their way towards the local vegetable stalls. As they went, they talked, with stallholders, other shoppers, admiring the produce, asking where it came from, buying some fruit as they went, setting the scene for when they came to their destination. In case there really was someone following them. By now Trout was convinced there was. He had seen the same face pop in their vicinity too often to be a coincidence.

Every sort of a vegetable imaginable was on offer across a number of stalls and right at the end a wooden arch proclaimed *Bluebell Farm, Organic Vegetables*. The writing was surrounded with extravagantly painted bluebells. Lauren went ahead while Trout browsed over a bread stall.

It was easy for Lauren exclaim over the sign and naturally this led to a conversation as to what they produced and where they were based. There was a wide variety of veg from every sort of salad leaves, to cabbage, carrots, potatoes, radishes, scallions, tomatoes, even a selection of soft fruits – luscious strawberries and plump juicy raspberries. She noted a pile of neatly folded jute sacks under the table and felt her heart thud against her ribs.

"Oh my God! They all look so amazing." She turned back to the two women, mother and daughter, as she had already found out. "Do you grow all this yourselves?"

"We do. Everything we bring to the market is seasonal, organic and fresh."

"How do you transport it all? It would take a truck."

"Not at all. We have an old pick-up and some days, if there's a right run on stuff, I give Hans a call and he makes an afternoon delivery as well." Her hands were busy rearranging the produce as she talked. "That suits me very well at times – he can take over the stall and I can pop out into the town for a couple of hours."

"Cork is so lucky to have such a fab market."

Trout approached, a large crusty loaf in a paper bag under his arm.

"There you are, dearie!" Lauren said. "What have you got there?"

"A crusty granary sourdough."

"Lovely! But look at this stall – all organic. I'd love to buy some but it wouldn't keep, would it? What a pity I already bought all that fruit! Maybe I should buy some of the salad stuff – just look how fresh it is!"

"Hang on a minute, poppet – we're travelling around, remember?" Trout gave Lauren as a pained a look as he could manage and with it issued a long-suffering sigh.

"Well, let's take some stuff for a picnic lunch, how about that? Some tomatoes, lettuce and chives. We can buy some of that goat's cheese we saw earlier and have a delicious lunch with your loaf of bread."

"Would you like one of our reusable bags for your purchases?" The stall-holder held up a jute bag with bluebells all over its weave.

"That's lovely. Yes, please."

"Pity you're driving – you could take a bottle of our country wine for the picnic." The woman didn't even try to hide her grin when she saw the way Trout picked up his ears.

"What type of wine do you have?"

Her hands busy packing the salads carefully into the bag, she answered off the top of her head. "We have blackcurrant and blackberry ready to drink. We have elderberry but realistically it needs two more years to be at its best, but when it's ready I'd put it up against any wine anywhere. Oh, and we have this year's elderflower champagne."

"That sounds interesting! What would you recommend for immediate drinking?"

"The elderflower is fresh but needs to be drunk fresh, so that's one. The blackcurrant is light enough, it's coming up to a year bottled and at the moment is delightful. The blackberry is richer and gorgeously fruity. It's very drinkable at the moment also. As I said, I'd give the elderberry a lot more time. We have a couple of customers that like to put it down themselves and have it on hand for when they want it."

"I'll take a bottle of each. If I like them and want more, do you have much quantity?"

The woman looked at him uncertainly. "When you say quantity, what do you mean?"

"I import wine and like to have a few speciality wines available in case someone is interested but I don't deal in wine that I haven't tasted myself. I find it's by far the best way to match a customer to what they want." He pulled his battered leather wallet from his back pocket, flicked through the cards and handed her one that read, *Tegan Wines*. "I deal mostly with small, local businesses and I can see a niche market for good quality country wines. If you're interested –"

"You promised me you'd forget work for this week!" Lauren butted in with a whinge in her voice.

"I'm not working, poppet, just giving my card to –" He quirked a questioning eyebrow.

"Fiona Deasy," the woman supplied.

"Where are you located, Ms Deasy?" he asked. "Maybe we could drop in and see your place – have a chat about the wines –"

Now it was Lauren's turn to emit a long-suffering sigh.

"We're out Belgooly way," Fiona said. "You'll find us easy enough. Ask anyone in the locality. We have an honesty shop at the bottom of our lane that we stock every morning – so look out for that as a landmark. You're more than welcome to look us up."

"Well, as you've got your wallet out you might as well pay for everything together," Lauren said.

"Anything for you, poppet," he responded with a grin.

He paid the stallholder and, carrying another of their reusable bags, with the bottles chinking inside it, bade her good-day, adding "We probably will drop in and I look forward to doing business with you in the near future."

CHAPTER 37

"Poppet! You're lucky I didn't clock you there and then!" Lauren flopped into the passenger seat, clutching a punnet of strawberries.

"Well, you started it." Trout had stowed the bags in the boot and now slid into the driver seat. "'Dearie', my arse! Couldn't you have come up with something more contemporary?"

"*Contemporary?*" Lauren's head shot a round to look at him. "Did you say," she started to splutter, "did you actually say *cont–contemp* . . ." Her spluttering evolved into full-scale laughter.

"What's so funny about 'contemporary'? It's a perfectly good word. In case you don't know, it means concurrent with the present time. My granny's sister used call me 'dearie' just before she'd wallop me for some imagined misdeed. Being called 'dearie' is a throwback to a less enlightened age . . ." Trout's lips began to twitch. "Come on, admit it – 'dearie' is the pits." He reached forward to insert the key.

Lauren was still laughing, leaning over, the strawberry punnet in peril of capsizing.

"Here, give them to me before you squash them." He grabbed the punnet from her unresisting hands. "Poppet." And watched her dissolve into more peals of laughter.

"I'm sorry," she spluttered. "I don't know what's come over me." She grabbed a breath. "Contemporary is a lovely word. It's from Latin so it's got sound origins. A dignified word – I shouldn't be laughing at it."

"You and your words!" His lips widened into a smile and in seconds he had his head thrown back and was joining in.

Soon enough Lauren lay her head back against the headrest, took a deep breath and stilled herself. "I have no idea why 'contemporary' struck me as so funny. But I needed that. A total release of tension."

"We both did. Only I didn't know it. And hopefully by now whoever is watching us is completely confused."

Lauren straightened herself and stared through the windscreen. "You think we're being watched?"

"I'm pretty sure of it." Trout fired up the ignition. "He's not as good at it as he thinks he is." He indicated and maneouvred into the traffic. "Unless he's working the old double bluff, where he's obvious, pretending to stay under the radar, while his pal stays in the shadows and is the actual tail." He watched the car in front with narrowed eyes. "We'll keep our eyes skinned for the same car or two turning up or keeping in the vicinity when we're out and about."

"I've a lot to learn, haven't I?" Lauren was completely serious now. "It didn't even occur to me to look out for a tail. Even if it did, I wouldn't know what to look for."

"Mark that for our first lesson when this is over. Shadowing, spotting a tail, that sort of thing."

"What about losing one?"

"That comes with the territory. As does figuring out if you actually want to lose a tail. Along with how you're travelling, whether you're walking or driving. Whether you find someone is following when you're following someone else. "

"*Whoa!* Why wouldn't I want to lose a tail?"

"Lots of reasons. Misdirection being the big one. You might want to lead a tail away from something, you might want to lead him or her into a trap, maybe to capture them. You might even want to simply get to a place where you felt safe enough to confront whoever was following you."

"*Cripes!* There's a lot more than I'd have imagined to it. So, this morning, what alerted you to the possibility that we were being followed?"

"Well, first of all it occurred to me that if we had thought of going back to where we finished last night so would The O'Carthy and his cohorts. I was watching out for someone from the time we arrived in the carpark."

"Investigation 101: presume the other guy is as smart as you."

"At least until you find out otherwise." Trout grinned. "Criminals are human too – they're as likely to presume as we are. That said, I reckoned the only vehicles in the carpark were workers in the port. They were all empty so it was as good a presumption as any. But, when we pulled out into the traffic, I caught a dark car pulling out from the kerb and noticed it stayed a couple of cars behind us all the way to the market."

"You never said."

"There was nothing to say. It might have been a bona-fide drop-off and simply going our way. And, in all fairness, when we turned in to park near the market it continued on as far as I could see."

"And that was it?" Lauren was disappointed.

"Not exactly." The amusement in Trout's voice warned her that he was fully aware she had expected more. "I kept a watch while we had breakfast and afterwards when we were wandering around. I noticed a face that kept popping up. Not overly obvious but nonetheless a face that appeared to take more than a little interest in us and our doings."

"You should have told me."

"And what would you do? You haven't enough experience yet, Lauren, to play it cool. Ninety-nine people out of a hundred turn to look when some says 'don't look'. They think they don't, but someone who knows what to look for can tell. That's something else we'll practise as part of the shadowing lesson. How to look without looking as if you are." He was moving forward steadily as the morning rush had given way to a marginally less congested thoroughfare. He frowned at the windscreen. "That's the Custom House coming up. Have a look at the map and see where we're going."

Lauren hauled the tote Marina had given her onto her lap. It was more than big enough and she allowed the leather was nice. The navy and pink, Marina had told her, was designed to work with any look and the iconic entwined silver LV made it, Lauren reckoned, worth more than all her bags together. She had only asked her for the loan of a bag that would keep all her bits together as her own was beyond redemption after using it as a weapon. She hoped the Louis Vuitton had as much stamina as her poor years-old Radley. She dug out her phone and accessed the map.

"We're coming up to the Kinsale Road roundabout. Where do we want to go?"

"Belgooly, wasn't it, Fiona Deasy said?"

"OK." She used her fingers to expand the map. "Take the Airport road and then follow the Kinsale road. I'll tell you when you need to turn left. It's roughly nineteen kilometres and it says here it will take twenty-seven minutes."

"Right. For some reason I thought we'd be going towards the coast but, from what you're saying, we turn inland. Keep an eye out for the turn-offs."

"She did say Belgooly and that's inland." Lauren turned to stare out the back window. "Any suspicious vehicles in the vicinity now?"

"Nothing that is raising any questions in my mind. We're making good time. Hey, look at this, we're out in the countryside already!"

"It's almost like home. On this one-lane highway we could be heading straight for the main street in Knocknaclogga, trees, hedges, the lot."

"Except look at the land."

"Tillage land. Potatoes, and that looks like maize."

"We're in land capable of growing the sort of crops that were for sale in the market in any case."

"Left here. This road is narrower and the ditches are wilder. Looks like there'll be an abundant crop of blackberries in the autumn."

"We're heading into hillier countryside."

"Still fertile though if we're to go by the lush growth everywhere."

"What exactly did you put into the route-finder?"

"Bluebell Organic Farm. *Stop!* Look! That's an honesty shop, selling fruit and veg. It says," Lauren squinted at the crooked lettering, "*'locally grown organic produce'.*"

Trout stopped the car. "What now?" He turned off the ignition.

"Now we find out if it's the one we're looking for." Lauren clicked open her seatbelt. "The farm must be nearby." She swung out of the car and rounded the front of it to look at the shop. It was a crude wooden shelter with rough shelves, holding a variety of vegetables – carrots, salad greens, beans, parsley and chives. There were long red leaves – she had no idea what they were – and further back, eggs and a punnet of strawberries. A steel cashbox with a slit for the money and a jar with some change in it were in the far corner. The shelves had the depleted look that suggested most of the produce was already sold.

The shop was set into a nook almost in front of a heavy iron gate that opened onto a track which meandered across a field dotted with sheep and curved out of sight around a grove of trees. She had no doubt the farm that served the shop lay over there, just out of sight.

Trout came to stand beside her.

"The farm should be over there beyond the trees." She squinted against the sun. "I could follow this track and see what way the land lies." She was half talking to herself.

"I'd imagine this road will bring us to the farm entrance, further along. It would be faster just to drive there."

"I suppose." She shrugged. "I guess I just fancied the walk."

"It would be nice to stretch our legs but at the moment time is of the essence."

"There's no guarantee that we're on the right track." Lauren hesitated. "I'm really afraid that we'll find all this morning has been a wild goose chase."

"Then the sooner we find out the better. Hop in. If this shop is linked to Bluebell Farm, we'll have some sort of answers in just a couple of minutes."

She nodded and climbed aboard while he rounded the car and sat in.

"Am I allowed to cross my fingers?" she said.

"Won't do any harm, so do." Trout let out the clutch and the Golf growled into motion.

CHAPTER 38

The turn-off for Bluebell Farm was around the next bend, two hundred yards from the shop but out of sight until you came to it. It was easily identifiable by the large wooden sign with the name and a riot of painted bluebells much the same as the one at the market. The road was little more than a rutted lane, canopied by large old beech trees. The Golf lurched and creaked its way to a wide gateway. The gate itself rested against a stone wall, while the opening was serviced by a heavy-duty cattle grid. They clattered over it onto a well-maintained farm road that ran between lush grass-covered fields where lazy cows chewed the cud and eyed them with complete indifference. Another turn brought them into the garden area of the farm. Two enormous tunnels and a smaller glasshouse sat contentedly there. A two-storey farmhouse, pink-washed with purple doors, stood solid and protective, flanked by various outhouses and sheds, overlooking the carefully laid-out beds and drills. Here and there, unidentifiable figures toiled diligently about the garden. A battered white pick-up truck, mud-stained and dusty, was parked on a semi-circular gravel parking area, facing the house. Trout pulled in beside it.

Lauren climbed out and looked around her with interest. It was much bigger than she had anticipated. She thought about the amount

235

of work her small back garden took to yield any sort of produce and marvelled at what she saw. From where she stood the cultivated area spread out from a post-and-rail fence to a grassy hill in the far distance. She moved slowly forward and saw a clear path of broken slate zig-zagging, between the beds and throughout the garden. Further on she saw fruit bushes that stood in ordered rows, the fruit no doubt set and ripening as she could see some of the bushes were draped with netting. The birds it attempted to protect the fruit from flitted and twittered all around. A mature orchard stood sentinel where a thorn hedge met the post-and-rail fence. Away to her left, two people were busy hoeing between drills of what looked like staked beans. Another someone was laboriously digging over an area of ground as if to prepare it for sowing. The whole place had an air of ordered industry.

From one of the tunnels a man emerged, a big man, made to look bigger by the large shaggy dog at his side. Lauren reckoned there was wolfhound in the dog but couldn't decide what other breed. Only for the size of him, she'd have thought he had the soft eyes of a spaniel. Man and dog padded silently towards them. The man watched them with curious eyes from underneath a well-worn western hat, from which straggled long wispy dirty-looking hair. He pushed the hat up with a clay-covered hand to reveal a high, rounded forehead. He was sporting a grey-white beard that would make him a worthy contender to play Santa Claus.

"Good morning – how may I help you?" His voice was low, diction precise, with an accent Lauren decided was German.

She heard Trout return the salute and smiled her own hello.

"We were in the English Market this morning and sampled some of your produce." Trout was feeling his way.

"*Ja*. It is good. You want more?"

"Perhaps. I was particularly interested in your country wines but haven't had a chance to taste the ones we got yet. I spoke to Ms Deasy and said we might drop in." Trout paused but the man just continued to look at him enquiringly. "But we have another reason to visit and I'm hoping you might be able to help us."

Still the man regarded him without a word.

Lauren found her tension levels mounting. Before she could stop herself, she blurted out, "Did two youngsters hitch a lift in your truck yesterday evening?"

Those curious, cow-like eyes turned on her. "No. They didn't hitch. They sneaked on board and stole a ride."

"They were desperate."

"So they said when I saw them and went to deal with them."

"What did you do with them?" Lauren heard the fear in her voice.

The man laughed. "I ate them, of course! Like the ogre in Hans Christian Anderson's tales." He had a rich, deep laugh and it transformed his face. He wagged an earth-encrusted finger at Lauren. "You had better tell me why you are looking for them and perhaps then I will tell you what I did with them." He turned away. "Come, I have some elderflower cordial on ice. It is refreshing on a warm day."

He led the way towards the house and around the side to where an open wooden veranda gave shade if not shelter. "Sit." He waved towards a selection of mixed wicker furniture. "I will bring refreshments." He glanced at the dog. "*Stay*." The dog plopped down on the ground in response to his master's command, effectively blocking them from leaving the veranda.

They likewise sat as they had been commanded and waited.

Trout leaned forward to examine the veranda rail. "Lovely piece of woodwork." He ran his hand along the smooth grain of the timber. "And look at this." He lifted up a flat square of board that was hanging from the rail, straightened it out, reached underneath and pulled two supports into place. "A built-in table. Isn't that the neatest idea?"

"Yes, it is." Lauren was staring at the big animal. "I've never seen such a well-trained dog."

"*Ja*. An intelligent dog like Bruder will learn anything you can teach him." He carried a bottle with a pressure cork in one hand and three tall glasses held by the base in the other.

Lauren noticed he had washed his hands and thought that he could easily fit another glass in the big broad paw that passed for his hand.

Trout stood up to take the glasses and place them on the table.

"You have found my table." He placed the bottle carefully beside the glasses and equally carefully manipulated the cork. "Too good to spill," he said. He glanced at Lauren. "You are my guests because Bruder didn't bark. He alerted me but didn't bark. Always a sign that a friend or a potential friend comes."

"Is he equally accurate with people who come to bring trouble?"

"I have never known him wrong in his assessment of a human. Other dogs . . ." He sighed. "If she is dainty and pretty, he cannot be trusted."

Lauren started to laugh then saw he was serious. "I imagine that could be a problem all right."

"*Ja.* For my poor Bruder and for the little one who is always equally smitten but, alas, it not enough when you are a giant and she is a fairy."

Trout cleared his throat. "The whole veranda is a fabulous piece of work. Did you make it yourself?"

Their host looked around. "Together we do all the work, Fiona and me. We bring the old house back to life. But enough!" He filled three glasses with a sparkling liquid faintly tinged with gold. "Sparkling Elderflower cordial. It has very little alcohol and is refreshing on a warm day." He handed the glasses around. "We must introduce ourselves. Hans Muller at your service."

Trout accepted a glass. "Thomas Tegan, Lauren O'Loughlin. We're looking for two young people and believe your two freeloaders are the ones we're looking for." He raised his glass. "*Sláinte!*"

"*Prost!*" Hans downed a long swallow, wiped his mouth with the back of his hand and said, "I didn't call them freeloaders."

"Will you tell us, please, what happened?" Lauren leaned forward. "Are they OK?"

"You will tell me why you want to know."

Trout in his turn took a long swallow. "Christ, this is good. Remind me to talk to you about your country wines before we go." He drank some more, looked at Lauren. "Is today only Thursday? It's like we've been trying to find Hannah for a week." He downed another mouthful and told Hans Muller the story of the past couple of days.

Hans listened, sipping his drink, occasionally nodding. When Trout finished, Hans lifted the bottle, saw it was empty and put it down again. "They told me they had escaped from a warehouse with the help of friends and had nothing but the clothes they were wearing."

He shook his head. "They had no phones so they had no phone numbers. Imagine, not one number that either of them knew in their heads!"

Lauren flicked a glance at Trout. Teenagers who couldn't remember phone numbers? Hardly likely.

"I could see they were frightened but they, or at least he, chose to be aggressive rather than ask for help." Hans stopped for a long moment, his head down. When he raised it, his face was troubled. "I did not mean to frighten them but I was startled when I saw in my mirror my sacks rise up and turn into people. I stopped and stormed out of the cab, demanding to know what they thought they were doing. They jumped from the trailer and stood there like, like, I don't know what. The girl looked like she was going to cry. The boy said they needed to get out of town and my sacks offered them a way of hiding as they did so. He was belligerent and protective of the girl. They said dangerous people were after them and they needed to get to their friends. I scoffed because they thought they could bamboozle me with tall tales. I did not have Bruder with me to show they were OK." The dog, hearing his name, stood and padded over to put his head on Hans' shoulder. A big hand came up to fondle his ears. "As I came towards them, they started to back away. I heard the girl whimper. The boy took her hand and they ran, fled from me who would do them no harm. I shouted but they were probably so afraid they took it as anger. I am ashamed that I didn't help your friends. That instead I added to their fear and worry." He stopped, looking abject.

"Where did you last see them?" Lauren kept her voice soft in spite of her anxiety.

"We were stopped on Brook Bridge. They ran up the hill towards Barrbán. I am more sorry than I can say." He shook his head. "I could not offer help then even if I wanted to. They were gone."

"What's done is done." Trout's voice may have fallen short of the philosophical tone he was aiming for, but he reckoned that at least they had a direction to go. "Can you give us directions to Brook Bridge and Barrbán and we'll be on our way?"

Brook Bridge was only a short distance beyond the honesty shop.

Trout and Lauren thanked Hans for the drink and his information. He pleaded with them to let him know the young ones were all right. Trout assured him they would and that they would fill in any other details when they came to discuss his country wines.

"The wines are Fiona's," he told them with a note of pride in his voice. He added he was sure she would be pleased to hear from them and they took leave of one another.

CHAPTER 39

Trout stopped on the bridge. They both got out and looked around. "Quiet. No houses in sight. You'd want to be a local to know where anything is around here."

"Just like home. At least we're used to it. How will a couple of Londoners survive?" Lauren allowed her eyes travel along the narrow road that Hans Muller had told them led to Barrbán. "I bet there's houses and habitations all the same. It's just a matter of finding them."

"The road is tarred and reasonably well maintained even if it is narrow." He indicated to Lauren to sit in. "Are those fingers still crossed?"

In seconds Trout was giving the Golf as much acceleration as it could manage on the steep and twisting way.

"Barrbán – meaning '*white top*' – of the hill presumably. I wonder does that mean that it's rocky at the top?"

"I don't know but this gradient is a challenge. I doubt if they got far, running up it. Keep your eyes peeled for a house."

"There. Across the fields, a two-storey dwelling. There's smoke so there must be someone there."

"A turn-off. It's well used so we'll chance going in."

Trout slowed and geared down. The road here was even narrower than the one they left, went straight for forty yards, curved left, then right, and went on for another hundred yards. After the turn the house came into view, sitting solid with its back to the road. Trout followed the way past and around the house and drove in between it and some whitewashed sheds, to a gravelled front yard.

It was an old house, painted and well kept. Two windows, one either side of a freshly-oiled teak door and two overhead, looked down and over a valley to some distant mountains. Directly in front of where Trout parked, an open-fronted shed protected a bank of turf and a neat pile of timber, cut and uncut, from the elements. It had all the appearance of old-fashioned prudence. Nothing ostentatious but more than enough with careful husbandry.

They got out, one each side of the car, and contemplated the view.

"What a fabulous place!" Lauren took a deep breath, turned to say something to Trout and caught sight of a woman standing in the doorway.

She was tall and thin with a narrow, ascetic face capped by dark hair cut close to her skull.

"Who are you?" She was neither welcoming nor unwelcoming, merely asked them a straight question and expected to be answered accordingly.

"My name is Lauren O'Loughlin and this is my friend Thomas Tegan."

"Another one of them friends. There's a lot of ye in the air at the moment." She stood tall and firm in the middle of the doorway. "What do ye want?"

"We're looking for a couple of youngsters we have reason to believe came this way last evening."

She straightened herself some more. "What was wrong with them?"

"Nothing. Except they had to leave Cork city in a hurry, without money or clothes or anything and we're trying to find them."

"Who exactly are ye again?"

"We're private investigators hired to find the youngsters but, more importantly for me, Hannah is my godchild and I'm worried about her."

"Ye'd better come in and hear what I have to say." She swung around and went inside without waiting to see if they followed.

Lauren followed her into a kitchen. It was basic but gave a sense of being comfortable. Directly opposite her was a Rayburn, radiating a gentle heat into the room, in spite of the heat outside. A green Formica-topped table stood on her right in front of a loaded dresser. Four brown chairs were pushed in around the table, two armchairs sat one either side of the range with a much-patched, faux-leather couch residing under the front window.

The woman waved them to take a seat. "Ye'll have a cup of tea. I'll have the kettle boiled in a minute."

Without waiting for a reply, she disappeared into a back area and almost immediately Lauren could hear the sound of an electric kettle starting to boil. She sank into the nearest armchair while Trout perched on the couch.

The woman bustled back in with three china mugs and a milk jug. It took Lauren a moment to register that she was talking as she set out the things on the table.

"They knocked on the door around eight o'clock. The boy was almost carrying the girl, she was that weak. He asked me for something to eat. He said he'd be all right but his friend was in a bad way for food." She went out again and returned with plates and a sugar bowl, talking all the time. "I asked him if they were on their own and he said they were. I checked. I left them there in the yard and went out along the road. I could see there was no car, nor any sign of anyone else. I figured she couldn't be putting on that paleness or that listlessness that showed she was suffering. I've seen it in calves and I reckoned she needed something fast." At that stage she disappeared again and came back with a packet of Rich Tea biscuits, still talking. "I looked at the young fellow. He was no bigger than myself and I thought if he tried anything I'd give as good as I got. I've got that blackthorn stick there in the corner and I can use it if I have to. I brought them in. The poor creature just slumped into that chair there." She pointed to the one at the end of the table. "And she put her head down and I thought she'd pass out. That's when I heard the lad call her Hannah. A nice old-fashioned name, I thought. I got the fresh loaf and the butter and a new packet of ham. The lad, he said his name was David, made her a sandwich while I made tea. She said she doesn't drink tea but I was having none of that. I told her straight out she needed a hot drink and one with sugar in it. I put two spoonfuls in and made her drink every last drop."

She went out and brought the teapot in from the back and left it on top of the range.

"Sit over to the table. I can make ye a sandwich if ye'd like."

"No, thanks. A biscuit will be fine." Lauren moved to the table, Trout following her. "We didn't mean to put you to any trouble."

"It's only a cup of tea. It's no trouble." The woman, who had yet to give her name, poured out three mugs of tea. "There's milk and sugar on the table, help yourselves."

"Did they tell you anything about where they were heading?"

"The silly goose said they were heading for Clare, where her godmother would know what they should do." She looked at Lauren with a shrewd eye. "That would be you."

Lauren nodded. "Her mother is my first cousin. She's the only child either of us have." Lauren felt the tears sting and for the life of her she couldn't figure why she had told this stranger such an intimate detail.

The woman was nodding. "I know how important that is." She was silent for a moment. "The creature was starving – once she started to eat, she could hardly stop. She made herself two more sandwiches and ate every bit of them. The lad, David, was reluctant at first but I told him not to be an *amadán*. I had enough food for the rest of the week and I'd be doing my shopping on Friday. Between them they finished the loaf and the ham and I don't begrudge them a bit of it. I was glad to see it did them both the world of good." She played with a teaspoon for a minute. "I didn't know what to do with them after that. It was getting late and would be dark in an hour. I couldn't turn them out. Where would they go? It's five miles to village and three to the top of the hill if they wanted to go somewhere on the other side. The lad David stood up to go. I could see the little girl was suffering and I made up my mind. I said 'Do ye give me yeer word ye'll not do me or what's mine any harm?" He was startled but she copped on fast. 'I promise,' she said. 'We both promise. Lauren always told me a person's word is their bond and my bond is to do no harm to you or yours'."

"How are we ever going to thank you for your kindness?" Lauren whispered.

The woman gave a big sigh. "The story's not over yet. The boy agreed and I said they could stay here for the night. I filled the range and got them blankets and an old quilt they could put on the floor there near the fire. They were right thankful. And what's more I slept like a babe in arms, never fearing a thing when they'd given me their promise." She shook her head sadly. "If that lump of a son of mine hadn't turned up before we'd even had our breakfast and created a hullabaloo, they'd still be here. He cleared them out as if I had no say in the matter, shouted at them and at me. The girl, Hannah, hugged me. She did, in spite of him. She hugged me and said she'd never forget my kindness. David said straight out 'You saved our lived, Mrs Moran' – that's my name, Josie Moran – 'and if there's ever anything I can do for you I will.' Bless him, he was as solemn as if he could do something. I gave them the eggs I had boiled and managed to slip her a packet of biscuits." Suddenly, she was raging. "The *luadarán*, he wouldn't be here if I needed him but he had to get up early to see a cow that was calving and thought he'd have his morning visit done by calling in before I was up." She looked up, twin blotches of regret on her cheeks, her eyes shiny with tears. "I'm right sorry that I couldn't have kept them for you."

CHAPTER 40

Josie Moran walked Lauren out to the road. Trout went ahead with the car and waited for them at the crossroads.

"We're halfway between the two villages here," she told Lauren. "The road, for all that it's narrow, can be busy enough. People use it as a shortcut. You'll only see the one house on the side of the road. The rest are hidden in little valleys and clumps of trees. Over the Barr and down to Bunnconic – that's the most likely way they went. At least that's what I advised them to do. It's well signposted."

"Bunnconic?"

"'Tis bastardised, of course. No doubt it was once '*bun an cnoic*' – the bottom of the hill, now some daft ones even call it Bunny. Mark my words the day will come when that's what they'll all say."

"I'm sure that's a long way off, if it happens at all." Lauren tried to inject a positive note into her voice but she was well aware of the line of least resistance.

"What possessed the creatures to think they'd get to Clare by coming to Cork?"

"They didn't really have much choice in the matter. I'm sorry we haven't time to go into the story now. I have to tell you we're not the only ones looking for them, only the others mean them harm."

"Oh!" Josie looked alarmed. "But ye'll come back and tell me how ye get on?"

"We will. I give you my word – whatever the outcome we'll come and tell you."

"Your word is your bond. You're the one told Hannah that."

Josie smiled and Lauren had a flash of the handsome girl she once was.

"I'll be saying a little prayer that all will be well. Good luck now."

Lauren slipped into the car and waved. She looked back at the first turn to see the tall erect figure still standing, watching them out of sight.

"To say they're meeting all sorts is an understatement of epic proportions." She recounted for Trout the conversation she'd just had with Josie. "Do you think we should just head to Bunnconnic? Is there any point in going off the road to make enquiries?"

"I doubt it. Even ones unused to country roads like Hannah and David would see they'd have a better chance of a lift on a busier road. What's that noise?"

"My phone. I'd forgotten all about keeping Marina and Karl updated. Not that there's much." She retrieved the phone from the depths of the tote. "Oh! Brendan."

She swiped for access and hit speaker. Brendan barely said hello before launching into his latest update.

"Slow down!" she said. "We can hardly make out what you're saying and Trout doesn't want to have to stop the car to listen."

Brendan gulped and started again. "I was keeping an eye out for communications on social media about our case. When I intercepted a funny sort of message. It's on FaceBook and I reckon that means someone older who isn't so up-to-date. It was a query about the reward and what exactly it was for. I kept the exchange refreshed and was able to follow when the chat was transferred to a private account." He was starting to get excited and speed up again. "A woman called Cleo Moran."

"*Moran?* Are you sure?"

"I have it right here in front of me."

"What did she say?" Lauren's heart was beating so fast she thought it would come out through her ribcage.

"She said two dirty youngsters broke into her mother-in-law's house last night and only for her husband routed them it's no knowing what they'd have done to her."

"The rotten liar!" Lauren fumed. "Was there a reply?"

"Yeah. It's been going back and forth. She's given them her address and Reward 101 – that's the handle the spooks are using – said someone will be with her asap. She wanted to know if they'd bring the money with them but they told her they'd have to verify her information before carrying such a large sum of cash."

"Cash?"

"Where did you get '*spooks*'?" Trout spoke over Lauren. "In my day spooks were spies."

Brendan laughed. "We can't see them, can we? And, generally, you can't see what spooks you, so it seemed like the perfect word."

"Good work, Brendan. Anything else we should know?"

"I don't think so. There's lot of chatter but that's the only bit of concrete information. You seemed to know the name Moran?" Brendan sounded tentative and hopeful at the same time.

"We've just left a Josie Moran who I'm pretty sure is the mother-in-law in question."

"*Holy shite!*"

"Language, Brendan!"

"Sorry but that's a low call. I don't think there's any way I can misdirect the chat. I'm staying under the radar so I can observe." He sounded regretful.

"Stay under the radar, Brendan. You've been a great help and we wouldn't have been as successful as we are, but for the fact none of the players know you're there watching them. Thanks, Brendan."

Lauren added her thanks and disengaged. "*Shit! Shit! Shit!*"

"Language, Lauren!"

"It's so frustrating. Every time we close the gap that shower of – of –"

"They're not worth thinking up a name for them. It's unfortunate Cleopatra liked the sound of the reward."

"Cleopatra?"

"She must at least have the Egyptian siren's ego and her drive for power to be vindictive enough to drop her mother-in-law into the shit-pile she's released."

"Should we warn Josie?"

"I don't see what we can tell her, seeing as all we know is that it's possible her daughter-in-law has tried to claim the reward for information. It's unlikely the spooks, as Brendan calls them, will resort to violence."

"Can we be sure? We saw what happened at the warehouse."

"I don't know, Lauren, but I'd say we have enough on our plate trying to find Hannah before Caligula. Especially now if he's wanted for questioning in a murder investigation."

"Wouldn't you think he'd cut his losses and get out of Dodge?"

"Ten million is a lot of money and it's possible the people who offered it will take a poor view of why they're not getting their money's worth. It's likely he's caught between a rock and a hard place."

"Am I supposed to feel sorry for him?"

"No. Just pointing out that he needs to succeed as much as we do. Only difference is the reason." He slowed to read a signpost. They were over the hill and coming down the other side without noticing. "Bunnconnic – five kilometres. So it's Bunny for short?"

"Don't you start. Apparently Bunnconic is bad enough without pre-empting its future calling, according to Josie."

CHAPTER 41

Bunnconic consisted of one street, two shops and two pubs. That one of them was a shop and pub combined didn't take from the numbers. Trout drove the length of the street, turned and came back to the shop with the fuel pumps.

"I'd better get a fill. Do you want to wait in the car or will you go in?"

"One might get more information than the two of us together. I'll sit here and watch the world go by."

Trout lifted the nozzle, realized the pumps were controlled from the shop, went to the door and asked the woman behind the counter to set him up for a fill. She examined him from behind thick-lensed glasses, smiled and moved to press a series of buttons on a machine behind her. Trout returned to the pumps and filled the Golf.

"Would you like anything?" he asked Lauren.

"Not really. We still have the fixings of salad for lunch but I suppose in the interests of starting a conversation you should buy something."

The shop was a typical country store with a bit of everything. Trout nodded to two men, deep in conversation at the end of the shelves, not so deep that they didn't give him a thorough once-over. He picked up a few bits and pieces and went to the counter. He judged the woman to be in her seventies. She had tightly permed purple hair and a no-nonsense air. She totted up his purchases, keeping up a running commentary on the weather, the state of the crops and anything and everything that ran into her head.

When she drew a breath, he took his chance. "We were to meet a couple of young friends of ours this morning on the other side of Barrbán but we must have missed them. Any chance you saw them? A girl and a lad, they were hiking across the hill, might even have hitched a lift."

"Can't say I've seen anyone like that this morning." She pursed her lips. "If they came through Bunconnic I'd have seen them." She indicated the big window behind her. "Maybe Pa saw them." She raised her voice. "*Pa!* Did you see any young strangers out and about this morning?"

The shorter of the two men turned, raised his cap, scratched his head. "I might have."

"This gentleman missed a couple of friends of his, young ones that he was supposed to meet on the road this morning."

"Well now, Nonie, I'm not sure but I thought I saw Marek talking to a couple of walkers when he was pulling out onto the road after collecting the milk. Do you know who'll know? Absko. He went after the cows to close the gate and he'd have a better view of the tankard than I would. I'll ask him." He was moving up the shop as he talked and before Trout could say a word, he was out the door.

Through the big window, Trout and Nonie watched him approach an ancient Land Rover. A face as black and gleaming as polished ebony with the whitest teeth Trout had ever seen appeared in the window.

"Absko is from Kenya. He's over here to learn farming." Nonie smiled indulgently. "He's a grand lad and a great little worker. We'll be sorry when he has to go back home but we're collecting a bit here and there and we're hoping to have enough to send five heifers and a bucket of straws back with him. He'll be able to inseminate them himself." She saw Trout's startled look. "Sure, we couldn't have it on our conscience to send in-calf heifers all the way to Kenya. They could slip the calf or anything. No, the straws are a better option. He's learning to do the AI with Pa and he can do it himself when he's back home."

It took Trout a few seconds to decipher the story and, when he did, he grinned. "That's a great idea. I'd like to contribute to the fund, if I may."

"You can indeed. I keep an account of all the money here. How much would you like to give?"

Trout still had his wallet in his hand after using his card to pay for the petrol. He flicked it open and extracted two fifties. "That's all the cash I can spare at the moment," he said. "Put it in Absko's heifer fund."

Nonie's eyes gleamed. "If you're sure, we'll be right thankful to you."

Pa bustled in the door, bristling with news. "Absko says that Marek stopped to talk to two people, a boy and a girl who were thumbing." He jerked his thumb to illustrate his words. "He's almost sure he saw them climb aboard."

"That's a milk tankard we're talking about?" Trout said.

"'Tis. He'll be heading for Charleville to off-load but he'd have a full round to finish." He scratched his head. "I'm his third pick-up on the round and he'll be full when he finishes – say three more farms. I know he aims to be pulling into the plant at one on the button." He glanced at the clock over the door. "It's twenty after twelve now, so he's on the last leg."

"How far to Charleville?"

"It'll be a straighter run for you – what is it, Nonie? About an hour and a half."

"Hardly. An hour-twenty more like."

"Either way you'd want to get on the road. You're going to miss them as it is and Marek does an afternoon run when he's had his lunch and a rest."

Trout thanked them profusely and hurried out to the car. As he closed the door, he heard Nonie tell Pa in an excited whisper about his donation to the fund.

"We're heading for Charleville. Have a look at the map and tell me the shortest route."

Lauren didn't hesitate, opened AA Route-finder and input Charleville and their location. When three routes popped on screen, gave Trout the directions for the shortest one.

He made a hard right at the end of the street, kept left at the V junction and pushed the Golf to the speed limit. As he drove, he regaled her with all he'd learned. She was interested in hearing about the young Kenyan, pleased to hear his reason for being in Ireland and delighted that Trout had given a generous donation to his cause.

"Nonie told me he'll be able to inseminate the heifers himself. That's why I was extra generous," Trout said casually.

"What? Back up! What did you just say?"

Trout did his best but he couldn't keep the laugh in. "That's what Nonie told me but I must have looked as startled as you because she added they intended to send a 'bucket of straws' with him. I figured that was farm-speak for artificial insemination."

Lauren laughed. "For a minute I thought –" The phone rang in her hand. "Landline. 021 local code, no name." She swiped to answer, said a polite hello and instantly hit speaker.

"They were here. I tell you they were here. Two of them in a black monstrosity of a van. But he must be a woeful bad driver – the front of it was all dented and damaged. They were looking for the young ones and they knew they spent the night here. Blast that one to hell and back, that she couldn't keep her nose out of my affairs! I told them I had nothing to say to them and to get out of my yard. The ugly one was inclined to be cross but the other one held him back. Said there was no point in making a bad story worse, that they had easier means of finding the runaways and not to be leaving a trail of destruction behind them. Thank God Fiachra came then and told them to leave or he'd call the guards. The skinny one said there was no need to be like that. They were going and his friend had just let the worry get to him. That he feared for his niece after that young fellow had enticed her away and he just wanted to find them. He apologized for the inconvenience. Inconvenience! A pack of lies. Tell me the young ones are all right? I'm going off my head with worry." And Josie at last drew a breath.

Lauren reassured her as best she could. "We haven't caught up with them yet but neither has anyone else."

Josie's heartfelt "Thank God!" prompted Lauren to add that it looked like the refugees had met with another good Samaritan on their journey. And that they were on the trail of that person at this very moment.

After the most minimal of pauses, Lauren said, "Josie, I want you to promise me you'll tell no-one you rang me. Not your son, not anybody."

"I promise. Gladly, I promise."

"Thank you. I'll just add it's for your own safety as well as Hannah and David's. Those two men are dangerous. You were lucky that the ugly fellow wasn't on his own."

"I got that feeling."

"I'm more than grateful you let us know. Now we can prepare ourselves for whatever's next."

"You mind yourself and let me know what happens."

"We will." The phone went silent in her hand.

"How the fuck did they get there so fast?" Trout said.

"And what did yer man mean when he said they had an easier means of finding out where we were?"

"*Shit, fucking shit!*" Tout slammed his hand on the steering, turned the car onto the hard shoulder and slammed on the brakes. "I knew there was something fishy about that tramp, but I couldn't put my finger on it."

Lauren was looking at him as if he'd lost the plot. She opened her mouth to say something but he was already erupting from the car. She quickly opened her belt and scrambled out. Trout had come around the back to the passenger side and was crouched down looking under the back wheel-well. He reached in and pulled out a small disk. "*A fucking tracker. He put a fucking tracker on the car.*" He threw it on the ground and stamped on it.

Lauren watched him with her hand over her mouth. She had never seen him so angry.

He leaned against the car. "We've been leading them right to them all morning. *Jesus Christ*, Lauren, why didn't I follow it up when I thought something didn't sit right with that tramp? No. I let it go and now they're right behind us."

He banged his fist on the roof until Lauren feared he would drive it straight through. Or at the least leave a dent they'd be responsible for.

"Now we know and you've dealt with it," she offered quietly.

"Yeah, I have," he said bitterly. "And those two yahoos will rock up to the shop in Bunnconic, spin Nonie a yarn and she'll say no bother, aren't they on their way to Charleville."

"Then I guess the sooner we get there before them, the better." She turned, saying over her shoulder, "I'll find a number for the shop and phone her while you're driving." She sat in, slammed the door and belted up.

Trout stared at her profile, the stubborn set of her chin, her eyes looking straight ahead, then saw her reach for her bag and extract her phone. He shook himself, slid into the driver's seat, started the car and pulled back onto the road. He jerked his shoulders, took a deep breath, but refrained from closing his eyes as he recalled he was driving. He felt himself settle.

"Have I told you lately that you're the best side-kick I've ever had." He gave her one swift glance, pushed the accelerator to the floor and steadied the Golf. He was glad the car had no problem driving way beyond the speed limit. "Let's go find Hannah and bring her home."

CHAPTER 42

They made Charleville in a little over an hour. Trout was pleased that they hadn't met any speed cameras or checks. They were turning into the Agri-Food plant by one forty-five. He reckoned that it was unlikely Marek would leave for his afternoon round before two o'clock. That gave them a good fifteen minutes to find him and ask him about his passengers.

Himself and Lauren had discussed their approach during the journey and agreed that they would need to be careful not to get Marek into trouble. As Trout pointed out it was unlikely that the company would approve of one of its drivers giving lifts to random hitchhikers. Their plan was to say they were looking for him to thank him for finding something they had lost. And to put a positive spin on it Tout had taken a couple of minutes at the ATM in Charleville and withdrawn six hundred euro, the maximum his bank allowed without prior arrangement.

"Holy cow! This place is huge. How will we find him?" Lauren was looking at the perimeter as they cruised along looking for the entrance. Eventually they came to a wide area with a roundabout and a sign directing them to Reception.

Reception came complete with a barrier and security guard. Trout pulled up and stood out to talk to the guard. He had the high colour and bulbous nose of a habitual drinker. He seemed sober at the moment and Trout reckoned that drinking on the job was not an option.

"We're looking for one of your drivers by the name of Merek."

"We don't give out information about our drivers. What did he do that you're looking for him?" The man's eyes gleamed with curiosity.

"He found something very valuable that we had lost and left it for us in a local shop. We'd like to thank him and give him the finder's reward."

The guard was looking at him with an expression that still showed curiosity but was underpinned with disbelief. "Pull the other one. Marek couldn't have found something you'd lost. He can barely find this place and he's been here two years."

"Whatever. He was outstanding this morning and I fully intend to commend him to the board but in the meantime I want him to know how much we appreciate what he did."

"Like, how much do you appreciate him?"

Trout smiled. "Enough that there's fifty in it for you if you page him."

"What makes you think I can page him?"

The man blustered a bit but Trout could see it was all for show.

"I'd say that paging system you have on your desk would make me think it."

The guard looked at him, a crafty sideways look. Trout extracted a fifty-euro note he had already placed in his pocket and looked at it thoughtfully. He watched the guard eye it hungrily.

"There might even be a twin if you could guarantee that you'll forget we've ever been here."

"What about the commendation?"

"That's for the board. No need to say we've already thanked the man for his help."

The guard licked his lips, reached forward and plucked the fifty from Trout's fingers. It disappeared instantly into a pocket. He turned and picked up a walkie-talkie-type instrument. "*Calling Marek Benes, Marek Benes you're wanted at reception. That is Marek Benes wanted at reception.*" The call echoed tinnily across the compound. The guard turned back to Trout. "I've a terrible time with my memory. Once I've done a thing, jumping janitors if I can't remember a damn thing about it!"

Trout produced the second note, which disappeared in the same direction as the first. He went back to the car but didn't get in. He could see the security watching him and speculating as to what he wanted with Marek. Well, if Trout had his way he wasn't going to find out.

After a couple of minutes, they saw a compact young man hurrying across the compound towards the reception. He was of slight build, medium height and had black wiry hair that foretold he would always have a dark shadow on his chin. He dealt with it by sporting a neatly trimmed beard. As he approached, the security guard waved and pointed to where Trout and Lauren waited. Marek slowed but continued towards them, his eyes wary but curious.

"Marek, my name is Thomas Tegan and this is my friend Lauren O'Loughlin. I'd prefer if you came closer so we can talk to you without our friend in the box hearing."

"Why you want to talk with me?"

"We want to thank you for one thing and to ask you a couple of questions for another."

Marek frowned at him. "Thank me?"

"For giving Hannah and David a lift."

The man stilled, then slowly walked closer, shaking his head. "I can't say I did that," he said quietly.

"I thought that might be the case. That's why I didn't broadcast our business around the compound."

Marek came right up to him. "Look, I'm due to take tankard out in," he pointed to his watch, "ten minutes. Checks all done but I leave on time. Very important. My job. Whatever you have to say to me, say it."

"Hannah is Lauren's godchild and we've been searching for her for the last two maybe three days. So much has happened I'm beginning to lose track of the time. There are also two unscrupulous individuals searching for her who mean to do her harm. We want to find her first and make sure herself and her friend are safe and reunited with their families. What you did this morning took them away from the immediate danger they faced and for that I've brought you a small reward but we need to know where they've gone from here."

Lauren was leaning across the driver's seat listening to the conversation through the open window. She handed Trout some folded notes. He tapped them against his fingers, being careful to keep them out of sight of the security guard. "This is yours no matter what. It's only a couple of hundred to show our appreciation, say thank you."

"I didn't ask for anything. I didn't give them a lift for any reward." The young man looked at the notes and raised his eyes to meet Trout's. "They were scared when they asked me for a ride. I know scared. I helped them. They said things, told me things. I think they had good reason to be scared. The girl said her godmother, Lauren, is in County Clare. Could I take her to Clare? I said no. Cork, Limerick, not Clare but my friend he goes to Clare. I said I will ask him. She cried. She was pleased." He indicated the car. "This is the godmother, Lauren?"

"Yes, and me, I am also a friend. We lost them in Cork and now have inadvertently led the others nearer than is comfortable. I'm hoping we'll be well gone with your information and you'll be out on your rounds when they turn up. That's all we have that will slow them down a bit."

"What you want to know?"

"Where do we go from here?"

"One of the guys goes from Tarbert on the ferry to collect milk in Clare. I said 'Filip, my friend, you take these two across in the ferry. Hide them, they have no money.' He asked did they break the law. I said no, he said no problem."

"Oh my God, that's brilliant!" Lauren leaned across to the open window. "We can't thank you enough."

"Where did you meet him? How did they meet him?"

"He was in a layby before Charleville. He has a rest there. Gets ready for the run to the ferry, Today I stopped and talked with him. He was agreeable." He looked at what Trout was holding. "I will share with Filip. He helped too."

Trout took out one of his cards, folded the notes some more and passed them to Marek. "If you run into difficulties here in Ireland, call that number and one of us will be there. We may not be able to help but we might know someone who is." He shook his hand firmly. "I'm thinking you should ring or text that number straight away and we'll have yours – then we can let you know how all this pans out. Thanks again." He waited until Merek was out of sight, to make sure the security guard didn't try to waylay him, then sat into the car. "Let's get out of here, before anyone else arrives."

CHAPTER 43

"Killimer. They've gone to Killimer. They might as well be gone to Timbucktoo."

"Hang on a minute, Lauren, that's a very nice part of Clare and they are going in the right direction."

"I know. I love the Shannon estuary but they have to get all the way over to East Clare, with no money and no food. Have you any idea how difficult it is, to get from West Clare to East Clare at the best of times?"

"They've done OK so far and in my experience the Clare people are just as friendly and kind as anywhere else. More so, I'm inclined to say, but I do acknowledge my bias."

"I get what you're saying. I'm just – where in God's name will we start?"

"Look up the ferry times. Then check which is the fastest way for us to get there, to Killimer that is." Trout was retracing the way back onto Charleville main street. "I'm going to pull in here and get us coffee at the bakery. We'll grab a bit of that grub in the boot. I don't know about you but I could do with some food." Trout indicated, pulled up and in one deft manoeuvre reversed into a parking space. "This place is a nightmare to back out of, with the traffic. At least this way we're facing forward," he muttered.

"I'll put a bit of bread and salad together while you get coffee, then I can look up the information while we're eating." Lauren got out as Trout exited the driver side.

A truck horn boomed. Trout looked back the street. "That's Marek on his way. So far so good. I won't be long and I know they do decent coffee here."

Lauren popped the boot and surveyed the bag of produce she had bought in the English market when she had imagined their picnic this morning. Only this morning, she thought. Luckily, Trout had had his granary sliced in the market. Fiona Deasy had thoughtfully included a handful of serviettes. She wondered what she would use instead of butter and remembered the country relish she had added to the purchases. There it was at the bottom of the bag. She unscrewed the lid, dribbled a good amount around each slice, lay a row of cherry tomatoes on top, no need to cut them, she thought their teeth could do that, added some mixed leaves and covered the lot with another slice of bread. She wrapped the sandwiches in the tissues, carried the lot back to the car and placed Trout's on the dash in front of the steering wheel. She sat back, took a big bite and, as the flavours burst in her mouth, opened the phone and looked up the ferry timetables. According to the website, the ferry crossed from Tarbet, every hour on the half-hour and took twenty minutes to cross. Next, she checked the distances from Charleville to Killimer. By road, through the Limerick Tunnel under the River Shannon, it would take one hour and twenty-six minutes. An hour and a half she thought, give or take. By ferry, one hour and fifty-nine minutes. Almost two hours. She did a quick calculation, if Marek handed over the two before he delivered to the milk plant, and his friend was preparing for the run to the ferry, she would presume he was heading for the half-two sailing. It was now, she looked at the phone – fourteen ten – they'd hardly have arrived there yet. That made the road, in her opinion, the only option. With that in mind she opened the map once more and took another bite of her sandwich.

Trout came out the door of the bakery, carrying two large take-out cups. He stood for a moment and examined the street in all directions. He stared back the way they'd come for an intense moment then hurried to the car. Lauren had leaned across, opened the door and he slid in. He handed her a coffee.

"A black Jeep Cherokee like Caligula's has just turned off main, going towards the milk plant." He placed his cup in the holder and started the car.

Lauren felt the food in her mouth turn to wood. She couldn't get her tongue to make the words, took a gulp of coffee to get some moisture in and burned her tongue.

Trout pulled aggressively out into the stream of traffic. The driver in the car coming towards him thought to give him the finger, thought better of it as Trout raised a conciliatory hand in apology and turned it into a resigned thumbs-up instead. Trout flicked the hazard lights in thanks and kept going.

"Have you picked a route?"

Lauren swallowed convulsively. "Yeah. And, with a bit of luck, we won't be far behind them. At least that's what I think." She explained her reasoning, was relieved when Trout agreed. "How did they get here so fast?"

"You have to remember they were more or less with us all the way until we found the tracker." Trout tried to sound nonchalant but an underlying anger gave a growl to his tone.

"It was a pity it took so long to find Nonie's number." By the time she phoned Nonie, Caligula had already spoken to her – and, of course, she had innocently chatted about Trout and Lauren and the generous donation to the heifer fund. She had excitedly told Lauren their friend had donated handsomely as well. Hearing the pleasure in Nonie's voice at the rewards garnered by her callers that morning, Lauren hadn't the heart to discomfit her and simply thanked her for her help and disengaged.

"Oh, well, what's done is done," Trout said. "We're heading for Limerick, right?"

"Yeah." Lauren tried not to sound despondent and failed.

Trout guided the Golf through the heavy traffic, snatching a bite of sandwich every time they ground to a stop. Even with the stop-go, they were soon out on the N20 and he opened the car to the maximum speed the road could cater for. It was a relief to swing onto the motorway and there he tested the Golf's power to the limit. Bit by bit the milestones were ticked off, by-pass Limerick, through the Shannon tunnel, counting down the exits to 12 and swinging onto the Kilrush road. They were lucky: they met no speed van or check-points and so far were ahead of the times given.

The spectre of the black jeep, equally fast behind them, was a constant worry.

"They won't know where they've gone," Lauren said. "The security guard knew nothing about the handover to Marek's friend."

"That's what we're banking on." Trout drove with fixed concentration. "The only other way they have of getting information is the reward on social media and Brendan will alert us if anything pops on that."

"Why is Caligula persisting? I know what you said before but surely by now he must realize that the gig is up and that he'd be better off removing himself from the very island of Ireland. Are we missing something?"

"I don't know. The possibility that he murdered the woman in London when she was supposed to be his partner in crime is another thing to take into account."

"Shyrl Baker. She must have been lonely, to take up with someone like Caligula."

"How do you know he hasn't some sort of charisma that's been hidden in our encounters with him?"

Lauren snorted. "When someone is trying to kill you it's hard to see their charisma. You'll be taking the next left."

"There it is. The signpost for the ferry." Trout turned on to the lesser road. "Jesus! They call this a road." He pulled into a gateway allow a car pass. "Are you sure we won't land in someone's back yard?"

"You saw the signpost. And the map has us going in the same direction as the sign. There's a right coming up."

"And there's the sea."

"And the ferry terminal."

Trout followed the sign on the road that said parking lane, turned towards the sea and parked where they had a clear view of the slipway.

Lauren looked at the incoming ferry. It was in the process of lining itself up for disembarking. There was a queue of cars and people already forming to board the four o'clock sailing. And an equal one onboard waiting to come off. An air of organized chaos prevailed.

"Now what?" she said.

CHAPTER 44

It was obvious that the main focus of the terminal was the ferry. And it was laid out to facilitate the most efficient way to embark and disembark, with plenty of extra parking, a gift and coffee shop with all the facilities a traveller might or might not need. Lauren was about to exit the car when Trout's phone rang.

"Mac," he muttered and swiped to answer.

She left him to it and wandered over to a nicely laid-out seating area to stretch her legs, get some air and look over the estuary. The ferry had stopped and was preparing to disembark. She allowed her eyes travel across the water, along the ferry, tracking the lane awaiting the passengers and cars about to set foot in Clare and the steadily growing queue of vehicles in the designated ferry lane.

As she turned, she saw a woman exit an old minibus that had pulled in two spaces over from where they were parked. The woman hurried across to stand on the green area at the curve of the road, where those disembarking couldn't miss seeing her. She was wearing working clothes, cargo pants that had seen better days, a loose top and soil-encrusted boots and carried a large cardboard sign. Lauren, her curiosity piqued, wandered over to see what was on it.

It was handwritten in large bold letters. *DO YOU NEED BED AND A BITE? WE NEED PEOPLE TO HARVEST FRUIT THIS EVENING. ASK ME FOR MORE INFO.*

Laure stared at the writing for a long moment before she approached the woman with her heart beating an uncomfortable tattoo in her chest. "Excuse me, did you come to meet the last ferry with that sign?"

The woman glanced at her and smiled. "Sure did," she said pleasantly. "Got five volunteers from it too. Are you interested?"

"Maybe. I'm definitely curious. Why the sign?"

"We have a fruit and veg set-up that we run with the help of Woofers – you know, workers that come to us through WWOOF, World Wide Opportunities on Organic Farms – and this week's contingent have been delayed. We're small enough but are building a reputation for reliability and Dromoland Castle have contacted us with a huge order. Imagine getting to supply Dromoland?" She looked into a magical distance where her fruit farm was supplying a five-star hotel on a regular basis. Then as reality returned she almost wailed. "They're looking for twenty kilo of mixed soft fruits for something they've on tomorrow and want it tonight or at the latest by six in the morning." She sighed. "We have the fruit – what we don't have is pickers. I put out a call on the socials and that got some, a good few actually, but if we had a dozen more, we'd be well on the way to meeting the order, in full and on time. I thought of the ferry, we have an odd few people wander in from it, we're only up the road, so I thought why not give people a nudge and see what happens?"

Lauren thought fast. "We were supposed to meet my goddaughter and her friend off the last ferry but got delayed and are trying to figure out where they might be."

The woman looked at her skeptically. "Why wouldn't they just wait?"

"They were robbed of all their possessions and got a lift on the ferry. They were aiming to get to us in East Clare and I don't think they realized how far away we are or that we might possibly come and get them."

"That was a tough break." She looked at the ferry where the heavy ramp was creaking open. "What are they like?"

"A girl, sixteenish, slight build, red hair. Possibly in dreadlocks. And a young man, around twenty, tall and skinny with a narrow face and an English accent."

"There are two young ones that might fit your description. "What are their names?"

What would Hannah use at this stage, Lauren wondered, and decided to chance it. "Hannah and David."

The woman nodded. "Yeah. We have them. Hang on until I see what this lot brings and I'll talk with you then."

"Thanks." Lauren moved to one side and left her to it.

Trout joined her.

She turned to him, trying to maintain a calm she was far from feeling. "I know where they are. At that woman's place. Had Mac any news?"

"A bit. The London police have requested that the Gardaí keep a look-out for Caligula who they believe travelled to Ireland last weekend. He wanted to know if the picture of the jeep's number plate was still valid. He's already passed it on and there're a BOLO on it, so that's good news. I told him where we were, that we'd last seen the jeep in Charleville but that otherwise we had no idea what Caligula and Co were up to. He said he'd let us know if anything popped."

Lauren's phone interrupted his narrative. She pulled it out and answered it quickly, "Hi, Brendan. Hang on, I need to move a bit away from the noise."

The cars exiting the ferry were filling the air with sound and fumes. She indicated to Trout to come with her and put the phone on speaker mode. Given the noise level she wasn't too bothered that they would be overheard.

"Lauren, there's been a lot of chatter on Insta about a ferry and a sighting, and the reward chat is pinging constantly. It appears, but I can't say for certain, that the Shark is waiting in Tarbert for a ferry and plans to meet someone who gives his name on Insta as Woof-Woof when it gets to Killimer. That's like only the other side of Ennis. Is it possible?"

"We're in Killimer ourselves at the moment. We got info that our two crossed on the ferry. We're trying to trace where they could have gone from here. Now, thanks to you we can be fairly sure Ca– the Shark is on the same trail. You've done good work."

"I'm working on tracing who Woof-Woof is. Or maybe getting a location hit. The minute I do I'll let you know."

"Will you do another thing, Brendan?" Trout spoke softly, directly into the phone. "You remember I gave you Mac's number? Give him a call and tell him about the possibility that the Shark is taking the ferry from Tarbert to Killimer. No need to tell him how you know, I doubt if he'll ask anyway. Ask him if he has any contacts in Clare and could he set us up with back-up if we need it. And thanks again, Brendan."

Lauren opened her mouth to say something about the conversation with Brendan but stopped when she saw the woman with the placard marching towards her, trailed by six stragglers.

"*I've done well!*" she called as she approached. She eyed Lauren and Trout and said cheerfully, "If yourself and your friend pitch in, we'll have no problem filling the order."

CHAPTER 45

"You signed us up to go picking fruit? *For fuck sake*, Lauren, what were you thinking of?"

"I didn't. You heard her at the same time I did. Why didn't you say something? Anyway, they're stuck and we have to go there to get Hannah and David, who I'm sure have agreed to pick fruit, so why not give them a hand?" She turned and cajoled him. "Frankie Owens is so excited about the order from Dromoland, I couldn't say no."

"Have any idea the work that goes into picking that quantity of soft fruit?"

"Well, I know when I pick the raspberries at home it's both time-consuming and dangerous."

"Dangerous? Now you tell me. Where did you get dangerous from?"

"Thorns and nettles to name two hazards and bending to pick strawberries is back-breaking. I've never picked blueberries. No, that's not true. I have out the mountain only we call them fraughans and they're tiny compared to the ones you buy."

"You forgot the blackcurrants."

"They shouldn't be the worst."

"Fruit picking. *Fucking hell!*"

"She did say we could have the yurt for the night."

"Do you actually know what a yurt is?"

"It's a dwelling the nomads use." Lauren saw his look and decided now wasn't the time for a history lesson. "Don't you remember? We saw the one Jazzer and V had in Nirvana. It looked fab and I'm sure they're very comfortable. Frankie says they give it to any couples who come woofing."

"It's a glorified tent. I never liked camping!"

"I'm sure it's really comfortable. I've read *Silverland*."

"What's *Silverland*?"

"Dervla Murphy's journey beyond the Urals. That looks like the turn-off Frankie told us about. Yes, there's the sign: Estuary Fields Market Garden."

Trout duly made the turn-off and soon they were driving along the banks of the estuary. The road curved to the left, away from the water and shortly after that they came to the entrance. A large board sign, with an impossibly blue depiction of the estuary surrounded by Estuary Fields Market Garden in vivid green, stood sentinel behind a rough post and rail fence. A matching, equally crude gate stood open onto a gravel driveway. Trout guided the Golf through and, up, up, up a steep hill, around a sharp bend and not far beyond it, into the cleanest concrete yard he had ever seen.

An old stone cottage stood, gleaming white on the left, weathered slate replacing the thatch he'd nearly expected to see on it. Beside it, an old-fashioned iron pump stood on a step overlooking a cement trough. Attached to it was a coil of hose with a wide nozzle pointing straight out at the yard. Behind it all was a substantial all-weather compressor, a yellow adapter showing where it too was connected to the hosepipe. An old hay shed held a few rows of round bales, stacked checker-board style in pink and black. A couple of bales, awaiting stacking, were across the near end of the shed. Directly in front of them, and set back from the yard was a round structure, covered with layers of tarpaulin, held in place by lengths of rope, three strands around it and two more crisscrossing the top. A low wooden door was held closed by a crooked stick, that fitted through a round latch and protruded either side of the jambs.

Lauren clapped a hand over her mouth but the laughter in her eyes gave her away. She cleared her throat. "You should never judge a book by the cover, you know. Nor a yurt by a stick used to secure the door."

Trout gave her a pained look.

"Come on, Trout, where's your sense of adventure?"

"Somewhere back in the early days of the last century." He eyeballed the makeshift-looking structure once more. "OK. I'll wait until I see the inside before I finalize my judgment." He panned his gaze further right and took in what was once probably an old barn, now tastefully repurposed into a dwelling house, with pigeon windows gracing the upper floor and the old stone steps originally leading to the loft now leading to what was probably the living area of the house. They were painted bright yellow and it looked like the main entrance was up there. This distracted Trout and caused him to ponder the prospect of going downstairs to bed as distinct to traditionally going upstairs. The battered old bus, last seen parked in the ferry terminal, was pulled in beyond the house. As Trout wondered where to park, Frankie Owens trotted around the corner and waved them into the space in front of the yurt.

"*Perfect timing!*" she trilled. "I've just sent in this current batch to Dom for feeding. Come along, he's serving lamb stew and I want my share." She waited until they joined her in front of the barn-house and added confidingly, "Dom makes a terrific stew. Not that I'd tell him, his head is big enough as it is."

She led the way around the house, past a closed door, set into the bottom storey, and on into a long low extension that turned out to house an industrial-equipped kitchen and a large oak table that could comfortably seat twelve. The six new recruits were already eating.

An extremely tall, thin individual turned from where he was stirring a simmering pot and smiled. "Welcome. I hear you've come to save the day among other things." He waved a hand at the table. "Sit. The labourer is worthy of his grub. Dominic Owens. Call me Dom, it's easier."

"Thomas." Trout, looking up at him, then around the table, threw out a hand. "And Lauren. Glad to be able to help." He pulled out a chair for Lauren and settled himself beside her while Frankie lobbed herself into a chair opposite.

Dom served them bowls of lamb stew that was worthy of a Michelin star. It was followed by a strawberry crumble that was amazing.

"That's mine, made first thing this morning." Frankie was making sure the due credit came to her. "It's the freshness of the produce," she added, basking in the fulsome praise from everyone around the table.

She wolfed down her share and stood up.

"Right. It's time to get picking. With all hands on deck we should be finished well in time. As we pick Dom will load and I'll deliver them once the van is full."

Outside she fell into step with Trout and Lauren.

"What do you want to do about your two friends?"

"They've agreed to work and we've agreed to work, so nothing immediately. But I would like a chance to say hello and reassure Hannah that we're here for her." Lauren looked at Trout, who nodded.

Frankie's relief was palpable. "That's no problem. I'll set you up near them." She pushed open a gate into a huge field and looked around with pride. "Welcome to Estuary Field Market Garden."

CHAPTER 46

"Christ on a bike!" Lauren couldn't help it. The field stretched in all directions, laid out for the most part in lazy beds, raised up from the ground and lush with growth. Off to the right rows of raspberry canes tangled and entwined with each other, paths at either side to facilitate picking with lightweight aluminum steps awaiting those who needed to reach the higher fruit. The blackcurrant bushes ran from the gate in a single row to the further end. They were pruned to shoulder height, laden with plump, shiny fruit and imbued the air with their distinctive cassis aroma. People moved diligently among the canes and bushes.

"Our regular local pickers are all in." Frankie sent two of the newbies to the raspberries and two to the blackcurrant bushes, calling out, *"New recruits! Annie, Paddy, show them the ropes!"*

Two young people detached themselves from the respective bushes and welcomed the newcomers into the fold.

"I set up Hannah and David on the strawberry beds. I'll take you there and," she turned to the other two, "you two can join the blueberry brigade. It's down at the very end."

Lauren, concealing her excitement at the prospect of seeing Hannah, asked her about growing the blueberries as they tramped between the raised beds, to an area further away from the yard. Frankie was delighted to expand on their work and explained how they had to dig out the bottoms and add peat to increase the acidity of the soil. She seemed oblivious to Lauren's lack of interest but broke off mid-sentence to hulloo at an elderly man in shorts, wellingtons and a bush hat complete with corks that twirled wildly when he jerked his head in answer to her call. She pointed to the two and shooed them towards him. He grinned and gave an enthusiastic thumbs-up.

"The strawberry beds are over here."

Lauren was amazed to see the high lazy beds were deeply topped with crackling, golden straw.

"We're organic, so it suits us to grow them in the traditional way. A lot of work but we're getting amazing results and we can mulch the straw and put in fresh stuff next year."

Lauren was scanning the beds, more interested in seeing if she could spot her goddaughter, when she realized that Frankie had stopped. She was indicating to where five young people were spread out across a row of raised beds, when her attention was caught by some activity in the far corner of the field. "*Bloody crows!*" she muttered, setting off at a run, waving her arms in the air, calling over her shoulder, "*Straight ahead, you can't miss them!*"

Lauren set her sights on a girl, wearing mud-stained jeans, boots that showed a flash of purple through the dirt embellishing them and a loose T-shirt, who doggedly and rhythmically leaned over the bed, plucked a strawberry, turned, deposited it in a shallow tray and did the same again. She had a ponytail of dreadlocks pulled through the back of an orange baseball cap that made her hair glow with copper tones. Sweat was running down her face and every now and then she swiped a sticky hand across it, adding tribal stripes of strawberry to her rosy skin. She plucked and turned with ferocious concentration, showing more willingness than skill.

Lauren called softly, "Hannah!"

The girl's head jerked up like a deer startled by a gunshot. She straightened herself stiffly, looked around her, saw Lauren, stared at her with a comical mixture of delight and disbelief before launching herself into her outstretched arms.

"*Lauren! How did you find us?* I knew I saw you at the warehouse but I couldn't be sure. Then we had to run again. David thought I was hallucinating. I'm so glad to see you!" she babbled, then cried, a short, relieved burst of tears, pulled back and brushed them impatiently away. "How did you find us?"

"We're investigators. That's what we do." Lauren laughed softly. "Apparently it's harder to cover your tracks than you think." She turned and brought Trout into the scene. "This is my friend Thomas. He helped me and now we'd like to meet David."

Hannah scrutinized Trout and, suddenly shy, said "Hello. You got us out of the warehouse." She straightened herself and said with a mature dignity Lauren didn't know she possessed, "We didn't get a chance to thank you."

"Pleased to meet you properly." Trout smiled. "We were all too busy for thanks that evening. Not that they were needed in the first place."

The young man working on the next bed had jerked upright and stared at them with a mixture of hope and apprehension. Now he came forward slowly, held out a hand to Trout and said shakily, "We owe you our lives. Hannah is right – we never thanked you but then things had got a little fraught by the time we left."

He tried a tentative smile that broadened into a grin when Trout shook his hand vigorously and said, "That's the understatement of the year if ever I heard one."

It appeared they were all aware of the public nature of this meeting. By mutual consent they had moved close together and now huddled, keeping their voices too low for anyone except themselves to hear.

"First off, Isla is doing well," Lauren said. "Her mother is over and it's expected she'll make a complete recovery."

"Oh my God, I'm so glad she's OK!" Hannah took a step back and glanced at David.

It seemed to Lauren she became more wary or perhaps nervous.

She was trying to decide which when Hannah asked tremulously, "Is there anything you don't know?"

"Lots." She turned towards the young man and held out a hand. "Pleased to meet you, David."

He took her hand and shook it, studying her without saying a word. Until he blurted out, "Lauren O'Loughlin, I presume."

Lauren moved forward and, with a gurgle of laughter, caught him in a friendly hug and said, "That should be my line, surely? I found you!" Out of the corner of her eye she saw Frankie turn and start back across the field. "Our hostess returns and is probably cursing the fact that she missed the grand reunion," she murmured.

Indeed Frankie was stomping towards then, her face alive with open curiosity. When she was near enough she said practically, "We've got fruit to pick." She eyed Trout. "I think you're a better fit for the raspberry canes. Come on, I'll take you back there and, if I don't get waylaid, I'll come back myself to work here."

"Grand. We'll meet up when the fruit is picked." He hesitated, looked at Lauren.

She nodded. "That's a plan." She leaned forward to give him a peck on the cheek, saying into his ear, "I'll explain the possibilities and probabilities."

"OK. Keep your eyes peeled and all that." He glanced at Frankie and added, "For nettles and briars and critters," nodded at the three and reluctantly followed Frankie back the way they'd come.

"We agreed to help pick the fruit for food and board," Hannah said earnestly to Lauren.

"So did we." Lauren's cheerful rejoinder seemed to settle Hannah. "But we'll want a full account before the night is out."

David mumbled something. Lauren turned her smile on him.

"You're not in any trouble. On the contrary, I'd say prepare yourself to be lauded to the heavens and back."

If anything, his expression became more glum.

Lauren looked between them and leaned in to say very quietly, "There's something you both need to know immediately. Can the three of us work together on this bed until it's and finished? I'd prefer if the whole garden didn't hear what I have to say."

Hannah and David looked at one another, then at Lauren. He came round to stand at the far side of where Hannah had been working. "I'll work from this side and we can huddle to talk." He raised his voice, "We'll show you what to do. We can all work together."

His accent had the lilt of London underpinned by a cadence Lauren couldn't identify. Now wasn't the time, she thought, there's too much at stake here. She glanced around. There were at least a dozen strawberry beds, laid out in four rows of three. Two of the beds furthest away were being worked on by young girls. She noticed the third picker, a man, two beds over, and one back from where David had originally been picking, watching them. He had a narrow foxy face with wispy blond hair straggling out from under a battered felt hat. He quickly bent to his picking when he saw her looking. She wondered could he be the mysterious Woof-Woof.

She smiled at the two. "Let's get cracking. What do I have to do here?" She lowered her voice. "We need to talk *really* quietly."

CHAPTER 47

As they plucked, twisted and filled, they kept their heads close together and talked in low voices.

The strawberry beds were densely packed with plants and the strawberries were large and plentiful. The straw kept them up off the ground and made them easy to see, A luscious red orb against the golden straw. They picked quickly into a low trolley with shallow crates stacked one on top of the other. Lauren shared Hannah's trolly. David had trundled his around the bed. The crates would be picked up by Dom as each was filled.

"I don't know if you're aware that Caligula has offered a reward on social media, for information as to your whereabouts," Lauren said, without looking at either of them.

Hannah moaned. "*Nooo!* After we left our phones turned off in case they could be tracked."

"That's why they were waiting for us in Cork." David sounded grim. "It must be substantial."

"Twenty thousand euro."

He tightened his lips. "I'd nearly turn myself in for that."

"David!"

"I said *nearly*, shrimp!" He glanced at Lauren. "There's more, isn't there?"

Lauren drew a deep breath, appreciating that he was going straight to the heart of the problem but not sure how she was going to frame it. In the end she said straight out, "We have reason to believe that someone saw you on the ferry and that Caligula knows you're somewhere about. Although I don't think he knows exactly where but it's only a matter of time."

"You think whoever grassed is here with us?"

"Yes."

"We need to get out of here, fast." Hannah's hands, reaching for a strawberry, trembled.

"And what? You have to stop running sometime and Trout and myself are here to keep you safe."

"And," David was teasing out a thought in his head, "I've heard loads of complaints since we arrived that there's no coverage here, phone or internet. Whoever it is can't immediately get word out as to where we are."

"They might have it done already?" Lauren said.

"I don't think so. Until we actually arrived, they would only have a general idea and I noticed a couple of people on the bus fiddling with their phones and going by the body language, getting no signal."

Lauren noticed that his words had a steadying effect on Hannah. Observant as well as practical, Lauren thought. "It has occurred to me that by standing our ground we can choose where to have the confrontation."

"You sound pretty sure there will be one."

"Caligula hasn't given up. Personally, I can't figure out what he has to gain by keeping after you. I would have thought ten million would be little enough to justify his persistence."

Hannah's head jerked up. "Where on earth did you get ten million from?"

Lauren lifted a full crate, carried it to the top of the ridge and waved at Dom who was crossing the headland. She moved back into position.

"It seems that Caligula was overheard telling Shyrl Baker there was a ten million payout for them if they succeeded."

"Yeah. But, Lauren, that was for her. Caligula's cut was going to be nearer a hundred and twenty million, if he got away with what he was doing."

The bitterness in Hannah's voice made Lauren pause and look at her godchild. Hannah was diving at the plants, her careful picking taken over by sudden, jerky grabs. In her agitation, she squashed a strawberry and swore.

"*Damn!*" She threw the offending fruit on the ground. "He was going to destroy my dad's credibility and all his investors would have lost their money and the world economy would have been affected. He even thought he could start a war in – in –" She was starting to hyperventilate.

"Hey, take it easy, shrimp! Lauren doesn't know any of that. Just keep picking and we can tell her about it." David raised his head. "You don't, do you?"

He sounded, Lauren thought, like an older brother, kindly but exasperated with his little sister's antics. "No. And, Hannah, I really would appreciate if you kept breathing." She made her voice cool and pragmatic. "And talking. The last thing we need is to draw attention to ourselves. As it is, I notice one guy over there doing his best to listen in on what we're saying."

"He's a good candidate," said David. "I noticed him watching us when we got out of the milk truck. It was like he did this double-take thing and then tried to pretend he hadn't seen us."

"Caligula posted a picture of Hannah. It doesn't look like you this minute, Hannah," Lauren put a smile in her voice, "but you would be recognizable from it."

"I noticed him." Hannah had gone from unnerved to sulky. "He smelled."

"Weed." David shrugged. "He's still here. So, either he hasn't been in contact with whoever or he's watching us for him." Again, he used that practical tone, while his fingers plucked strawberries and deposited them in his crate.

Lauren thought about what Marina had said about David intervening between his sister and her father and wondered what was the full story of his falling-out with his family. Probably the step-dad wanted him out of the way to have a clear run at Isla and engineered it to happen. No doubt they'd find out but, right now, it wasn't the most pressing problem. "We're nearly finished here and the next bed brings us nearer to Worzel Gummidge over there."

Hannah giggled. "That is so cool – you've got him to T."

"It's always easier to deal with someone when you know their name."

"Well, even if his name isn't Worzel Gummidge, I'm going to call him that." Hannah had her rhythm back. "He looks like a scarecrow and I can deal with a silly old scarecrow." Her tone said 'So there!'.

Lauren drew a careful hand over the plants, parting the leaves. "I don't see any more ripe ones here." She hesitated – at the moment she needed to know what exactly they were up against with Caligula. "So, before we move on, troops," she said, leaning in between Hannah and David, "any idea why Caligula is determined to find you?"

"Yeah," said Hannah. "I guess I do."

"Well?" Surprised, Lauren waited expectantly.

Hannah looked at her sideways and went back to searching the leaves for ripe strawberries. "I stole his data-stick," she muttered. "The one with the access codes for Dad's investors. And I guess it also has the details of his own account in the Bahamas where the one-hundred and twenty million is."

CHAPTER 48

It took all Lauren's considerable will-power not to react to Hannah's mumbled confession. "I guess that would concentrate his mind on finding you all right."

She hoped she managed to sound mild and non-judgmental. Her head was spinning. She took a deep breath, counted three and let it out slowly.

"Come on, you two," David said, raising his voice to a peevish mutter. "We have my bed to do yet and we've two more before we finish. God, I don't think I'll ever eat a strawberry again!" He added under his breath, "Worzel isn't even pretending not to be interested in us." He grabbed the handle of his trolley and trundled it around to the bed he'd been working on before joining Lauren and Hannah.

The women turned and having only the width of the trench to travel, started harvesting the ripe berries immediately. The three of them worked diligently and in silence.

Lauren was trying to figure out what the next move was. She squinted along the length of the bed which seemed twice as long as the first one. She badly wanted to talk to Trout. As it was, her mind was hopping and fizzing while she was acutely conscious of the sideways looks from the scarecrow lookalike. They absolutely needed to get out of here. They needed to make Hannah safe.

"*Shit!*" She leaned close to Hannah's ear and hissed, "Where's the data stick?"|

Hannah turned. "I don't know. New York maybe."

"*New York!*"

"I didn't want it." She turned back to the strawberry plants. "I put it in an envelope and posted it to Dad's office in New York."

Lauren felt her knees go weak. "But, Hannah, it could get lost in the post! Or, or anything!"

"I don't care." Hannah hunched her shoulders. "All I wanted was to get it away from that horrid Caligula. He gives me the creeps. I didn't want to throw it away in case it could be used as evidence against him." She rounded on Lauren. "*You* told me the best way to get rid of something small you didn't want on you was to put it in the post."

"Well . . ." Lauren had a flash of a weekend in London after she had helped Trout solve a case involving murder and mayhem, and regaling Marina and Hannah with their exploits. She sighed. "Did you send an explanation of what it was, with it?"

"No. Just a note saying '*You need to see what's on this*'." She perked up. "I signed it *A Friend*."

"It's probably encrypted," David said quietly from the other side. His hands were parting the leaves, long lean fingers searching for fruit.

He has musician's fingers Lauren thought as her mind searched for their next move. "Do you play music?"

"Piano," he mumbled.

"David won a scholarship to the Academy," Hannah said proudly.

"That was before." He looked at Hannah. "I've told you," he spoke with quiet dignity, "we have to deal with what is, not with what we'd like it to be."

"And I've told you *my dad* –" Hannah began hotly, her voice rising.

"*I think we're finished here!*" Lauren said loudly. "Where did you say the other beds are, David?" She flicked her eyes right, where the Worzel Gummidge character had stopped picking to look at them.

"Down the back there." David indicated behind and below him. "This tray is full. I'll leave it up top for Dom. What have we left? I have one empty tray."

"We have one empty and this one half full." Hannah glanced at Lauren. "When all our trays are full and delivered to Dom, we'll be finished with the strawberries." She turned and grabbed the handle of the trolley. "We'll head over."

Lauren stretched her shoulders. "Right behind you. God! I never knew picking fruit was such back-breaking work. I'll never take a punnet of strawberries for granted again." She trudged after her godchild, aware of the way Wurzel's eyes swivelled after them and that he tracked their path to the further strawberry beds.

They exchanged greetings with the two young girls there, who appeared old hands at the game, judging by the quick and efficient way they plucked and filled their trays.

"Supper time soon!" one of them called cheerfully.

"Really. What time is it?" The evening was still bright but now Lauren thought about it, the heat had dissipated, leaving a more benign warmth behind it.

"Quarter to eight." The second girl consulted a tiny fob watch on a chain, which she pulled out from where it lay hidden inside her T-shirt.

"Cool watch."

"My mum's. She insisted I bring it because we can't use our phones here."

"No cover." The other girl gave vent to her disgust with such primitive conditions.

"And we have to be ready when she calls for us at nine," the other continued undaunted. "I'm Rosie and that's 'Vette."

Presumably Yvette, thought Lauren.

"You lot newbies?"

"Are we that obvious?" Lauren groaned, hamming it for all her worth. Even as she thought, there's no need for hamming – I could groan a lot more, only I wouldn't give it to say to these young ones.

"I'm Hannah." She grinned in synch with the two girls. "The geriatric relation is my godmother, Lauren."

"*Hey!* Who are you calling geriatric?"

And with the good-natured ribbing lightening the mood, Lauren and Hannah pulled into the next ridge and started picking. They weren't long at it when Lauren heard Rosie say, "Hi" in a low sultry tone. She looked up in time to catch Hannah's scowl and hid a smile as she heard David return the greeting with a hearty "How's it going, girls?"

He beckoned to Lauren to step aside with him. Hannah followed.

"Worzel is gone," he said in a very low voice.

"Gone?" Lauren said. "Maybe he's sneaked off to have a smoke."

"I heard him telling Frankie that he was going for a piss but I saw him heading for the lane leading into this place."

"Probably going to look for coverage," Hannah said. "Is there anything we can do?" Her voice shook.

Lauren made a face. "I don't know. We could do with having a conference with Trout."

"Who's Trout?" David asked.

"Thomas. His nickname is Trout."

David grinned. "He doesn't look like one." He became serious as fast. "Lauren. You said about choosing our place for a confrontation?"

"Yeah. What are you thinking?"

"I'm thinking there are a lot of people here that shouldn't be exposed to any shit we might bring to them."

Practical *and considerate*, she thought. "I know. We've agreed to help get this job done so we need to get this fruit picked. Then we can decide our next step."

They returned to their picking.

Lauren turned to the girls. "Any hints as to how we can speed up the picking without damaging the fruit?" she asked hopefully.

CHAPTER 49

There were no shortcuts when picking soft fruit. The two girls had laughed when Lauren asked them for tips and Yvette said, "You get faster, the more you do."

They settled down to work and bit by bit the trays were filled. The two girls helped them with the last bed and together they headed for the yard, pulling the trolleys with the final laden trays. A haze of blue smoke and the smell of grilling food hung over the yard.

"Goody, Dom has the barbie out." Rosie perked up and increased her pace.

"He'll have our burgers ready for us to take with us," Yvette predicted confidently. "Look, there's Mam, she must be early."

Rosie consulted her hidden watch. "No. We're late. We'd better hurry. Dad needs the car in twenty minutes and we need to get home."

Frankie came to meet them. "I'll take those, girls, your mam's here. Run and get some food. We'll see you tomorrow."

"Thanks, Frankie." The girls handed over the trolleys and ran.

"That was a great evening's work." Frankie beamed at the tired faces trudging along beside her.

"What now?" Lauren asked.

"I'll get these stowed and head for Dromoland. Nick and Ivan will come with me to unload. They're two of our Woofers. They've already eaten."

They had reached a small refrigerated truck. Frankie trundled up a makeshift ramp into the wide body of the truck, where rows of trays packed with fruit were stacked with a commendable use of available space. She slipped the last of the trays into place, hauled the trolly down and closed the door.

"There's no point in hanging around with them. Best get them delivered and out of the way. Dom got a message that the others will be here tomorrow, now that most of the work is done!" She laughed. "Not entirely true. We have to prepare for the Saturday and Sunday markets. But that's only small fry compared to this."

Lauren couldn't resist asking. "What do you do with the fruit you can't sell?"

"It hasn't happened yet but we've been making small batches of jam and conserves. Now that we've a proper kitchen set up that will be easier." She dusted her hands on her jeans. "We've been getting good feed-back from the markets with what we were doing on a small level. So, we're hopeful." She crossed her fingers.

"I don't how you do it. The sheer amount of work is mind-boggling."

"You have to love it, otherwise you'd go mad." Frankie laughed again. "Maybe we are a bit mad anyway but it suits us. And we're lucky. We get to meet the nicest people. Go on, go get some grub. I need to get this thing moving. I'll thank you properly in the morning."

I wouldn't be too sure about that, Lauren thought grimly. There was a serious possibility they would have brought trouble to the door of Estuary Field Market Garden well before morning came. Nonetheless the smell of food was tantalizing and she followed Hannah and David as they hurried towards it, like sniffer dogs that had picked up the scent and intended to follow the trail to the end.

Lauren went straight to Trout, ignored his reproachful look as he held out his hands for her inspection.

"Are you going to complain about a couple of scratches?" She flopped onto a chair beside him. "We have a lot bigger problems than scratches at the moment."

"You reckon? You haven't felt my pain."

"About an hour ago Worzel Gummidge went for a piss and hasn't been seen since."

"Worzel Gummidge?" Trout turned fully to look at her. "Has the sun got to you, Lauren? Or are you just hungry? Either can cause hallucinations? Here, have this." He thrust the fully loaded burger that was in front of him into her hand. "I'll get another one."

In spite of herself, Lauren smiled. "We christened the guy that was taking too much interest in in us after the scarecrow. After all, he did look like one." She gave in to the delicious aroma and took a big bite. "This is good," she mumbled around the mouthful of food, chewed and swallowed. "We think he went to find enough phone coverage to report where we are." She took another bite and watched Trout as she chewed.

"*Bloody hell*! They'll arrive sooner rather than later so."

"We need to alert Dom to the possibility. At least Frankie is gone with the delivery but, Trout, there's still too many people here who could get hurt." Her appetite suddenly gone, Lauren lowered the remains of the burger. "What are we going to do?"

"It's too late to get out of here. We'd only be leaving the place vulnerable. Finish your food, you'll need the energy. I'll go and talk to Dom."

She watched Trout walk over to Dom, pick up a barbeque fork as if he was assisting him and lean in to say something to him. Dom gave him one startled look, then went back to flipping burgers even as he kept his head angled towards Trout. Lauren wondered at his lack of reaction, the cool listening and careful concentration on tending the barbeque. She picked up her burger and resumed eating, contemplating the possibility that Dom wasn't as hapless as he let on to be. After all, she reasoned, in spite of its size the market-garden enterprise was laid out and run with military precision. Dom stood tall and straight, his shoulders square, his knees loosely locked. Very few people that tall held themselves well. Not without training or making an effort to maintain their posture. The mountain pose would do it, she thought, if he was a devotee of yoga – otherwise a man trained to stand for long periods with little or no movement was the best possibility. She swallowed the last bite, surprised to see she had eaten the whole lot and looked to see where Hannah and David were.

They were in a bunch with the remainder of the pickers. Hannah was talking animatedly, moving her hands in all directions. David offered a few words here and there. As she watched they went into a huddle, six heads of various hues and shapes. For all the world they looked like they were planning an almighty prank. She wondered what they were up to but decided it was so good to see Hannah carefree in spite of the circumstances that whatever bit of fun they were planning was best left alone.

Trout reached to pick up a platter of burger buns from the table and started to lay them on the shelf at the back of the barbeque. It dawned on Lauren that the buns were also made fresh, here on the farm. She determined she would have to have another burger and this time she would pay attention to the freshness and flavours of the contents. She rose and went to join the men.

"You want to eat or help?" Dom smiled at her.

"Can't I do both?"

The smile became a grin. "Good answer that." He reached behind him and jangled a decorative cowbell Lauren hadn't noticed until now, dangling from a wooden trellis at the back of the barbeque area. "*Grubs up!*" he called.

The youngsters gave a last titter of laughter, broke ranks and hurried towards the table. There were bowls and plates of the fresh produce grown by Estuary, waiting to be added as each built a burger to his or hers liking. Lettuce, tomatoes, onions, a couple of types of relish that were in jars with home-made labels and a large bottle of a well-known brand of mayonnaise. In minutes the table was depleted and a fair amount of the food loaded onto buns and plated. The youngsters moved back to benches, still near enough to get more food but far enough away to continue their own chat. Lauren kept one eye on them as she regarded their surroundings for possible hiding places.

The cottage, she had learned, was the bunkhouse for the Woofers – it was behind the benches and to their left. Rosie had told them that its two bedrooms were repurposed as respectively male and female dorms. Its big central kitchen was used as the communal living room. Yvette had added Dom didn't hold with this couples' lark. Genuine couples got to stay in the yurt and they had to have told them beforehand if they needed it. Lauren had smiled at the thought of Dom laying down the rules with adventurous young ones but she could see the sense of it. Beside it, the water pump with its modern additions abutted the row of pink and black wrapped bales, awaiting hoisting up on top of the others. The yurt looked serene but she couldn't see what hiding place a one-room glorified tent would have to offer. She gave up her speculations, loaded a burger with everything and prepared to indulge herself.

The growl of a high-spec engine climbing the hill pounded through the air and shattered the evening calm. Every head shot up. Every eye turned towards the entrance as a big, black Jeep Cherokee, with a damaged front grill, roared into the yard.

CHAPTER 50

The jeep lurched off the gravel, onto the cement and slammed to a stop. Three doors opened as one, Caligula swung down from the passenger side and two unknowns hopped out of the driver door and the back passenger side respectively. All three carried guns, and held them pointing straight out in front of them. At the young people, nudging each other and watching them avidly, at Trout and Dom standing by the barbeque and at Lauren, behind the table, frozen in the act of picking up her burger.

"*Shit!*" Trout swore softly. "They're all packing SIG Sauers."

"Yep, the Magnum 22 Automatic by the looks of them," Dom whispered, then raising his voice, called, "*Welcome! We're just having a barbeque. Would you care to join us?*"

Caligula, interrupted as he was about to talk, snarled something unintelligible, raised his voice and shouted, "*We'll give you a barbeque you won't forget in a long time!*" His gaze landed on Lauren. He curled his lip. "Nobody gives me a black eye and gets away with it." He squinted along the gun and smiled, a cruel twist of his lips. "I've something special planned for you." He panned the gun across to aim straight at Trout. "Hand over the girl and we'll let all these other people go."

"I'm afraid I don't have your capacity for believing in fairy tales, Caligula." Trout kept his voice low and pleasant. Out of the corner of his eye he saw the youngsters move to stand in front of Hannah and David, blocking them from view of the gunman covering them. They were still nudging each other and giggling. He wondered what in tarnation they were playing at. Didn't they recognize a gun when they saw it? He turned his attention back to Caligula. "The gig's up, Larry, you might as well call it a day and vamoose while you can."

"I want the girl. The stupid bitch has caused me enough trouble – it's well time she answered for her interference. Where is she? We know she's here." From his stand fair square between his two recruits he kept the gun trained on Trout, clicked his fingers at each of his side-kicks in turn and indicated for one to go through the fruit-pickers and the other to go after Lauren.

The lad heading towards the Woofers was not much older than themselves. He started to pad towards them, his eyes gleaming with anticipation.

There was a shout of "*Fore!*", the youngsters scattered and a pink bale began to roll towards the gunman, leaving David where it had stood, his hands outstretched, his face a study in consternation at the power he had released. The gunman hesitated, stared at the pink sphere that was rolling towards him, gathering momentum with every turn, threw his hands up in the air, spun about and ran. The bale hopped and bounced after him. He yelped, tripped and dived head first into the drain carrying the run-off from the yard across the field. The bale gave a final hop and settled itself across the drain, over its fortunate victim who, while trapped at least wasn't squashed.

Meanwhile, two of the Woofers grabbed the power hose from beside the pump, while a third cranked the compressor. A mighty jet of water hit Caligula in the middle of the chest, sweeping him off his feet and sending him sprawling onto his back. The gun discharged upwards, sending a flock of crows into the air protesting raucously. The two with the hose advanced, the pipe jerking in their hands with the power of the water, all the while keeping the stream of water raining down on him. Trout jumped the railing, skidded to where Caligula lay flailing about in an attempt to get up. and grabbed the gun off him, getting drenched himself in the process. He checked the chamber; another bullet had automatically loaded. He tutted "Dangerous yokes these guns," and turned it casually towards Caligula's head. "I have him covered," he told the two braves. "Ye can turn off the water now."

The third guy paid no heed whatsoever to the chaos reigning around him. His eyes were locked on Lauren and he loped towards her, picking up speed and licking his lips. "Boss says you're all mine," he chortled. "We're gonna have fun, babe!"

"Oh, for heaven's sake!" Lauren sounded thoroughly pissed off. She grabbed a breath, shouted "*Geronimo!*" and with a mighty heave turned the table over. The gunman ran full tilt into it and hung for a minute half over it, winded. Dom grabbed the meat tongs, reversed it to use its heavy wooden handles and clipped the guy firmly behind the ear. He went limp. The gun slipped from his fingers. Dom scooped it up and engaged the safety lock. He turned to Lauren and held up a hand for a high five. She obliged.

Hannah was standing with her hands over her mouth. The young people joined hands and did a victory dance, chanting, "*We are the champions! We are the champions!*" They turned as one and ran to Lauren. "Do we get the prize?"

"The bad guys didn't win. We must have got the prize!"

"Prize?" Lauren turned bewildered eyes towards Hannah. She came forward slowly.

"Ah, Lauren, I might have told them that we were acting in a reality TV show and if the ones playing the bad guys didn't get the better of us, they'd win a prize."

"You what?"

Lauren surveyed the scene around her. Her assailant was still draped across the sideways table, Dom standing over him with the tongs. The enormous pink bale was looking picturesque against a hedge of red and purple fuchsia. There was no sign of its captive, possibly still under it, counting his lucky stars. Trout was crouched with the gun still pointing at Caligula, who lay stranded in a puddle of water. Lauren met Trout's eye. He smiled. She felt her lips twitch in response, and knew if she gave into laughter, she was in danger of becoming hysterical. *Bloody hell!* A reality TV show!

"That was a brilliant idea," she said quietly. "But, Hannah, it could have gone terribly wrong. We could have all been killed."

"Well, we weren't!" Hannah's eyes flashed. "You're always telling me that the biggest thing stopping people from achieving something is fear. So, I took away the fear by saying it was a reality TV show and look what we achieved. Anyway," suddenly her face crumpled and big tears slid down her face, "I was scared enough for all of us."

"Oh, Hannah!" Lauren caught her godchild in a tight hug. She took a deep breath, reckoned there was nothing to be gained by further reprimand in this moment and whispered, "You can bet there'll be a prize."

She turned to the crowd. "Well done, everybody! You are all well-deserving winners."

There was another round of dancing and cheering and a conga line back to the benches where the group fell on the remains of their burgers with renewed appetite.

Lauren turned to Dom. "I'm so sorry about the food."

"No worries. Nothing will be wasted. The hens and pigs will dine well tonight and, let's face it, the possibility of telling people how we overcame a bad guy with a table full of lettuce and tomatoes will give me pleasure for many a day."

Again, the sound of a car powering up the hill cut through the revelry, relative calm or whatever one calls the aftermath of a battle.

Heads turned. All except Trout's who saw Caligula's eyes narrow as he calculated his chances of getting away. Trout said softly, "Just try it. I'll make sure not to hit a vital organ but it would give me great pleasure to cause you a great deal of pain."

A Garda car and a motorbike swerved to a stop beside the jeep. Two Gardaí climbed out and looked all around them.

"Mac said we'd probably be too late," one of them remarked. "Looks like I'll be buying him afternoon tea in some fancy Cork hostelry."

"As long as it's Barry's tea, he'll be happy," his colleague quipped as they headed further into the yard.

CHAPTER 51

Lauren was trying to shoo the overexcited fruit-pickers off to bed, while laughing uncontrollably, when Frankie trundled the game old truck into the yard. The black jeep was still in situ, and four police cars lined the periphery, three of them with their engines running, preparing to leave.

"I'm so glad you're back." Lauren ran over to her. "The children won't go to bed for me. Even though I've told them there'll be no slacking in the morning, especially as you're going to be short four pickers tomorrow." She was aware that she was behaving like an over-excited child herself but justified it by telling herself it was the relief of, you name it, finding Hannah, seeing Caligula in custody, generally losing of the tension of the past few days. She knew there would be stories to hear and to tell, and that she'd have to run the gauntlet of what, she had no doubt, would be Marina's fluctuating moods. Although she consoled herself that Karl might be a mitigating factor there.

Frankie stared at her, speechless. Looked around her yard, her home, with bewildered eyes, and said faintly, "What did I miss?"

"Send them to bed and we'll tell you all about it." Lauren lowered her voice. "The boys have started on the country wines without us."

"What country wines?" Frankie, suddenly got mad. "They can't drink the wines! I've only just put them into the demi-johns." She made to storm towards the barbeque area where people were sitting on the benches or standing around, conversing intensely. Someone, possibly Dom, had lit giant citronella candles to deter the midges. And these added a halo effect to the yard lights that spotlighted the tableau.

Lauren caught her arm. "It's all right. It's ours. We had some in the boot." She spluttered into laughter again when she saw Frankie looking even more confused. "Come on, I'll explain."

Beside them the Garda cars, one by one, revved-up and left. Together, Lauren and Frankie turned to look. As they passed, they saw the incumbents, handcuffed, their demeanor telling its own story. One was leaning back against the seat with his eyes closed. Perhaps he was repenting the error of his ways. His sojourn under the pink bale and subsequent rescue had knocked the arrogance out of him. It had taken a bit of time to figure out how to move the bale without crushing him and he was in the drain for longer than was comfortable. In the end Dom had produced a coil of rope and a decrepit yellow tractor – with the tractor pulling and Trout and one of the Gardaí pushing, the bale was moved and towed to where there was no danger of it moving again. Dom lamented that they would have to rewrap it but concluded it was a small price to pay for the work it had already done.

The second car held a dazed and dejected-looking fellow, who given the way he moved his head was probably suffering with a headache. He was staring at the handcuffs as if he was wondering what they were.

"I never knew that barbeque tongs were such lethal weapons," Lauren murmured as she watched the car pass. "But I was ever so glad to find out how effective they can be."

Frankie turned astonished eyes on her. "Barbeque tongs?" she murmured faintly.

The third car held Caligula. He glared at Lauren with enough fury to scorch her skin if she was of a mind to let him. He had tried to bluster his way out of the situation, claiming that the fruit-pickers had attacked him, that he had only drawn his gun in self-defence, that Trout had threatened him with bodily harm, on and on until Inspector Bodine, as he introduced himself, said, "We take attempted murder of a Garda very seriously here." He turned his back on him, ordered his sergeant to take him out of his sight before he forgot that his brief was to uphold the law.

By then reinforcements from Kilrush and Ennis had arrived and the miscreants were in various stages of detainment.

Lauren and Frankie watched the car out of sight, turned and joined the group on the benches. Trout held out his hand and drew Lauren close to his side.

"Mac did the needful for you, Tegan," Bodine said. "He called me and gave me the lowdown on what was happening. He's some operator. He must have put two-thirds of the Force through his hands. And we're all the better for it. They're saying he'll finally have to go next year."

"Yeah." Trout agreed. "He's used up his extension and his negotiated contract at this stage. He was a one-off, was Mac. I don't know what he'll do when he finally retires."

"The Force was his family for so long. But he's got friends everywhere. By the time he's visited us all, he'll have had a chance to settle." Bodine gave a nod to himself and added, "His head's-up set the scene but it was young Crilly who really got us here on time."

"We have a lot to thank you for." Trout turned to the leather-clad young man who was standing silently, listening. He said to Lauren, "This young man was trying out his new motorbike this evening." He glanced at the young man. "A Honda Gold Wing, I believe, nice bike."

The young man grinned. "It's only second hand but she sure moves."

Inspector Bodine took up the tale. "Crilly has been posted to Clare recently and we're glad to have him. As you say he was off duty and taking his bike for a spin when he saw the black Cherokee, remembered the alert on it and rang it in. That coupled with Mac's call gave us the momentum to get moving. Especially as Garda Crilly had the ball–" he cleared his throat "*Ahem*, what was I saying – oh yes, the guts to follow the jeep, and keep us posted as to exactly where it was."

"I only did what any of us would do," Crilly said.

But they could see that the young man seemed pleased with the attention.

Lauren thought, with an indulgent smile, that he'd go far with that mix of initiative and self-effacing pride.

"*Hey, if you tell us where you go clubbing, we'll buy you a drink!*" the distinctively American voice of one of the Woofers called.

This reminded Frankie that her workers were still up and she needed them fresh for work in the morning. She started to shoo them off to bed.

Hannah came forward to give Lauren a hug. A big smile split her face. "Thank you."

Lauren returned the hug tightly and went to shoo Hannah towards the cottage. Then she started and clapped her hand over her mouth. "*Crikey!*" she said. "We never told Marina and Karl what was happening."

CHAPTER 52

There was a flurry of activity. Frankie insisted the youngsters at least go into the cottage, which they did, albeit reluctantly. Inspector Bodine, with Crilly in tow, had taken his leave, telling Trout he'd be in contact, possibly the next day or the day after.

Once Lauren had mentioned Marina, Hannah had pleaded to say hello to her.

"Except," as Trout reminded her, "we have no coverage here and we forgot to ask where the nearest signal point is."

Frankie, returning from riding herd on her workers, overheard and said, "We have a dongle we use for our own business-networking. I'm sure you could use it for a facetime call. Only, Lauren, it's two o'clock in the morning. Surely you don't want to disturb them at this hour?"

"You don't know Marina. We won't be disturbing her."

Hannah was nodding like a puppet on a spring beside her.

"I'll get the laptop. We might as well stay out here while the candles hold." Frankie shook her head and loped up the steps into the house.

As predicted, Marina and Karl were awake and judging by the immediacy of the call being answered were anxiously awaiting an update.

Hannah pushed her head in front of the screen, gave a little wave and said, "Hi, Mum! Hi, Dad!"

Marina gasped, held out her hands and burst into tears. "*Oh my God! Hannah! Oh my God!* Where are you? We'll come and get you. Won't we, Karl? Just tell us where you are and we'll be right there."

"Good to see you, Hannah." Karl was calm but he swallowed convulsively as he tried to maintain some degree of dignity in the face of his overwhelming joy.

"Lauren says it's late and I have to go to bed but I just wanted to see you for a minute and tell you I'll be with you tomorrow."

Lauren winced at Hannah's choice of words but let it flow.

Hannah blew a kiss towards her parents. "See you tomorrow!" Then she allowed Frankie to lead her away.

"Hi Marina, Karl," Lauren said. "I know it's late but I just wanted to reassure you that all is well." She herself was drooping with tiredness.

"Where are you? What happened? Is Hannah really OK? Karl says that fellow Caligula is wanted for murder. Did you see him?"

Even if she wanted to answer Marina, there was so many questions Lauren had lost track of them by the time Marina drew a breath.

Trout draped an arm over her shoulders and nudged her to one side. "All is well – but everyone is pretty exhausted. We'll get a night's sleep and make our way back to Cork tomorrow."

"But –"

Karl shushed Marina and said in a reasonable tone, "Or we could come to you in the morning? If you thought it would make things easier."

"To be honest with you, Karl, we need a rest and bit of space to think after the day we've had."

"Which included four hours picking strawberries," Lauren interjected.

"Picking what?" Marina looked shocked.

Before she could say anything else, Lauren added, half thinking out loud. "You'll need to get Hannah some new clothes. We'll probably be able to pick up a few bits in Kilrush in the morning but, at the moment, she's only got what she wearing and –"

"*Kilrush?*" Marina screeched. "What are you doing in Clare? How did you get there? You're supposed to be in Cork!"

Lauren turned imploring eyes on Trout.

"Lauren is sleep-talking, thinking she's awake," Trout said quietly. "Maybe we can just leave any decisions until morning"

"But where are you?" Marina ignored Karls attempts to shush her. She batted his hands away. "There's something they're not telling us and I want to know what it is."

"We're in Clare. Our journey to find Hannah brought us here. There's a lot we're not telling you. Mainly because we're all exhausted." Trout spoke staccato, each sentence short and clipped. He softened his voice. "For the moment, Marina, it has to be enough for you to know Hannah is fine. You'll see her tomorrow."

Marina burst into noisy sobs. Karl put his arm around her and turned her into his shoulder. "We are content to know that. Thank you, Thomas and Lauren. We'll talk when you've rested and decided on the best course of action. Good night." And without waiting for an answer Karl disengaged.

"Night," Trout just managed before Karl and Marina disappeared from the screen. He sighed. "That went about as well as you'd expect." He ran his fingers through his hair and turned the laptop over to Frankie. "Thanks. It was better to let them know."

Dom was sitting quietly beside Frankie, his long legs stretched out in front of him. He had produced four, delicate long-stemmed glasses from the house and placed them on the table. "I think a nightcap is in order, a little relaxation, a little distraction. Why don't we sample your blackcurrant wine. All that vitamin C will help us sleep or something." He smiled a lazy, inviting smile at Frankie.

"I've never heard that vitamin C was good for sleep." Lauren perked up. "But seeing as it's good for everything else, I'm willing to try it."

"Especially if it's delivered in alcohol." Frankie said smugly. "Who wouldn't want to try it?"

"Dom, will you do the honours?" Trout smiled. "Fifteen minutes to unwind and then bed. Sounds good."

Dom peeled the foil from the bottle, wrestled the cork free and poured the deep-purple liquid into the glasses. They each reached for one.

Dom raised his. "Here's to successful conclusions and potential friends!" he said.

The others answered him in tones from anticipation, to relief, to pleased.

"*I'll drink to that!*"

"*Sláinte.*"

"*Amen.*"

They drank with sleepy pleasure.

"This is good. What do you think, Trout?" Lauren said.

"You keep calling him that silly name. Where did it come from?" Frankie spoke languidly and almost immediately continued. "You're right though, this is good. If I can get mine anywhere near it, I'd say we'd be onto a winner." Frankie turned to Dom.

He tipped his glass towards her. "We might have to do a good bit of tasting before we get there." He smiled at Trout. "I doubt if the nickname is an allusion to your drinking habits. You don't have the look of an old soak."

Trout laughed. "Far from it. A childhood incident with a dog, a river and an old fellow with a fishing rod. I might get to tell you sometime. But what I can tell you right now is that this is good. I would be delighted to have it on my inventory for special customers."

"The potential for friendship keeps growing," Dom said dreamily. "Only that I have to be up in a couple of hours, I would pursue it this minute. As it is, I can feel the vitamin C working already. I'm for bed." He stood, lifted the bottle and divided it equally between the four glasses, taking care not to tip the lees into anyone's glass. "Take your wine with you. The bed is ready. Goodnight."

CHAPTER 53

The yurt may have looked primitive but it had one of the most comfortable beds Lauren had ever slept on. She willingly admitted that spooned against Trout, with his arms tightly around her added to the comfort. Plus, they were able to bring the security stick in with them and hang it, spar-like, across the door from one specially constructed holder to the other. It was primitive, but both effective and secure. She woke early, realized there was no rush and stretched luxuriously. Her thoughts ranged over the events of the previous evening and the delight in finding a proper bed in the yurt. It wasn't pitch black and she dreamily watched the shadows and thought about primitive conditions and primordial urges. This funneled her mind into the intoxicating thought of how she could use those same urges to very good effect. She turned, sliding sinuously against Trout, to find him smiling at her.

"Good morning."

She pressed closer and feathered a row of dreamy kisses across his bare chest. "I get the feeling it just got even better," she murmured.

A determined *rat-tat-tat* woke Lauren the second time. She sat up groggily. "What? " She squinted around the shadowy room, trying to figure out where she was. The knocking was getting more frantic. "Lauren, Lauren, you have to get up!"

"Hannah?" She catapulted herself out of bed, realized she was naked, grabbed the throw that was dangling half-on, half-off the end of the bed and wrapped it around herself. She stumbled to the door and with difficulty lifted the stick, dropped it one side and opened the door a crack. "Hannah, what's wrong?"

Hannah was leaning against the yurt, panting. Lauren looked past her. The morning was bright but she could still see the glisten of dew on the grass outside the door. Still early, she thought, so whatever had roused her goddaughter must be serious.

"Lauren," she whispered. "Marina – Mum's here."

"What? *No!*" Lauren found herself whispering back.

"I heard her talking to Frankie. I thought I was dreaming, but I wasn't. They're both here. Mum and Dad in a silver car with a cute driver."

Lauren groaned. "Why the heck couldn't she have waited until we got back?"

"I don't know. What'll we do?"

"I need to get dressed and, by the look of things, " she eyed the skimpy T-shirt Hannah was wearing, "so do you."

"I don't think either of us is going to pass muster, whatever we do." Hannah giggled. "You've got no more passable clothes than I have."

"*Brat!*" Lauren went to swat her godchild but her makeshift cover started to slip so she grabbed it instead. "We'll get dressed anyway. Come back to me when you're ready."

She closed the door and after a minute's contemplation, replaced the stick and waddled back to the bed.

"What was that all about?" Trout, looking tousled and sleepy-eyed, sat up and grinned at her. "Nice robe." He patted the bed invitingly. "Come back in and we can keep each other warm while we make plans for the day."

"Our plans for the day have just got short shift," she said, rooting on the chair beside the bed to find her clothes. "It appears Marina and Karl have arrived." She pulled on items of clothing as they came to hand.

"How could they have arrived? They don't know where we are!"

"It seems they do now. Hannah says they were talking to Frankie out front, five minutes ago."

"And we aren't even prepped with coffee."

The urgent *rat-tat-tat* came again.

"That's Hannah now. I'll go and prepare the way. Only try not to leave me too long without back-up." She rose in one fluid movement.

"Hey!" Trout caught her hand. "A little booster to stiffen your spine for the task ahead." He kissed her hard and fast, dropped her hand and gave her a little push. "*Fágh a' bealach!*"

"Clear the way? Surely that's what you should be doing?" Lauren attempted to pass off the shaky breathlessness in her voice as annoyance then decided to hell with it, threw her head up and unfastened the door.

Hannah was hopping impatiently from one foot to the other as she waited for her. She was wearing her mud-stained jeans, the T-shirt she had slept in and had tied a colourful scarf over her dreads. Lauren grimaced.

"Frankie must have brought them into the kitchen," she whispered. "There's no sign of them outside."

"Why are we whispering?" Lauren whispered back.

"I don't know." Hannah gurgled a laugh. "It feels like we don't want to get caught."

"We're up now, so we can stroll in as if we're coming for breakfast and act surprised when we see our unexpected visitors." Lauren looped her arm through Hannah's. "Cool scarf."

"I borrowed it from one of the girls. I don't see the point in giving Mum any more ammunition than is necessary."

"Good plan. Come on, we'll present a united front."

They headed around the house.

The silver-grey Mercedes Lauren had last seen outside the Village Inn was parked in front of the house. The driver, Eoin if she remembered correctly, was standing looking around him with a delighted grin.

"Hi, Eoin!"

"Hello, Lauren – Miss." He pulled his hat off his head and blurted, "This place is so cool. I'd love to spend my holidays here."

"I'm sure they'd love to have you. They use Woofers all the time."

"It's a bit basic but it's super-cool." Hannah chimed in. "We picked strawberries for our bed and board yesterday. Dom does fab food."

"I suppose Marina and Karl are inside?" Lauren couldn't help sounding hopeful that he might, just maybe, contradict her.

He beamed. "Yeah. They only had the area, around Kilrush, and that you can pick strawberries in it and I got them right to the door."

"Very enterprising of you."

"Ah, thanks, Lauren, but really Estuary Fields is the only registered market garden in the area. I said we'd try here first and hit pay-dirt!"

Hannah had her hand clamped over her mouth in an effort not to laugh out loud. Lauren mock-glared at her. "I wouldn't be too sure it's a laughing matter until we've bearded the lion."

"I know. And I'm sure we smell – even if we don't, Mum'll think we do!"

"Come on. We'll face the music in solidarity with each other."

"Wish us luck, Eoin!" Hannah said.

Arm in arm, they marched around the house and into the kitchen.

CHAPTER 54

Marina and Karl were ensconced at the top of the big table, with steaming cups in front of them. Dom straightened from taking a large pan, which gave off the most tantalizing smells, from the oven. He smiled with what Lauren could only describe as relief when he saw them.

Marina turned to see what he was looking at, surged to her feet, rushed forward and crushed Hannah in a vice-like hug, wailing, *"My baby, my baby!"*

Hannah allowed herself be patted and petted until her mother pulled back and Karl reached to draw her into a tight hug. Over her head Lauren could see his eyes were shiny with tears. She had a lump in her own throat watching the reunion.

"I'm sorry for causing you so much worry." Hannah had big, fat tears rolling down her cheeks. "I should have told you. I should have tried harder to make someone listen."

"You were frightened. In hindsight, what you did was brave and very clever." Karl spoke quietly. "Especially now that we know how ruthless Caligula is."

"It nearly didn't come off. Only for – oh my God – David. You have to meet David. He was brill." She caught her father's hands, lifted shining eyes to his. "Only for him I'd never have got off the roof."

Karl drew her into a chair between himself and Marina.

Lauren moved to sit across from them. Dom silently placed a mug of coffee and a jug of milk beside her, and went back to his cooking.

Karl lay a hand on Marina's arm as she went to speak and shook his head. She sat back, her eyes devouring her daughter, and remained silent.

"Tell us what happened, Hannah," Karl said.

Trout padded into the room, nodded at Dom, who immediately produced another mug of coffee and placed it on the table as Trout slipped into a chair beside Lauren. She smiled at him – nobody else paid any attention – and turned back, as eager to hear Hannah's story as the rest of them.

Hannah took a deep breath and plunged into speech.

She had been in the stationary room in the London office of KOE the week before, looking to borrow a ream of paper for her school project, when she heard Larry Caligula and Shyrl Baker enter. She wasn't sure what made her hide, but her abhorrence of the security man was such that she didn't want him to find her there and perhaps give him ammunition that he could use against her. At first, she feared they were there to make out and she curled herself into a ball and covered her ears, but then she realized that they were discussing something that they didn't want anyone to know about. She heard her father's name mentioned and pricked up her ears. Caligula was talking about throwing a spanner in the works of the monetary commission talks by destroying Karl Offenbach's status as an honest broker. He told Shyrl that he had acquired the details of certain accounts, and was in the process of redeploying the funds into an account in the Bahamas in such a way that Karl himself would be held responsible for the losses. He went so far as to boast that he was setting the great Offenbach up for the fraud case of the century. He told Shyrl there was a ten million payout with her name on it. All she had to do was to hold a data stick he would give her in a couple of days in her secure drawer and bring it home with her on the following Thursday evening. She protested a bit, saying how could she be sure of keeping it safe. He told her she was the PA's secretary and as such was above suspicion. He would see her later and they would go over it again but he was sure he'd have everything ready by the following Monday and they would make their move on Thursday. When Shyrl asked him how he intended to get Karl to London, so the fraud could be brought to light, he had laughed and said he would kidnap his bitch of a daughter and hold her to ransom.

Hannah gulped. "I was so scared. I stayed there until I was sure nobody was around, then I got out as quick as I could. I thought and thought over the weekend. I knew JoJo was going away and I thought if I told Mum I was going to you, Dad, she'd go away for the weekend and that would give me a chance to, well, I thought I'd go to Ireland and ask Lauren what I should do." She smiled a watery smile at Lauren. "I thought I had better continue as usual so I called in the office most days, hung around with Angela and Shyrl and on Thursday I was in Shyrl's office when she was called out to sign for a delivery. I couldn't believe it – she had left the key in her drawer. I didn't even think it through – I opened the drawer, saw a data stick, grabbed it and left. Oh, I made sure to lock the drawer but I was shaking so much I was sure someone would notice. I didn't know what to do then but I thought of Lauren telling us about putting secret documents in the post. So, I went to the post office, bought a padded envelope and sent the stick to your office in New York, Dad. I marked it private and personal so I knew only you would open it."

It was hard to know who was the most aghast, Karl or Marina.

Karl cleared his throat. "So what happened then?"

"I'm not sure. I suppose Shyrl told Caligula that the stick was missing and he must have got wind that Mum was away. Either way he turned up at the Mews early Friday morning. I was terrified and I just ran."

She went on to recount the full story of her flight that morning. How Caligula had arrived, how she had forgotten most of her money in her desk drawer as she rushed to escape. How she had met David on the roof and he had hidden her and confronted Caligula, and later got her off the roof. How they went to get his young sister, Isla, who feared her father was going to barter her to pay off a debt and what had happened to Isla when they were attacked by a gang.

"We had to leave Isla in Waterford. David thought she'd be safer if we took away her things, so that she couldn't be identified too fast. In case her father found her." Hannah twisted her fingers together in distress.

Marina gently pried them apart and held her hands. "We've met Isla. Her mother is with her and she's safe," she said softly. "They're coming to stay with us in Cork for a few days until Isla is fully ready to travel. Her mother knows everything and has taken steps to protect her."

"Oh, David will be so pleased! He was really worried about her, especially as his stepdad had already messed up his chances of going to the College of Music when he threw him out. Everything David owned was on the roof, apart from what he kept in his ruscksack. That creepy Caligula probably destroyed his things out of spite when we escaped."

"He may not have had the time to do that," Karl reassured her. "But we'll find out and make sure everything is restored to him. By the way, how did he, actually, get you off the roof?"

"It was cool. David had this rope hooked over the ledge of the railing. We just slid down, he flicked the hook off, rolled up the rope and we ran."

Marina clamped a hand over her mouth and whimpered.

Karl smiled reassuringly. "We'll have to meet this enterprising young man of yours. Where is he, by the way?"

"He's still asleep. Everyone was allowed a lie-in this morning because we pulled off the stunt with the reality TV thing."

"Reality TV?" Karl raised an enquiring brow at Lauren.

Lauren hesitated. "Eh . . . I think we'll leave that for the moment . . . we'll talk about it later."

"I see we still have a lot of catching-up to do," Karl said. "Some of it we can do on the road. Dominick has kindly invited us to breakfast. I propose we eat and set out as soon as possible."

"Except Hannah and Lauren need to get into some proper clothes." Marina hauled Hannah to her feet. "Come, Lauren, show me where you can change."

"Change into what, Marina? These are the only clothes we have."

"The only clothes?" Marina wrinkled her nose. "What is that dreadful smell?" She sniffed at her daughter's headscarf and shrieked, "*Your hair, your beautiful hair. What have you done?*" She reached trembling fingers to pull the scarf off.

"Chill, Mum. They're only dreads."

"*Dreadlocks!*" Marina actually moaned as if in pain.

"Yeah. Aren't they great, saves all that washing and brushing and everything. I'm thinking I'll keep them."

"Keep them?" Marina said faintly. She looked at her daughter and rallied. "*Over my dead body.* We're going to hairdresser's tomorrow. Our more immediate problem is some decent clothes."

Dom cleared his throat. "I'd say breakfast is a better objective. Especially as the hordes will descend on us in about fifteen minutes. Frittata anyone?"

Everyone tucked in with gusto. Halfway through, David rushed in looking for Hannah, only to skid to a stop when he saw the party at the end of the table. He started to back out but before he had gone a few steps, Karl stood up, walked over to him and caught him in a hug. "How can I thank you for keeping my daughter safe? We were about to go looking for you. Your breakfast is ready and we'll leave soon afterwards. Your mother and sister should be in Cork by the time we get back."

"You've seen my mother?" David sounded wary.

"I have indeed. And I have made my most suitable lawyer available to her. You need not worry about her or your sister again." Karl guided David to the table. "Marina, this is the young man who has kept Hannah safe."

Marina likewise rose to hug him and thank him and fuss over him. He endured her fussing stoically.

Hannah grimaced and mouthed "Sorry."

Lauren stood up. "Sit over here, David. I'm finished and I want to go and have a chat with Frankie." She started towards the door.

Marina called after her, "Don't be too long! We need to go to Kilrush on our way back!"

"That's in the opposite direction to where we're going, Marina," Lauren said.

"So? Neither you nor these two children can travel without some appropriate clothes."

"The two children have survived tempest and pestilence," Lauren said dryly. "I'm sure they'd manage to get the Cork in the clothes they're wearing."

"Really, Lauren, you have no concept of the niceties of life."

Trout winked at Lauren and she felt her initial aggravation dissipate. "I'll tell Eoin come in and have some breakfast, Dom. If that's OK with you."

"Absolutely. The more the merrier. You can give a holler to the rest while you're at it."

"Will do."

CHAPTER 55

Marina went through Kilrush like a dervish. She picked a man's shop she deemed appropriate and shooed Trout and David in with orders to find and put on clean clothes and dump what they were wearing. Karl refused to have hand, act or part in it. He stayed in the car, telling Trout he would set a few things in motion while he waited for them.

"Is she for real?" David muttered to Trout. "Dumping perfectly good clothes just because they need a wash?"

Trout winked at him. "We don't have to do everything she says. The thing to remember is, she's paying so we can get anything we fancy. Hear that, Pat?" He turned to the salesman who was watching them with a bemused expression. "The lady says we're to be kitted from the skin out. What do you fancy putting us into?" He looked around at an array of multi-coloured pants. "Within reason, of course."

It took longer for the girls. Mainly because Marina insisted on visiting every ladies' clothing establishment in the place. On the other hand, she did spread her custom between them all and by the time they were finished Lauren and Hannah were fully clothed, from underwear to outer wear to shoes, all to Marina's satisfaction. The proprietors of the establishments were left reeling from the whirlwind that blew through the town.

Lauren, after her initial resistance, decided co-operation was a small price to pay for the generosity of her cousin. At least, they had managed to persuade Marina that, under a fresh scarf, Hannah's hair could wait until they had more time. And, finally, they set out for Cork.

Trout, in answer to David's mute appeal, had insisted that the lad ride with him and Lauren. They would travel in tandem but, if they were separated, they would meet up at the apartment when they each arrived in Cork. There, they could regroup and plan the next move.

Lauren had suggested that they could come to Knocknaclogga while they were in Clare but Marina had pooh-poohed the idea. They would be better off in Cork where they had all the benefits of a modern society available to them. For a moment after that conversation, Lauren had felt her temper flare. Then she reminded herself who she was dealing with and left well enough alone. She contented herself with a phone call to Lucy and a promise of a full disclosure of their adventures when they got home. Up to a point anyway, Lauren amended to herself when they had rung off.

Trout had spoken to Inspector Bodine. He informed him they were returning to Cork and asked after any new developments.

Caligula was being transported to Dublin that afternoon. Officials from the British police were coming over to interview him and the thinking was he would be extradited to England to stand trial for the murder of Shyrl Baker. The attempted kidnapping and intent to extort money from Karl Offenbach and the possible fraudulent removal of monies from KOE International were also under consideration. The fraud, in Bodine's opinion and much to his disgust, was being considered in the same category as the murder. The bottom line was, he told Trout, that Caligula was well held. He had added that since the attempts to extricate himself in the Estuary Field's yard had failed, Caligula had clammed-up. Bodine had said, with a certain relish, "He has to remember that his erstwhile pal The O'Carthy is in the sidelines. And that's one gent I wouldn't like to have on my case. Too many unforeseen accidents happen in his vicinity, especially if the same lad feels threatened. Caligula might even feel safer in England, if you get my drift."

David was mostly silent on the drive back. He had answered their questions but volunteered very little information. At one stage he said "A lot of people helped us. I'd like an opportunity to thank them properly and I'm sure Hannah would too."

Lauren reassured him and talked about the various people they too had met. The same people who had helped Hannah and David and how both herself and Trout had promised to return and let them know all was well. A short discussion had ensued on the best way to go about it. Lauren was of the opinion that Karl had something planned and figured there was no point in preempting things until they knew how the land lay.

They all arrived at the Elysian more or less at the same time. Eoin decanted the Offenbach family at the main entrance while Trout drove into the high-rise car park and parked near the elevators.

To Lauren's surprise, when they arrived in the apartment, three rucksacks were leaning against the wall, inside the door.

"*Our bags!*" David stared at them as if he was seeing things. "How did they get here?"

Hannah rushed towards them. "Look, our bags! The security guy at the door gave them to us. He said someone left them in, saying that they had found them down by the docks and to give them to the Offenbachs when they returned. How weird is that?"

"The O'Carthy washing his hands of Caligula more likely," Trout said sotto-voce in Lauren's ear.

She nodded her agreement as she watched Hannah and David eye the bags with a mixture of apprehension and gratefulness. "You might as well check them out," she suggested after getting tired of waiting to see what they'd do.

Hannah dropped onto her knees beside them. David bent down and straightened his, then crouched beside it. Tentatively he reached into the front pocket and pulled out a black hard-cover notebook. He stared at it for a long moment.

"Your music!" Hannah breathed.

He nodded, a dazed look in his eyes. "I thought it was gone forever."

Like a spell had been lifted, the two young people went through the bags, quickly and thoroughly.

"Everything is here. My passport, phone everything." Hannah sat back on her heels and looked at David. "What about yours?"

He nodded. "Looks like it. Isla's as well."

"Mum phoned Isla and her mum from the car," Hannah said softly, still looking directly at David. "They've decided to stay in Waterford for a few days and Dad got them the loan of a holiday cottage a friend of his owns. They're going to be OK, David."

"Yeah, I hear you." David sounded choked. "Thanks to your dad and mum.",

"Dad says Eoin will drop you over when we've had a bite to eat and he's finalized a few things."

"It's nearly all too much," he muttered, dashing a hand at threatening tears.

"It'll never be too much again, after the last week," Hannah said solemnly.

"Oh, Hannah!" David laughed, shook his head. "There will always be things that are too much."

"No," she said mulishly. "I've decided – what's the phrase people use that I thought was rubbish before?" She wrinkled her brow and thought furiously. "Oh yes! Don't sweat the small stuff! That's it. I'm taking that as my motto from now on."

"Yeah, right."

And like flicking a switch they were back to two bickering teens.

Lauren smiled, turned to Trout and as she did so caught Karl beckoning them over. He motioned them onto the balcony and closed the doors behind them.

"I contacted Clive Ramsbottom while we were in Kilrush. I asked him to visit the mews and have a look at the roof next door. JoJo knows him so he was able to fill her in at the same time. Hannah has already chatted with her and I've arranged for her to come over tomorrow." His tone became grimmer. "Clive's just got back onto me. Hannah was right, everything was destroyed. He found the remnants of a tent and the mangled remains of the young man's belongings. He also," Karl balled his hand into a fist and growled through his teeth, "found the marks where a grappling hook had knocked off the paint and scored the stone of the rampart. Only for that enterprising young man . . ."

He drew a long breath through his nose. "To think I trusted that – that – " He shook himself. "I am going to make damn sure Caligula pays the full price for his actions."

Lauren, looking at the fire in his eyes and his set face, had no doubt he meant exactly what he said.

CHAPTER 56

Lauren and Trout had stayed an extra day in Cork to tie up a few loose ends. In reality TCLI's brief was to find Hannah and return her home. That was done but Trout felt he needed to follow-up on the fallout and this he did.

Now, only two days later, they had travelled to Ardmore where Karl had arranged a thank-you party. He claimed Ardmore was the perfect location as it was where David's family were domiciled, in what turned out to be Seamus Eacrett's holiday home. And, as Lauren well knew, one of Karl's favourite hotels in the world was located there.

Brendan came with them, almost bouncing in the back seat in his excitement. Trout had debated the merits of calling him up on his hacking skills, then considering that they had been more than willing to use the information he had uncovered, decided on a different tack. They had ended up having an in-depth discussion on internet safety with Trout showing him a couple of tricks he hadn't yet worked out for himself. Brendan had pointed out, reasonably Trout thought, that anyone who knew how the commands worked should be able to figure out how to access any if not all sites on the net. On that logical summing-up, they had rested their exchange, to each other's satisfaction.

"Karl seems to have tracked down just about everyone we met over the course of the investigation." Lauren was looking at her phone. "Hannah has been sending me updates. He's sent minibuses, limos, even organized B&B for people who are travelling any great distance and, wait for it, gifts to the ones who can't make it." She shook her head. "Hannah sounds as excited as a kid at a birthday party. I have to hand it to him – if you want all the stops pulled out, Karl's your man."

They finally arrived in Ardmore and took the Cliff Road, enjoying the bird's-eye view over the sea and the amazing round tower dominating the skyline.

"I'm so glad I don't suffer from vertigo," Lauren murmured. "I'd hate to miss out on this spectacular view."

Hannah was watching out for them on the terrace. She rushed to give Lauren a hug, swung around to include Trout in the welcome and indicated a much more relaxed and smiling David, following in her wake. He greeted them with a certain diffidence and invited them to come and meet his mother and sister. Brendan hung back, his normal loquaciousness quelled by his surroundings and the vivacity of Hannah. He was duly drawn forward and introduced.

"You're the computer geek!" Hannah gave an excited squeal and rushed to give him a hug in turn. "You did a cool job finding us. Come and meet Isla. The two of you will probably understand each other's language. She's a computer geek too."

And in spite of Brendan reddening to the tips of his ears, the ice was broken and the three young people moved off chattering like magpies.

A dark petite woman rose from where she was watching the exchange with an interested gaze. "Helen Slocombe." She held out a hand first to Lauren, then Trout. "David didn't get around to introducing us after all."

Lauren thought she had the saddest face she had ever seen and she gently held the fragile fingers between her two hands. "It's a pleasure to meet you, Mrs Slocombe. You must be very proud of David and the good sense he has shown over the past week."

Trout added his compliments as the woman murmured, "Helen, please. I'd revert to my own name, only I don't want to add to Isla's distress at the moment."

"Isn't this the most amazing place?"

"And we're so lucky to have a little house, practically on the beach, just over there." Helen indicated across the water to where a scattering of houses could be seen a little way over from the village. "It's given Isla a chance to heal and helped David come to terms with himself."

"I'm so glad," Lauren said simply and sincerely.

They moved towards where Helen had been sitting under the shade of a large blue-and-white-striped umbrella. As Lauren went to sit down, Marina, in a swirl of pale-yellow silk, rushed onto the terrace.

"Hannah said you'd arrived!" She gave Trout a perfunctory peck on the cheek. "I'm glad you're here, Thomas. I'll sent Karl out to you – he's like a lost soul in there since he has finished arranging everyone." She caught Lauren in a quick hug, stood back and eyed her cream capris and fitted top with disfavour. "I knew it," she said. "Really, Lauren, that is no outfit for a party. Come along, I've just the thing for you."

"Hang on, Marina."

Her cousin grabbed her hand. "Hurry. Our guests will be arriving soon. You need to be ready." She towed Lauren away, up the stairs and into a luxurious bedroom with floor-to-ceiling doors open onto a sunny terrace that allowed the gentle sound of waves ride a soft sea-breeze into the room.

"What a gorgeous room."

"It's yours. Yours and that delicious man of yours. Change quickly. Oh, I forgot the shoes! Back in a mo." And Marina darted away.

An array of silk underwear and the most gorgeous dress Lauren had ever seen were lying on the bed. She stared at them for less than thirty seconds because she knew that when Marina was in that mood, she'd be fast and then she'd have an audience as she dressed. So, without ado, she slipped on the sensuous garments and was wriggling into the dress when Marina returned.

Marina helped Lauren pull the dress into place, zipped it up, dropped a pair of nude, kitten-heeled sandals in front of her, and ordered, "Slip those on." Marina stood back and eyed her cousin critically. "Brush out your hair." She scurried away. She was back in seconds carrying a fine gold three-strand chain. "Turn around and I'll tie it for you." Lauren felt the cool touch of the gold encircling her neck and falling to rest just above her breast bone. "That should do it." Marina pulled open the wardrobe door to reveal a full-length mirror.

"Oh!" Lauren stared at her reflection. The dress was silk jersey in the fresh green of a Tiger Aloe. The skirt fell from a ruched waistline that emphasised her hour-glass figure. The cross-over bodice hinted at décolleté. The strands of gold glittered slightly, drawing the eye to the creamy column of her throat.

"I – I don't know what to say."

"Nothing. Nothing at all." Marina gave Lauren a quick, tight hug. "I can't thank you enough for what you've done." She turned so the two of them were reflected in the mirror. "Looking good, cuz. Come on, let's show everyone what the two most amazing girls in Knocknaclogga can do."

"We're not teenagers anymore." Lauren was laughing as she protested.

"I know. The thought of what we can get up to as adults is so delicious to contemplate."

EPILOGUE

The party was a resounding success. The food was delicious. The wine, or whatever your tipple was, flowed freely. Seamus Eacrett, looking like he'd lost weight, brought a tall, robust wife who treated him with off-hand deference and almost immediately abandoned him to join the women. He was still pale, but set up court in a corner where he was joined by Con McMillan, his cousin Dougie, Jarlath Considine and Bob Rackett.

Trout wandered over, laughing as he said. "Garda&Ex convention, I see!"

Pamela O'Leary looked like a model in a gold sheath dress and sky-high sandals. Lauren detached her from the Garda convention and brought her to meet Marina and Helen. "Don't mind that lot," she told her. "They haven't an eye for beauty between them."

Ken Cahill and Zoe Long came with their parents. After initially being overwhelmed, they were soon ensconced with the rest of the teens and, judging by the hilarity issuing from that direction, a good time was being had by all.

The staff and little girls from the Holly Unit arrived, excited and apprehensive and chattering non-stop. Hannah and Lauren were soon in the middle of them, answering questions and telling them how much they had enjoyed meeting and spending time with them in Tramore. Bernadette was tearfully grateful that they remembered them and was fulsome in her thanks for the generous donation Karl had made to the Home.

Josie Moran had exited the car Karl sent to bring her with a regal dignity and an honest pleasure in being there. Both Hannah and David had rushed to greet her and thank her and introduce her to everyone. She had confided to Lauren after a glass of sherry that she was lucky the outfit she wore to her son's wedding was such good quality. An occasion such as this required one to be dressed appropriately and wasn't Lauren looking lovely? That colour really suited her.

Romeo Ingels turned up in a white djellaba, looking more prophet-like than he did on the hill. Himself and Bruce McTeggert struck up an unexpected alliance over the Greenway, and remained deep in conversation for most of the evening.

When everyone was settled with drinks, relaxing while waiting for the much-anticipated food, Karl stood up and waited until there was quiet.

"My friends, and I call you all that in the light of your help to my daughter and her friend in their recent ordeal. I welcome you and endeavour to try and thank you all for the kindness and generosity you've shown, without thought of return." He looked around, continued quietly, "You all played a part, but there is one person I must single out because it was his bravery and prompt action that initially saved Hannah's life. David, I am told you are a gifted musician. The management has kindly made a piano available to us. I would like you to play for us."

David went red then white. "I – I –"

"Please, David," Hannah said softly. "Play the piece you've been writing."

David looked at her. He moved as if in a trace over to the white piano in the corner of the reception area, sat down and stared at the keys.

An expectant hush had fallen over the gathering.

A long moment passed. David raised his hands, held them poised and played a run of scales. Then seemingly satisfied, he began to play. Softly, sadly at first then swelling into a heart-thudding run of notes, softening again, He played on, varying the tone and rhythm, the beat and speed. As he became lost in the music so did his listeners.

"*Oh my God!*" Lauren whispered. "He's telling the story of their flight. He's put it into music."

He ended with a light, happy run of chords, stopped, raised his hands and let them fall on to his knees.

There was complete silence for a moment and then the applause thundered out. Karl, unashamedly emotional, cleared his throat and said, "Congratulations, David, you have just claimed the annual KOE Bursary for Further Studies. We'll discuss the details of it another time." He walked over and placed a hand on David's shoulder. "That was an amazing piece of music. Does it have a title?"

David looked at him, a dazed expression on his face. He looked over at Hannah. "I've been calling it *The Journey* but I think, I think now it's going to be known as *Finding Hannah.*"

The End